NEVER PURSUE A PRINCE
The Wedding Vow, Book 1

Copyright © 2021 by Regina Lundgren
Published by Edwards and Williams

Cover Design and Interior Format

© THE KILLION GROUP INC.

THE WEDDING VOW

BOOK
ONE

Never Pursue a Prince

REGINA SCOTT

2 1 6 6 3

To you—your enjoyment of my books keeps me writing. And to the Lord, for making a path in the wilderness and directing my steps.

CHAPTER ONE

Chelsea Palace, outside London, England, May 1825

A T TIMES, LADY Larissa Dryden found being the daughter of a duke highly inconvenient. Take now, for instance. She would have liked nothing better than to herd her younger sisters and dearest friend into the reception hall to meet their illustrious host. But that, alas, was not the gracious act of the daughter of the mighty Duke of Wey. So, she studiously maintained her best smile as she inched along nearly at the end of the receiving line of five hundred of London's finest.

Simple enough to mark her progress. The gallery walls in the mansion the Batavarian court had leased were paneled in gilded medallions. She was fairly sure she'd just passed the eighth. Only a dozen more to go to reach the reception hall.

If only her progress in fulfilling her goal was as easily measured. There, she felt as if she were perpetually stuck on the first step.

"This," Belle said with an approving swish of her white satin skirts, "is what is known as a tremendous crush."

Her youngest sister was right. All up and down the line, ladies smiled, giggled, and attempted to look interesting. Their fans wafted away the warmth of a May evening, made even hotter by the hundreds of candles flickering in the massive crystal chandeliers overhead. Every marriageable miss for miles must be here.

That was not going to help matters. On their other side, their middle sister, Callie, sighed so deeply she also set her rosy skirts to swinging. "Perhaps we should go."

Over Larissa's dead body.

"Now, what would His Majesty think?" Larissa said with a smile to her sister. "He was so kind to invite us all."

"Even me," their friend, Petunia Bateman, said from just behind. "And that's saying a lot."

"You have every right to be here," Aunt Meredith soothed. A good friend of the family, she was standing in as their chaperone until their family could return from their country seat in Surrey. Though she was not titled, being the wife of a prominent solicitor, she looked as if she outranked every other lady in the line, with her raven hair done up in a sophisticated arrangement on top of her head and her lavender satin evening gown embroidered all along the neck and hem with green vines.

"Yes, you do," Belle agreed. "We all do. We must remember our vow. This is Larissa's night to shine." She nodded to Larissa, golden curls bobbing.

Belle was nothing if not an optimist.

"And what vow would that be?" Aunt Meredith asked, dark brows up in question. Her eyes, the same shade of lavender as her gown, swept from Larissa to the others as they all moved forward again.

Eleven medallions to go now.

Callie sidled closer to Larissa, who slipped her arm about her sister's waist in support. Callie had been wont to blurt out every word ever uttered in her presence, whether by servants murmuring in the corridors or their father practicing one of his speeches for the House of Lords. Her sister had learned to control her tongue as she grew older, but nerves or pressure tended to squeeze the truth out of her. And she was not about to share this secret. Neither was Larissa.

Belle saved the day. "Larissa, Callie, Petunia, and I are resolved to have a marvelous Season this year," she said with her winsome smile that set her jade-colored eyes to glowing.

"Ah," Aunt Meredith said, but by the way she cocked her head, ostrich plumes in her hair waving, she saw right through the half-truth.

Callie's gaze dropped to her pink satin slippers, and she clamped her mouth shut.

"Yes," Larissa said, keeping her voice serene, as her late grandmother had taught her. A lady had no need to raise her voice, particularly when she was protesting her innocence. "We intend to make a difference this Season. That's why Callie and Tuny are supporting the new Society for the Prevention of Cruelty to Animals."

Callie lifted her head and nodded.

"Commendable," their chaperone said. "And what is your goal, Larissa?"

"Larissa's going to marry a prince," Belle announced.

Heads turned; frowns aimed their way.

A lady also quelled any unpleasant rumors about herself. "It was a silly thing I said when I was a child," Larissa explained, pitching her voice to carry. "Doesn't every girl grow up hoping to marry a prince?"

That statement at least made the gossips turn the other way. She did not like thinking how they would react if they knew the whole.

The vow had been Belle's idea, and none of them had been proof against her will. But then, no one ever was.

"Larissa has always helped us," Belle had said when she'd announced it. "Now it's our turn to help her."

They had all been gathered in Larissa's bedchamber, as they often did after an evening out. With her brother and sister-in-law's permission, this Season Petunia was staying at Weyfarer House, the duke's home in London.

Her family hoped she might have a better opportunity to meet a suitable gentleman. Larissa intended to make certain of it.

"I'm game," Tuny had said, leaning back against the carved headboard on Larissa's four-poster bed, her straight blond hair hanging down onto her lawn nightgown. "What do you suggest?"

Belle held out her hand. "We all vow to see each other married, and married well, before harvest arrives in September."

Tuny met Larissa's gaze. They both knew the excitement, and the disappointment, of a London Season. It was easy for the eighteen-year-old Belle to make such a vow when she was lovely, talented, animated, and on her first Season. Callie, Larissa, and Tuny were on their third. It would have been longer for Larissa, if she hadn't insisted on waiting to come out until Callie was old enough to join her. At the distinguished age of three and twenty, Larissa and Tuny were beginning to hear whispers about being on the shelf. So was Callie at one and twenty.

Then again, Belle's vow matched with Larissa's personal goal to see them all happily settled, so she said nothing. A lady knew when to speak and when silence was the most beneficial for achieving her aims.

Callie was watching Belle. "Do you really think we can manage that?"

"I do," Belle said with a determined nod. She wiggled her fingers. "Come on, hold hands."

Callie stuck out her hand and took her sister's. She offered the other to Tuny, who took it and held out her left hand. They'd all looked to Larissa.

She'd grasped Tuny's hand with her right and Belle's with her left, completing the ring. "Very well, Belle. Let's try."

Which is why they were now standing ten medallions away from where King Frederick of Batavaria and his two unmarried sons, Crown Prince Otto and Frederick Archambault, were holding a reception on their first week in England. As of yet, few had so much as caught a glimpse of the Royal Court.

Still, no matter what her sister remembered from their childhood, Larissa had no intention of marrying a prince or anyone else until she knew the others were well on their way to a happy future. Squiring them about might have been easier if she had been married, but she no longer had the luxury of waiting for the perfect suitor to appear. If they all worked together, this Season would see all their goals achieved. Perhaps one of her sisters or Tuny would catch the prince's eye this very night. Rumor had it that Crown Prince Otto was dashing, handsome, and well spoken. He might even be good enough to meet her mother's and late grandmother's expectations.

Even if none of the gentlemen she'd met had been able to meet those expectations.

For some reason, that thought caused her smile to slip. Unacceptable. She was the oldest daughter of a duke and the granddaughter of two. Noble blood ran through her veins. If she decided on a course, she would not be stopped. Her mother and grandmother had instilled that knowledge in her from the day she had been born, and her stepmother, Jane, had only reinforced it. Belle had said they would all find excellent matches this year. She was not going to allow a momentary melancholy to make her lose sight of their vow.

What she needed now was time away from prying eyes and listening ears to regain her composure. Other guests had broken from the line to promenade up and down the gallery or greet friends. Her absence would not be remarked upon, if she made it brief.

"Excuse me," she murmured to the others before slipping into a corridor that opened to the left.

The warmth of the gallery cooled to something more

refreshing as the conversations of the other guests faded behind her. Larissa drew in a breath. Now, this was more like it—elegance, order. Chelsea Palace had been built by a wealthy family some years ago, but the current generation saw little use for it, according to the London papers, so they had been persuaded to lease it to the visiting court. Shaped like an H, it held public rooms along one wing and private rooms along the other. This corridor must link the two.

Like the gallery, it was suitably impressive, with marble statues in the Greek style interspersed with massive paintings in gilded frames. For a few moments, she might forget Belle's vow, her own childish preoccupation with marrying a prince, and her concerns for Callie and Tuny. She wandered farther, footsteps muffled by the ruby-red carpet running down the center of the polished wood floor.

The largest picture in the group was positioned high on the wall opposite double glass doors that must lead out into the garden. She stopped in front of it, mindful of her party in the gallery behind her, and gazed up at the man standing with head high, shoulders back, and meaty arms akimbo. His sandy hair streamed out around a strong-boned face, and he glared at the world as if determined to conquer it.

"They say it doesn't do him justice."

Larissa whirled to find that a gentleman had joined her. No, not a mere gentleman, for gold cording crossed the black uniform on his chest, where it wasn't covered in medals. She'd seen similar guardsmen flanking the front entrance of the palace, gazes alert for any mischief. They had seemed stalwart, seasoned. He could not be much older than her, perhaps by five years or so, yet he'd managed to earn a gold sunburst of a star, a silver cross embedded with a ruby, and a host of other ribbons and gems.

But their sparkle was nothing to the gleam in his silvery-blue eyes, as if she were gazing into the depths of a diamond.

"Forgive me," she said. "I didn't mean to intrude."

"No intrusion," he assured her with a nod of his head that caused the candlelight to dance along the gold in his curly hair. "His Majesty would hardly hang a picture if not to have someone admire it."

His voice held a curious accent, not unlike that of the French ambassador, who had spoken to her and her father at a recent Society event, but there were harder notes as well. German, perhaps? Batavaria had borders with both countries, as well as Switzerland. A shame she could not question him. A lady did not linger with a fellow to whom she hadn't been introduced. Besides, he had his duty, and she should not keep him from it.

Tilting her head, she saw Callie watching her. Tuny, Belle, and Meredith were already out of sight. In another few moments, she would be alone with this man.

But she could not seem to convince her feet to move. Could she not, just for a moment, pretend she had nothing more to do than to converse with a handsome gentleman?

"So, this is the king?" she asked, forcing herself to look at the painting instead of him.

"King Frederick Otto Leopold the Fourth of Batavaria," he agreed. "Just before he became a father. They called him the Lion of the Alps."

Larissa smiled. With that defiant look, it was easy to imagine him roaring at his enemies.

"Of course, that was before the Congress of Vienna," he continued. "In their great wisdom, the leaders felt it best to entrust the wellbeing of the citizens of Batavaria to a greater power. The lands are part of Württemberg now."

Though he had spoken as if telling a story, she heard

the bitterness beneath the words.

"But they allowed the king and his sons to keep their titles," she said. "And their wealth." She turned to look at him.

His smile was tight, his posture equally so. "There is a blessing in that."

Beyond him, Callie waved a hand before disappearing from Larissa's view. Disappointing, but there was nothing for it. Her own duty called.

"I should go," she said, starting to edge around him.

"Wait," he said, smile turning up. She was certain someone had added more candles to the chandeliers. "May I have your name, to tell the king?"

Something in his look told her it wasn't just the king who might be interested in the answer to that question. A shame a guardsman was in no way the fit consort for the daughter of a duke. She need only state her name, and he would know it too. How sad it would be to see the light of interest fade.

She inclined her head. "Lady Larissa, daughter of the Duke of Wey."

"An honor, your ladyship." His smile didn't waiver, nor did he bow.

Her position didn't trouble him? Well, of course not. As a member of the Imperial Guard, he would be accustomed to dealing with royalty.

Suddenly, his smile winked out, and he grabbed her arm. Really! That was entirely too familiar. She tried to pull away, but he dragged her behind the closest statue, then put a finger to his lips, eyes begging her to be silent.

To her credit, the lovely Lady Larissa did not protest further. She scowled fiercely enough to frighten off the French army, but she nodded agreement to his silent plea. He tipped his head to the corridor, and she squeezed closer to him behind the statue to peer out. Her dark blond hair, crimped in curls around her long face, glittered in the candlelight. Was that the scent of orange blossoms? Leo didn't dare shake his head to clear it. It was hard enough to concentrate knowing what might be at stake. His future. The king's life. No one had believed him when he'd suggested the reception might be a perfect time for their enemies to infiltrate the palace. Perhaps that's why his brother had insisted that he roam the corridors. It had been a way of humoring Leo while keeping him safe. Now he had the satisfaction, and the thrill, of knowing that he must be ready to lay down his life for his liege.

But the fellow strolling toward them didn't look particularly dangerous. He wasn't well built, and his tight-fitting evening tailcoat offered few places to hide a weapon. He might have been one of their guests, stepping away from the line for a breath of air. But, unlike the lady beside Leo, the stranger did not seem disposed to admire the paintings or statuary. With a single glance over his shoulder, he lowered his dark head and strode for the opposite end of the gallery, which gave into the rooms reserved for family.

No one was there at the moment. The king and his court were in the reception hall, and all servants were tending to the festivities. What was this fellow seeking?

The stranger slipped through the glass doors at the end of the corridor and disappeared.

Leo straightened. "I must follow him. Go back to the reception, Lady Larissa. Tell the first Imperial Guardsman you see that his captain requires his attention in the king's rooms. He will summon others."

Her eyes, a potent mixture of dusky green and warm brown, like the fir trees of his beloved country, blinked before she nodded again. "Of course. Please, be careful."

She squeezed out from their hiding space, lifted her blue skirts, and hurried down the corridor.

A grin escaped him. A redoubtable lady. A rarity among the women who generally pursued the prince. Squaring his shoulders, he followed the intruder.

At least this manor house was more easily navigated than some the king had chosen to lease from aristocrats with too many properties to care. The one in Italy the first five years after Batavaria's dissolution had had corridors that twisted and turned as much as their enemy's strategy. The one in the German confederation the last few years had been dark and drafty, with far too many rooms for the guards to protect the king and his sons easily. This house had straight lines, which allowed Leo to catch sight of a black tailcoat disappearing around the corner the moment he entered the private apartments.

Making for the Thames' end of the palace. If the intruder was intent on theft, why not stop along the way and pillage the salon or the crown prince's suite? Was he planning to hide in the king's bedchamber and catch him unawares?

Cold seeped through the black wool uniform he'd been proud to don. He'd been trained to fight since the age of ten, eighteen years ago now. He'd devised strategies to fend off French cavalry and Russian raiders alike. It was only since the kingdom had been taken from them that he'd had to determine how to thwart spies and assassins instead. Some of their enemies, like King William of Württemberg, his ministers, and his favorite spy, Mercutio, feared the king or the crown prince would attempt to retake the monarchy and their ancestral lands.

And they would be right. Leo had been working since the Congress of Vienna to see it done. No stranger would take that from him.

Keeping his back to the wall, he drew his sword and advanced down the corridor. A shame the blade was more ornamental than purposeful. The king insisted on pomp and ceremony for these affairs. Still, it was sharp enough, and he was skilled enough, that he should be able to stop one man.

If he could find the fellow!

He passed the study the king used more as a retreat than a room of business. The lamp was out, and moonlight trickled into the space from the window. No sound, no movement. He edged his way forward, past the smaller dining room, the bedchambers where the off-duty guards slept at night, and the antechamber to the king's suite. A glimmer of light showed under the door leading to His Majesty's bedchamber.

His other hand was on the latch, breath coming fast, when footsteps thundered down the corridor behind him. Stealth had no more use. He threw open the door and barreled through, just as the other members of the Imperial Guard burst into the antechamber.

At the sight of him, they clattered to a stop, brows and swords up in question.

Leo stared at the open glass-paned doors to the terrace overlooking the garden, where curtains blew in the breeze. "Search the grounds. Bring anyone you find to me."

They did not question his right to order them about. The six of them streamed past him into the night. Two would have remained at the doors, and two would be guarding the king.

Ten men against, what? A battalion from Württemberg could be hiding in the shadows. But surely their plunderers would not send so many. With Charles soon to be crowned king of France, the monarchists had the upper hand on the Continent. Their enemies would have to send someone secretly to stop King Frederick from petitioning England's King George to see his lands restored. They might even enlist powers in England to help.

The delightful daughter of a duke, perhaps? She had

been in the right place at the right time to distract him from his duty. Was she even who she claimed?

Perhaps he should learn more about this Lady Larissa, after he explained to the king that danger had indeed crawled closer.

CHAPTER TWO

"WHO ARE YOU looking for?" Callie whispered as she and Larissa waited in yet another line to be introduced to the king and princes. Meredith, Belle, and Tuny were several groups ahead of them, but Lady Lilith, wife to Mr. Villers, had agreed to allow them to join their party after Callie had lagged behind to cover for Larissa's disappearance.

Larissa turned to face forward. "The Imperial Guard. Shouldn't they have returned by now?"

Callie glanced back too, fine pale hair a flash of platinum in the candlelight. "You said there was only one stranger. It shouldn't have taken them all to subdue him. They looked rather formidable."

They had indeed. Though stationed around the vast reception hall, they had been easy to spot. Here too, many of the walls had gilding on them, whether on the frames of paintings, the glowing sconces, the chairs scattered along the silk-draped walls, or the threads of the tapestry draping the high-backed chairs where the king and his crown prince sat, with no sign of the second son. The black uniforms of the Imperial Guard had stood out like shadows in the sun.

She'd only begun talking to the guardsman closest to the reception hall doors when the majority of them had converged and surrounded her. To a man, they'd towered over her, eyes sharp and bodies poised for battle.

Larissa had refused to quail. After all, they couldn't see her legs trembling below her shimmering blue skirts or hear the hammering of her heart beneath the beribboned bodice. A lady appeared serene, always, no matter how much she quaked on the inside.

"Your captain needs you," she'd said, raising an imperious arm to point to the gallery. "Someone is attempting to enter the king's chambers."

One had glanced toward the dais, then tipped his chin, and the others had streamed out.

"Thank you, my lady," the remaining guardsman had said, bowing so deeply she might have been the queen.

Or a princess.

"How can you possibly be cold in here?" Lady Lilith asked now, as if she'd noticed the shiver that had gone through Larissa at the memory. "It's positively sweltering." She waved a painted silk fan in front of her emerald-green gown.

"What one must endure for a moment with His Majesty," her husband agreed, gloved hand brushing at the air. Then he latched it firmly onto his wife's arm. "Shall we, darling?"

Lady Lilith moved forward with a presence few managed. Tall enough to dwarf her dark-haired husband and a good number of the men in the room, she had been called an Amazon. A shame *she* hadn't met the Imperial Guard. She had the exact amount of haughtiness necessary to order them about. Larissa had probably sounded breathless, despite her best intentions. But they hadn't hesitated.

Callie was hesitating now. She glanced from side to side as if trying to determine an easy escape. Larissa threaded her arm through her sister's.

"You are the daughter of an English duke of impeccable lineage," she reminded her. "You have no need to fear meeting anyone."

Callie gave her a grateful smile. "You are always so supportive, Larissa. Thank you."

Larissa gave her arm a squeeze. "What are sisters for?"

Then Lady Lilith and Mr. Villers stepped aside, and it was her and Callie's turn to greet the king and remaining prince.

The Lord Chamberlain on the king's right hand was tall and gaunt, with white hair that showed gaps of pink skin. He had been present when they'd first arrived, accepting their cards from Meredith and comparing them to the list he now held in his gloved hands.

"Lady Larissa and Lady Calantha, daughters of the Duke of Wey," he intoned in a voice as cold as stone.

Her nerves fluttered like the wings of a dove launching from its nest, but she dipped a graceful curtsey, head bowed, as Callie curtsied beside her. As she rose, she smiled to the king. Lines crossed his noble forehead and ringed his deep blue eyes. The sandy hair had turned iron grey, with silver streaking through it like falling stars, and those strong cheeks were partially covered by a grey beard and mustache. Still, his head was just as high, his chest in the crimson coat as broad as in the picture she'd seen in the corridor.

"Ladies," he said, voice booming with the same accent she'd heard in his captain of the guard. "Welcome." He looked to his left.

Larissa turned as well, then had to force herself not to gasp. She knew that tousled sandy hair, those diamond eyes. They looked a shade darker now, as if the candlelight hadn't touched them, and the crimson coat with its gold facings was far brighter than his uniform.

He inclined his head. "Ladies. You are the fair flowers that adorn our court."

Even his voice sounded deeper. An intruder in the palace indeed. Had it all been a game? Surely he had better ways to amuse himself!

Callie nudged her, and she realized the king and his horrid son expected a response.

She might be hideously disappointed and on the verge of calling him a scoundrel, but she was a lady born and raised. And a lady never let a gentleman gain the advantage.

"It is an honor to welcome you to England," Larissa said. "We hope your stay will be enjoyable."

"Very likely it will be," the prince said, already looking bored.

The chamberlain nodded, and Larissa and Callie moved aside to make way for the next couple.

Larissa led her sister to where Meredith and the others stood near a white stone fountain that bubbled in the corner of the opulent room.

"Did you dazzle him with your wit?" Belle asked as Larissa's skirts brushed hers.

Callie cast Larissa a look. "She barely said two words to him."

Belle frowned. "Why? He's a prince."

Larissa glanced to where an elderly earl and his countess were greeting the prince, who managed a nod. "Some princes are more noteworthy than others."

Tuny was frowning as she too looked back at the young man they had waited so long to see. "He didn't seem all that lacking. What didn't you like about him, Larissa?"

She wasn't about to go into the whole story with Meredith watching.

"Perhaps I am merely fatigued," Larissa allowed. "It was a long wait, in stifling heat, for a short introduction."

Belle swished her skirts again. "But a grand reward. When we met the prince, he said he would call on us."

Callie's head came up. "Us? All of us?"

"You, me, Larissa, and Tuny," Belle promised.

Larissa shook her head. "Is there no one who won't bow to your whim?"

Belle beamed. "None. So, you see, you have another chance to attract his attention."

As if she had ever truly wanted one.

Still, Tuny seemed to accept her explanation about fatigue, for she patted her hand as if in understanding. Meredith went so far as to request that the carriage be brought around. Larissa couldn't help glancing down the corridor as they passed through the gallery, but she caught no sign of the Imperial Guardsmen. The two at the door remained stoic. Surely they couldn't have been happy with their prince's performance. Or perhaps they were accustomed to dealing with his mad starts.

She should have known she could hide nothing from Callie, however. Her younger sister might be quiet and nervous in company, but she was bright and clever, and she missed little. Their maid had just finished changing Larissa for bed when her sister padded into her room.

"You did for yourself," Anna scolded her.

Callie turned as pink as her flannel nightgown. "Belle helped."

"Thank you, Anna," Larissa said. "That will be all for tonight."

The young maid bowed her head and slipped from the room with a look to Callie. Larissa's sister came to plop herself down on the poster bed, the color of her nightgown a contrast to the blue and white furnishings Larissa loved.

When they were little, before Jane had come into their lives, Larissa and her two sisters had had separate bedchambers, and no one had even imagined intruding on the others. Thanks to Jane, they knew such times were no intrusion but a chance to share secrets and plot perfection.

"You saw something tonight in the prince," her sister said now. "What?"

"Remember the man I met in the corridor?" Larissa

asked her, tucking her stockinged feet under her nightgown as she sat beside her sister.

Callie nodded. Her pale hair had been let down into her night braid, and her blue eyes looked huge. "A member of the Imperial Guard."

"Did you see his face?" Larissa asked.

Callie shook her head. "He was turned away from me."

Larissa sighed. "It was the prince, though I didn't know it at the time. What is it about these Batavarians that one son thinks to masquerade and the other hides entirely?"

"And the newspaper editors have been sneering all week about the Batavarian tradition to only name the firstborn son a prince," Callie said. "But it's not really all that different than King George's brothers being given the title of duke."

"At least most of them are better behaved these days," Larissa said.

"I've heard the stories," Callie said. "They were scandalous."

"I'm sure Prince Otto would have joined in," Larissa told her. "Tonight, he wore a uniform and sent me running for reinforcements when he claimed to spot something nefarious. I've never been so embarrassed in my life."

Callie frowned. "But when we were introduced to him, he acted as if he had never met you."

"Exactly." Larissa made a face. "What sort of gentleman amuses himself by toying with others? Not one with whom I want any of you to associate."

"Of course not," Callie said. "Still, it's rather odd. No one mentioned him appearing in the reception hall late. Others greeted him before we did. How did he move from the corridor to the throne so quickly?"

Larissa threw up a hand. "Perhaps there's a secret passage between the two areas. All I know is that he lied to me and made me a fool in front of his guards. I won't give him a chance to treat any of you the same way."

"Well," Callie hedged, "he is one of the only unmarried princes close to a reasonable age. And he's rather attractive, if you like that curly-haired look."

She'd liked it well enough. How might it feel to thread her fingers through those curls?

She raised her chin. "Exterior attractiveness is not the same as character."

Callie grinned. "You sound like Mother."

She meant Jane. Callie and Belle were too young to remember the mother who had borne them. They knew nothing of her instruction, her insistence that her daughters were to be ladies of the highest order. Like Larissa, they remembered their late grandmother, the dowager duchess. Her Grace had been a force of nature, and she had had equally high expectations for all of them.

Callie and Belle had been eight and five when Jane had come into their lives, and they'd latched onto her with a hunger Larissa understood. At eleven, she'd been the only one who'd struggled to call Jane her mother. It seemed a betrayal somehow. And Jane was…Jane. Warm, wonderful, and whimsical.

"She's right, you know," Larissa said, reaching out to tuck a loose hair behind Callie's ear. "I could wish for every gentleman who comes calling to excel in character. But your character is unassailable. I wish I could convince you. You have no need to hide."

Callie ducked her head and studied her toes where they peeked out from below the hem of her nightgown. "I know. I truly do. But sometimes, like tonight, don't you feel a little…small?"

No. Her mother and grandmother had taught her that her place lay among the nobility. She only grew frustrated when someone questioned that about her sisters or her. And sending her running on a wild goose chase was perfectly calculated to do just that.

"We are the daughters of a duke," she told Callie. "We deserve such splendor."

Callie's face puckered as she looked up. "But what if we don't want it?"

Larissa cocked her head. "Then what do you want, Callie?"

"A nice library," she said, raising her brows as if in hope. "A cup of chamomile. A pup at my side and a cat on my lap. Good friends like you and Belle and Tuny."

All simple requests, but not what was expected of any of them. "And is there no gentleman in that picture?" Larissa pressed.

Callie sighed. "Not one that fits well."

And there lay the problem. Despite the love Jane had lavished on them; despite Belle's encouragement, Tuny's friendship, and Larissa's support; Callie was on her third Season, with no suitors to speak of. She could not seem to rise to the occasion.

"They whisper about us, you know," Callie said, proving she had followed Larissa's thoughts. "I hear them at balls and such. They call us polished, pretty, and well positioned. Why will no one offer for the Duke of Wey's daughters?" Her head snapped up at last. "And don't you dare say it's Mother's fault."

Larissa grimaced. "It isn't her fault, precisely. Only a few high sticklers refuse to acknowledge her. They can't forget she was our governess first."

"And the widow of a cavalry officer," Callie reminded her. "Any gentleman worth his salt would be honored to have her as a mother-in-law."

"Now, why can't you show that kind of spirit in public?" Larissa teased.

Callie laughed. "Well, it would certainly make life more interesting." Her merriment faded. "Will you really turn the prince away when he calls?"

"*If* he calls," Larissa said. "He lied about one thing. It

follows he will lie about others."

But if he did dare show his face, she fully intended to give him a piece of her mind. Above all else, a lady protected those she loved. A gentleman who lied was not finding his way into her sisters' or Tuny's hearts. And there was no room in hers.

"What were you thinking?" King Frederick demanded as he stormed into the private side of the palace, the prince and the captain following. "Did you think no one would notice?"

Fritz, Captain Frederick Leopold Archambault, wandered to the sofa and sat, stretching long arms across the curved back. "No one *did* notice, Father. They seldom do."

Their father thumped his chest, setting the metals pinned there to bouncing. "I noticed. When I tell these English my son will be beside me, I expect my son beside me."

Fritz raised an eloquent brow.

"You know what I mean," his father thundered. He pointed a thick finger at Leo. "So do you. I thought you outgrew this game when you were children."

Crown Prince Otto Leopold Augustus, still in his uniform, strolled to the cabinet on the wall and poured his father a glass of claret. He had dismissed all the servants except their valets, who were waiting in the suites beyond. The mirror on the cabinet door showed him a face too like his own watching from behind him.

"It was a matter of necessity tonight," he told his father. "I warned you both you might be in danger. Now we have proof."

The king's massive chest deflated, and he sank down on the sofa next to Fritz. "Danger? From whom?"

"That would be the question." Leo brought him the

glass and glanced to his twin brother, who waved a hand to forestall him pouring another.

Their father took a cautious sip. "I saw the guard storm out. What was amiss?"

"A stranger breached the private apartments," Leo supplied, going to sit on the chair opposite them. "But we lost him in the garden."

Fritz stiffened, but Leo shook his head at him. This was no time for his brother to grow overly protective again. For once, Leo had the matter in hand.

"Ah." The king rolled the crystal between his palms. "No harm done then, I suppose."

"Would you have preferred he was waiting when you entered tonight, alone and unarmed?" Leo asked.

"I will station a guardsman in your chamber," Fritz said.

Their father bristled. "I can defend myself. When I cannot, it will be time to talk of abdicating."

"No talk of abdicating," Fritz told him. "You know you would never step down willingly."

The king leveled a finger at him. "And you should have been chasing after intruders instead of pretending to be your brother. You know why we came here."

Fritz's jaw hardened, but he leaned farther back and crossed one leg over the other as if he couldn't care. "So you can spread your largesse to another worthy country?"

"So we can convince King George to support our cause," Leo put in as their father's face turned a vitriolic red that boded no good. "To win back our kingdom."

"And that went so well when we tried it in Italy and the German confederation," Fritz reminded them.

"Italy was self-absorbed and the Germans self-seeking," their father grumbled. "The English king will understand us, once we become better acquainted. His sister may be married to King William of Württemberg, but he has not shown a strong preference for that kingdom. All the more reason not to alienate him by pretense."

Fritz put a hand on his chest and thrust out his lower lip. "Oh, Father, am I not a true son of Batavaria?"

"Not a very good one when you take your brother's place," he said.

"I disagree," Leo said. "Fritz took my place because I insisted on assessing this threat."

"But you accomplished nothing except endangering yourself," the king complained, pausing to take another sip of his wine. At least his color was coming down.

"I will look into the matter further," Fritz promised their father.

Reinserting himself again. The role only grew more rankling with time. How could Leo restore the kingdom if everyone was intent on cossetting him?

"No need," Leo told his brother. "I've already begun investigating. An English family may be involved."

Fritz's foot came down, and the king lowered his glass. "Oh?" their father prompted.

"Did you meet a Lady Larissa, daughter of the Duke of Wey?" Leo asked.

Fritz shrugged. "I met three daughters of the Duke of Wey. Lady Larissa seemed tolerable, if a bit too aware of her position. Lady Abelona, now, she has potential."

By the appreciative light in his brother's eyes, her potential had nothing to do with Leo's investigation.

"And the third?" Leo probed.

Fritz frowned. "Do you know, I can't recall. That doesn't speak particularly well of the girl, does it."

"No matter," their father said. "The Duke of Wey did not attend the Congress of Vienna or any of the others since. I understand they call him the Hermit Duke because he prefers the company of his family and friends at his estate in Surrey. He is unlikely to protest the re-establishment of a kingdom on the Continent."

"We cannot know that," Leo argued. "He could have conspired with others who were involved in one of the

Congresses. Lady Larissa should have been in line with the other young ladies clamoring for a moment with the prince, but I discovered her in the corridor leading to our private apartments, just before the intruder appeared. They could have been planning to meet. I say we look further into the family."

"I agree," Fritz said. "I believe I made some vague promise to call on them. Which means you have a right to go as Prince Otto Leopold. I will accompany you."

Leo straightened his uniform, determination stiffening his fingers. "My attention should be sufficient, but I will go as Captain Archambault. I earned the position, same as you. Besides, until we know more, I have no intention of allowing Lady Larissa to realize a prince is pursuing her."

Fritz narrowed his eyes, as if prepared to argue, but their father spoke first.

"Perhaps a prince should pursue her. Tonight was a good beginning, but these English keep their own council. If we are to gain the attention of their king, we must force our way into Society. I will write to the woman chaperoning the duke's daughters and ask them to be your escorts as you tour London. That will give you entrance to other amusements that might benefit our case. And it will give you both the opportunity to determine what secrets they hide."

CHAPTER THREE

"**Y**OU FOUR MADE quite an impression last night."

Meredith Mayes set down her teacup and glanced at her charges seated around the breakfast table at Weyfarer House on Clarendon Square the morning after the reception. Though she had kept busy over the years with her employment agency and her mission to find places for gentlewomen and gentlemen down on their luck, and her husband Julian's law practice had flourished, they had never been blessed with children. These were as dear to her as if she had birthed them herself. Even Julian had agreed she must move into Weyfarer House to chaperone them while Jane was unavailable. The tickle of a feathered tail against her ankle told her Fortune, her cat, was strolling the ranks just as proudly.

"The prince made an impression too," Belle said. Her look to Larissa was nearly as bold as the color of her apple red walking dress, the cunning tucks along the bodice drawing attention to her figure.

Larissa lifted her teacup with all the poise of a future duchess, the delicate green plaid of her gown at odds with the strong thrust of her chin. "We stood in line for an interminable amount of time to spend a few short moments with the king and His Royal Highness. I doubt we made any kind of impression, and I also doubt that's much of a loss."

Petunia tugged at the red and blue plaid scarf tied around the neck of her white cotton bodice and leaned closer to Meredith. "You might have noticed Larissa took the prince in dislike."

As if she had had something to do with the matter, Callie sank deeper into her seat, the tassels decorating her signature pink gown trembling.

Meredith allowed herself a frown. "And why would that be?"

"No particular reason," Belle put in. "As Larissa said, our time with the prince was entirely too short. We must find another opportunity to become better acquainted."

Meredith glanced from Larissa's calm face to Belle's determined one. "Then it's a good thing the king requested your escort on his sons' tour of London. Underhill brought me the note this morning."

Petunia and Belle sat up taller at the report, but now Callie's tassels weren't the only thing trembling. There was a decided slosh in Larissa's tea.

Interesting.

Jane had no concerns that her girls would find their matches when they were ready, but Meredith could not be so sanguine. Belle was a charmer. She'd taken London by storm, but she hadn't shown the slightest preference for any of the young men who came pouring through the front door. Callie had always been introspective, the Observer, Julian called her. The more Larissa, Belle, and Petunia encouraged her to take part in Society, the less she seemed inclined to try. Petunia viewed the world with a mixture of wonder and skepticism that seemed to keep everyone except close friends at a distance. And Larissa's focus had been on her sisters and Petunia, as if she could find each of them a wonderful husband by sheer force of will.

Perhaps touring London in the company of two presentable young gentlemen would do them all some good.

Larissa's toe tapped under the table, and she felt a thump as Fortune must have pounced on her slipper. So, like the prince, the king expected them to dance to his tune. He would not find her groveling. She had a goal this Season, and wandering about London with an odious prince did not further her cause. A lady knew when it was time to plot strategy.

Meredith generally took Fortune for a walk around the square after breakfast. The grey-coated cat was the only one Larissa had ever seen with a jeweled collar and leash, though Fortune didn't appear to like either much. Still, it was the perfect time to sequester herself, her sisters, and Tuny in the library.

It took only a moment to explain to Belle and their friend what the prince had done last night. Belle was shocked and Tuny indignant.

"What game was he playing?" Tuny demanded. "Someone should have taught him better."

"Agreed," Larissa said. "And I would be only too delighted to instruct him. We cannot allow him to assume that English ladies accept such treatment, simply because his father is a king."

They all nodded.

"What do we know about this prince and his brother?" Tuny asked, brown eyes narrowing. "Besides what was in the gossip rags."

Callie popped to her feet. "Father has a book on the monarchies of the world. Give me a moment, and I'll find it." She bustled to the shelves, pink skirts flapping.

"Are we sure this was a game?" Belle asked, jade eyes turning down as they did when she was disappointed. "Perhaps it's a mistake. Perhaps he didn't have time to introduce himself properly and was embarrassed to admit it."

"He had time," Larissa assured her as Callie hurried back with the book.

Her middle sister's head was buried in the cream-colored pages. "The Royal House of Archambault," she read. "Hereditary rulers of Batavaria. The last entry is for King Frederick Otto Leopold the Fourth. No mention of his sons." She tipped the book to look at the spine. "I wonder how long Father has had this book."

"Perhaps the second son was ill last night," Belle said, as if determined to give the prince the benefit of the doubt. "Perhaps His Royal Highness had to shoulder both responsibilities."

"And change clothes to change roles?" Larissa scoffed. "Doubtful."

"But what if there's a good reason to pretend to be someone he's not?" Belle protested. "What if he's in danger? Perhaps someone else thirsts for the crown and seeks to harm him."

The statement came perilously close to the excuse he'd used last night.

"But if he's in danger, why did he run toward it instead of away?" Larissa asked. "He should have been the one to summon the Imperial Guards, not me."

A cough from the doorway drew all their gazes to Mr. Underhill, the butler Jane had hired years ago after they'd moved their beloved housekeeper, Mrs. Winters, out to Castle Wey. Anyone coming to their home would find him suitably tall and imposing to serve as the head of a duke's household. But Larissa, her sisters, and her brothers had quickly learned that he was willing to unbend for them with a twinkle of his blue eyes. Now he inclined his sable head.

"I beg your pardon, your ladyships, Miss Bateman, but a Captain Archambault is here to see you, and he is not content to wait until Mrs. Mayes returns. What would you like me to do with him?" This time the light in his eyes all but begged them for an excuse to throw the interloper out.

Larissa exchanged looks with her sisters and Tuny.

"Archambault," Callie said, gaze returning to the book. "Their family name."

"The second son?" Tuny guessed.

Larissa squared her shoulders and turned to the butler. "Show him into the withdrawing room, Mr. Underhill. We'll meet him shortly. And please send a footman for Mrs. Mayes. She should be here to see our triumph."

Leo rocked from the toes of his polished black boots to the heels, gaze sweeping the room. The walls were the color of spring grass, with a portrait over the wood-wrapped hearth of a dark-haired woman surrounded by three girls and two boys. Lady Larissa's mother and siblings, perhaps? The camelback sofa and the chairs opposite it were upholstered in fine fabric. The carpet held the same delicate colors unique to France's Aubusson workshops. Similar carpets had graced the palace in Batavaria. It was all very warm and welcoming. Why did he feel as if the enemy waited around the corner?

Then Lady Larissa glided into the room, head high and gaze distant. Today she was dressed in a fetching plaid gown that would likely make her eyes look more green than brown. He had to force himself not to peer closer to confirm that.

Three other ladies accompanied her. From Fritz's description, the petite one in red, with the golden curls, must be Lady Abelona. The taller one with the thick blond hair and narrowed eyes, gowned in a simple dress with a white bodice and blue skirts, did not match his brother's vague memories of the third sister. Her height and militant stance would make her difficult to forget. So the third daughter of the Duke of Wey must be the one with the paler hair and pink skirts, who came in last.

They fanned out along the wall beside the door, as if determined to keep him from escaping. He wasn't sure what he'd done to earn their wrath, but he could tell succeeding in his mission today was going to take every ounce of diplomacy he possessed.

He inclined his head. "Ladies. Thank you for seeing me."

"I am surprised you'd dared to be seen," Lady Larissa said, making no move to take a seat. "After all, you did all you could to hide from me last night."

No one had ever spoken to him that way before. He wasn't sure whether to be annoyed or intrigued. He settled for a simple question. "Hide?"

"You lied about your identity," she accused. "You're not Captain Archambault. I saw you on the throne beside your father's. You're Prince Otto."

He should have realized she'd wonder about the resemblance. Only his father, mother, and a few trusted friends could tell him and Fritz apart easily. He wasn't sure why he was disappointed she wasn't one of them.

He spread his hands. "I am His Majesty's second son, Frederick Leopold, Leo to my family. I bear some resemblance to the crown prince."

"Some!" she sputtered.

"He's right."

She blinked, then turned to look at the middle sister Fritz had so easily dismissed. Intelligence sat in the light blue eyes that regarded him.

"That's not the prince we met last night," she said. "This is a different man."

Lady Larissa frowned, but some of the stiffness left her frame, as if she could not bring herself to argue with her sister.

The lady with the militant stance stepped forward. Her

eyes were a warm brown, and they crinkled around the edges as if she'd found the last exchange amusing.

"Allow me to make the introductions," she said in a voice that sounded just the slightest less polished than Lady Larissa's or her sisters'. "You met Lady Larissa last night. Lady Calantha, Lady Abelona, this is Captain Archambault. And I am Miss Bateman, their good friend."

The other two dipped curtsies, and Leo bowed. He'd hadn't used the correct response last night, he realized. A prince might not bow to the daughter of a duke, but a captain of the guard should.

"Ladies, a pleasure," he said as he straightened.

Lady Larissa seemed to have recovered her poise. She motioned gracefully to a chair. "Won't you join us?"

He waited until they were seated—her two younger sisters and Miss Bateman on the sofa and Lady Larissa on a chair—before taking the chair she'd indicated.

"Did you discover who was sneaking into the king's room?" Lady Abelona asked.

Surprised, he glanced to Lady Larissa, who smiled apologetically.

"I told them everything about our meeting last night, Captain," she confessed.

At least she was willing to believe he was a captain. The thought that he was purposely misleading her made the chair feel harder, but he forced himself to answer her. "I see. I am sad to report that our unknown visitor escaped into the garden, and we were unable to find him. There have been threats against the king, so of course we must take every precaution."

They all expressed outrage that anyone would seek to harm a king.

"You must tell King George," Lady Abelona insisted, little chin up. "He can lend you a detachment of the Home Guard."

The last thing he wanted was to make their king think

his family too weak to defend themselves. They'd hardly look like the sort to re-establish a monarchy. And he still wasn't sure how these ladies or their father figured into the stranger's presence last night.

"We would not dream of inconveniencing His Majesty, King George," he assured them. "It is a matter best dealt with ourselves."

Lady Larissa's face tightened, and she seemed to sit a little taller on her chair.

"You disagree with me, Lady Larissa?" he guessed.

"I would never be so presumptive," she assured him. "But when someone we love might be in danger, we must do all we can to protect them."

His brother certainly subscribed to that belief. Leo was still surprised he'd been able to convince Fritz to remain at the palace and not send a pair of guards with him.

"Well said," he told her. "Perhaps you'd care to put action to the sentiment."

She regarded him as if he'd spilled tea all over her lovely carpet. Oh, right. A mere captain shouldn't challenge the daughter of a duke. How did Fritz navigate such matters?

Her youngest sister leaped to his aid.

"Why, certainly we would want to ensure King Otto's safety," Lady Abelona said with a flutter of her lashes.

Lady Larissa inclined her head as regally as a queen. "Although we must refuse his kind invitation to accompany you about London. It is the Season, after all. We have obligations."

Someone squeaked as if in protest. He glanced to the sofa. Miss Bateman was regarding Lady Calantha, who appeared to be staring at the carpet as if she found the flowered pattern more fascinating than the conversation. And Lady Abelona was looking at her oldest sister, green eyes surprisingly hard.

She must have caught Leo's gaze on her, for her smile turned up sweetly. "What my sister means is that we'll have to consult our schedule before we can determine a day and time to accompany His Highness and you."

Lady Larissa's smile was far less sweet. "You must excuse my sister, Captain. She is on her first Season and doesn't realize the number of expectations she must meet."

"Does the prince have somewhere he'd particularly like to see?" Lady Abelona asked Leo as if her sister hadn't spoken.

"I'm sure we could find someone who is more familiar with it than we are," Lady Larissa said.

He remembered moments at the negotiating table, when Batavaria had been caught between the desires of France and the German states, that had been less fraught.

"I will be sure to ask His Highness," he hedged. "In the meantime, allow me to suggest another sort of help that should not interfere with your obligations. With your standing in Society, you must see things, hear things. Is it possible some have taken us in dislike?"

If her father was involved, surely Lady Larissa would dissemble, but, for some reason, they all looked to her middle sister.

Lady Calantha visibly swallowed before meeting his gaze. "All I've heard is sympathy that your kingdom was taken from you."

Lady Abelona nodded. "English gentlemen are chivalrous and high-minded that way."

Lady Larissa coughed. It sounded suspiciously like a snort, but surely she was too much of a lady to utter such a sound. "We may have one or two who wouldn't mind meddling where they shouldn't, if it profited them in some way."

"Beau Villers," Lady Calantha suggested.

Leo stiffened. "Villers? He was on the guest list last night."

"He was," Lady Larissa admitted. "We saw him there. He is the husband of Lady Lilith, sister to the Earl of

Carrolton, and Mr. Villers' sister is married to Viscount Worthington. But he wasn't the man you and I saw in the corridor. And I doubt he would go so far as to hire anyone."

"He doesn't much like spending his wife's money," Miss Bateman explained. "Unless it's for his own pleasures."

"What of his relatives, then?" Leo asked. "Carrolton, Worthington."

"More devoted lords you will never find."

The loyal statement came from a dark-haired woman, who stood in the doorway. Leo rose as propriety demanded as she swept into the room. She was of the previous generation, with an elegant demeanor and, he saw as she came past him, eyes the color of lavender. Just as striking was the grey-haired cat that stalked beside her, a band of white fur encircling her neck like a cravat. She stopped to regard him with copper-colored eyes, as if she could see inside him to his darkest secrets.

Lady Larissa nodded. "Mrs. Mayes, our chaperone, and Fortune, allow me to present Captain Archambault of the Batavarian Imperial Guard. He is the brother of Prince Otto."

He could understand introducing him to her chaperone, but she seemed to be including the cat as well. Mrs. Mayes had no issue with the matter, for she inclined her head. "Captain."

"Mrs. Mayes," he said, offering her a bow, then belatedly added, "Fortune."

"Why would you impugn the honor of our dear friends?" the chaperone challenged as she went to take a chair near the sofa. The cat circled around to stand beside Lady Larissa, whose fingers stole down to stroke the fur.

"I meant no disrespect," Leo said, wondering if he should wait for the cat to sit as well. "It is my duty to protect the king, and therefore to question everything and everyone."

The answer did not seem to satisfy her by the way she pressed her lips together, but she did not argue further, and Fortune sank onto her haunches next to Lady Larissa, so he allowed himself to return to his seat.

"Captain Archambault believes someone is out to harm the king," Lady Larissa explained. "He has asked for our help in identifying anyone who might have taken His Majesty in dislike."

"We would do anything to support the prince," Lady Abelona put in brightly.

Leo nearly sagged. Not another one. It seemed a truth universally acknowledged that any unmarried lady longed to become a princess. Was it too much to ask that he be admired for what he'd accomplished, the man he had become, rather than his title?

But he must remember at the moment he was pretending he had no title. He nodded to the lady. "Thank you."

"You are very welcome, Captain," Lady Abelona said. "Perhaps you and His Highness could meet us in Hyde Park, at the southeastern end of the Serpentine, tomorrow to learn what we gather. Say three?"

Once more Lady Larissa's face tightened, but she didn't offer an alternative.

"Perfect," Leo said.

Mrs. Mayes adjusted her skirts, which were the same shade of lavender as her eyes. "There is one more matter." She looked to her cat. "Fortune?"

Lady Larissa, her sisters, and Miss Bateman stilled, their gazes fastened on the cat. Why? Surely the animal wasn't dangerous. Their chaperone would hardly allow her in good company if she tended to claw or bite. But he had never felt more like running, not even when faced with the prospect of arguing with his king, as when the feline rose to her feet and padded toward him.

He could not take his eyes away from the pools of copper that regarded him. Fortune had her head down and gaze focused, studying him as if he were a mouse that had crept into her domain. He would not have been surprised had she pounced on him.

Instead, she straightened and began winding her way around his boots, purr audible.

"Well," Mrs. Mayes said with a pleased smile. "Feel free to call any time, Captain. And we would be delighted to show you more of London."

Lady Abelona and Lady Calantha beamed. Miss Bateman shot him a smile. He glanced at Lady Larissa.

Her color had fled, and she was staring at the cat as if she had lost her last friend.

CHAPTER FOUR

"FORTUNE LIKED HIM," Belle said proudly after Captain Archambault had taken his leave.

Larissa still couldn't credit it. He might have spun a tale of casual similarities between him and the prince, and he was certainly making an attempt to safeguard his family, but he had a tendency to order action and expect capitulation. How could Fortune give him her approval?

The cat's ability to know a person's nature was legendary in their family. It had been her acceptance of their father that had convinced Meredith to install Jane as their governess. The cat had matched Tuny's brother with his wife and oldest sister with her husband, too. To Larissa's knowledge, Fortune had never been wrong, but the darling was older than she appeared. Had her perceptions dimmed?

As if Fortune knew Larissa had doubts, she prowled over to her and leaped up into her lap to knead Larissa's skirts with her paws before settling for a nice nap. Larissa ran her hand down the silky fur.

"What did you see that I missed?" she whispered as her sisters and Tuny debated their next steps.

Fortune closed her eyes and purred, the rumble vibrating against Larissa's thigh.

"Larissa?" Callie ventured. "What do you think?"

Larissa blinked and glanced up to find all gazes on her. She put on her polished smile. "We have calls to pay today, but I see no reason why we cannot ask questions that would aid Captain Archambault as we do so."

The list of possible acquaintances who might know something of use to the captain took up an entire page. They decided to divide and conquer. Larissa had been out long enough that it would not be shocking for her to accompany her youngest sister on morning calls. Meredith accompanied Callie, and Tuny had a footman escort her to her brother's home near Covent Garden to enlist the help of her sister-in-law, Charlotte, who was the daughter of a viscount and welcome in certain circles. They would all meet back at Weyfarer House later to compare notes.

"We should be able to pay at least four calls," Larissa said, plaid skirts swinging as she and Belle headed down Clarendon Square. Theirs had been one of the first establishments built at one end of the fashionable area fifteen years ago. The house hadn't had a name, then. Belle had christened it Weyfarer House, a play on their family name and the manner in which they moved between the castle in Surrey and the house in London. Now a row of white-fronted townhouses with wrought-iron rails edged the pavement along both sides of the park in the center.

Belle adjusted the long-sided, lace-trimmed cap she wore under her wide-brimmed hat. "Can we at least avoid Mrs. Netherbough? She sneered at the roses on my ballgown the other night."

Larissa reached over and gave Belle's hand a squeeze. "She came out with Callie and me. She is insufferable about the fact that she married before we did. But she is well connected, and our father was a good friend to her late father."

Belle brightened. "If we're going to visit Father's friends, we should stop and see what Lord and Lady Worthington are up to."

"They're down in Cornwall to learn more about a miniature steam engine to power balloon flight," Larissa said. "Charlotte confided in Tuny."

Belle sighed.

Larissa could not be so concerned. She generally enjoyed the tradition of morning calls, paid early in the afternoon. Chatting with acquaintances, seeing what other ladies were doing for fashion and decoration, learning who was interested in whom—it was rather satisfying, and it gave her insights into how she might better present her sisters and Tuny. And now she had another reason for visiting: to see what she might learn for Captain Archambault.

She was not surprised that the visit of the Batavarian court was on everyone's tongue. Many of the people on whom they called had been at the reception last night, and those who had not been so fortunate were eager to share what they'd heard from others and quiz Larissa and Belle on their impressions.

"I heard Prince Otto was utterly charming," Lady Ellen warbled, fingers clutching the arms of the Oriental chair at the second call they paid.

"And handsome," her younger sister put in. "What did you think, Lady Larissa?"

"I found him tolerable," Larissa said. "A shame we know so little about his family."

"Tiny country," Lady Ellen's mother said with a sniff. "Not really more than a valley high in the mountains. And even that belongs to Württemberg now. I'm not entirely sure what he's prince of." She tittered, and her daughters joined in.

Belle bristled, but Larissa merely smiled. "Good breeding and proper behavior transcend borders." She was enough her mother's daughter that her sarcasm went over the top of their fussily curled hair.

It was worse at the Countess of Wellmanton's home. Her two daughters were both out now, and they soon had their heads together with Belle.

"So kind of you to chaperone your sister," the fastidious Lady Wellmanton said, as if Larissa could have no other role now that she approached spinsterhood. "But you were kind to look out for Lady Calantha as well. I wish my girls had an older sister to help. The social whirl is so tiring when they are so popular."

Larissa smiled. "Ah, but who could ask for a more devoted mother? Were you not at the reception last night? I thought I saw Lord Wellmanton and your son."

She wrinkled her nose. "They went at the request of the secretary to the Württemberg Envoy. Lord Wellmanton has always supported diplomatic relations."

Larissa was about to ask for clarification when Belle's voice grew louder. "I tell you, you needn't set your cap at Prince Otto. He isn't at all pleasant."

"Well, at least he isn't simply a captain like his brother," one of the sisters retorted.

"I don't know," the other said. "Belle said the brother was very handsome. He might not be a prince, but he moves in the same circles."

Larissa's fingers twitched in her lap, as if she would grab Captain Archambault and wrest him from their control. How ridiculous! Despite Fortune's endorsement, she hadn't even decided she liked the fellow.

"I thought you were on Prince Otto's side," she told her sister after she had pried a few more details from their hostess and they had taken their leave.

"I am," Belle said, chin up and gaze bright. "But I'm even more on your side. If anyone is marrying a prince, it will be my sister."

"I'd far rather see you and Callie marry a prince," Larissa told her with a smile. "And Tuny too."

Belle sighed. "There simply aren't enough princes to go around."

Larissa laughed. "In that case, perhaps we can agree to

forego touring with this one."

Belle's chin jutted out. "No. This is an opportunity. Everyone will be watching him, and we'll attract notice too."

She hadn't thought of that. The prince was already the talk of the *ton*. Having him beside them might be just the thing to bring Callie to others' attention.

"Very clever," she told her sister, and Belle preened.

As her sister had predicted, their greatest challenge lay in their last visit. Caroline Netherbough's tastefully decorated withdrawing room was crowded when they entered, every satin-striped chair taken. But the ladies rose and excused themselves at the sight of Larissa and Belle. Larissa wasn't sure whether they didn't wish to monopolize their hostess or were glad to make their escape. In any event, she and Belle soon found themselves ensconced on the flowered sofa, with Caroline on a curved-back armchair across from them.

She had always been lovely, with the sleek blond hair, guileless blue eyes, and willowy figure some gentlemen favored. Her family was well respected, if not particularly wealthy, but she had managed to marry a man of some standing. Her lustring gown, bedecked with ribbons and silk flowers, proclaimed her new status.

"Dear Lady Larissa," she crooned. "It's been an age. And darling Lady Abelona. Are you enjoying your Season?"

"Yes, a great deal," Belle said. "It's so exciting to meet new people and see new things."

Caroline's smile slid over them like butter on a warm scone. "Yes, I'm sure it seems so to you. Your sister and I have been around long enough to know the importance of permanence."

A lady did not sink to the level of her adversary. Her return must be subtle, the whisper of a saber. "I didn't see you at the Batavarian reception last night."

Caroline brushed down the sleeve of her fine gown.

"Horace had to stay late in the city, but it seems I didn't miss much by not attending. I understand the reception was dreadfully dull."

"Likely it would have seemed so to you," Larissa said. "All that tedious waiting for one's turn to see the prince."

She waved a hand. "I have in mind to invite him to my own ball. A shame Horace says their visit will come to naught. Too many are aligned against them."

Larissa met Belle's gaze before raising her brows at their hostess. "Why, whoever would align themselves against the Batavarian court?"

"People who have business dealings with Württemberg," Caroline informed them archly, as if she knew all about the matter. "Not that Horace is in trade, mind you. He occasionally deals with those who dabble. And some of them have the ear of our king."

"Oh?" Belle asked sweetly. "Who would that be?"

Caroline's gaze danced away from them. "I'm sure I'm not at liberty to say. Now, what do you plan to wear to Lady Carrolton's soiree next week? Of course you're going."

Of course they were. Lady Carrolton was another of Meredith's former clients, and her husband, the earl, had gone to school with their father. The Countess of Carrolton was unlikely to snub them by leaving them out of one of her famous soirees.

So, Larissa allowed the conversation to wander into commonplaces. By the time they left, Belle looked mutinous.

"Why didn't you question her?" she demanded as they started back toward Clarendon Square. "She obviously knew something."

"She knew next to nothing," Larissa assured her. "She had bits and pieces picked up from overhearing her husband's conversation with other gentlemen. If she'd been able to name names, we would never have heard the end of it. However, what she said is of interest. And you can be sure I will mention the matter to Captain Archambault when we see him in Hyde Park."

Belle wiggled her shoulders. "Then we will give the prince a tour?"

"Yes," Larissa said with a smile, "if he's available on such short notice."

It was all perfectly logical, no more than her duty, really. What she couldn't understand was why she could hardly wait.

The king had meetings with the members of the English Privy Council later that afternoon. Leo put on the scarlet and gold and joined him, with Fritz in uniform against the rear wall. The older lords made a number of conciliatory noises, but in the end none committed to presenting the Batavarian cause to King George, who, as yet, had not granted Leo's father an audience.

"Making us wait," Fritz complained when the three of them regrouped in the private salon.

"A king's prerogative," their father insisted.

A prerogative designed to put the waiting party at a disadvantage. Leo could only wonder the reason in this case.

"At least I had some luck with Lady Larissa and her sisters," he said. "It begins to look as if they have no connection with our intruder, but they may be able to give us insights into our true adversaries. We are meeting them in Hyde Park tomorrow at three."

Fritz raised his brows. "We?"

"The captain and the crown prince," Leo clarified.

Fritz shook his head. "Too many crowds. I prefer to keep the advantage. The fewer who see the two of us together, the more likely we can continue to change places as needed."

"Very well," Leo said, trying not to sound too eager. "Just play my part at the ball Friday night. I want to keep an eye on the apartments."

Fritz sighed. "I really despise being put on display."

"Since when?" Leo quipped.

"You will both come," the king commanded. "We have only invited those needed to support us, the most powerful men and women in London. We must show a united front."

"Even at the expense of protecting you?" Leo asked.

His father thumped his chest. "We are the Royal household of Batavaria. I need no coddling. And as for this English king, he should be the one suing for an audience with us!" He dropped his hand and stomped from the room.

Fritz tipped his chin to beckon Leo closer. "I interviewed Lawrence, Matterone, and the rest of the staff while you were out. None of them saw anything out of the ordinary last night."

He should have thought of that. The Lord Chamberlain, Lawrence, and their Steward of the Treasury, Matterone, had come with them from Batavaria, as had most of their staff, leaving friends and family behind. They would understand what was at stake to find an intruder in the palace. Since arriving in England, they'd added kitchen staff, a bevy of chambermaids who came in daily to their otherwise all-male household, a coachman, stable hands, and a few gardeners. According to Lawrence, who managed the staff, all had come highly recommended.

"Thank you," Leo said.

"I also changed stations and shifts among the guard to confound anyone who might have been studying our movements," his brother reported. "We will continue to be vigilant."

Leo nodded. What else could he do? It had been ever thus since they had been boys. He was supposed to focus

NEVER PURSUE A PRINCE   51

on strategy and vision. Fritz was supposed to keep him safe. The roles were becoming far less satisfactory than they had once been. At times, his title felt like a tight-fitting coat, hampering his movements. He could only hope Lady Larissa, her sisters, and Miss Bateman had had better luck in discovering some clue to the unseen enemy he and his family faced.

It must have been that hope that made his spirits lift the moment he sighted them. He and the rest of the king's household had attended services at the church nearest the palace before he'd ventured into the city. He had driven by Hyde Park several times since arriving in London, but he still found the place fascinating. Batavaria consisted of a long river valley surrounded by mountains, with only two cities of any size, located at either end. What need had they for a park when the wonders of nature were all around? Here, Hyde Park was a welcome swath of green among the stone and brick buildings.

Though, at this time of day, it was immensely crowded, as Fritz had predicted. Good thing Miss Bateman was difficult to miss. Her height was accentuated by the plumed black hat she wore above the royal blue walking dress. Beside her, Mrs. Mayes was once again in lavender, and he wasn't sure whether to be pleased or disappointed she had not brought her cat with her.

Lady Abelona was all in white, and her gown had so many pleats, tucks, and lace it was a wonder she moved so well. Her broad-brimmed white hat was trimmed in sky-blue ribbon. Lady Calantha wore green, from her flowered hat to her swaying skirts, as if she was trying to blend in with the bushes.

Even among so fine a set of females, Lady Larissa was notable. Head high in her silk-lined bonnet that matched the bluish-grey of her gown, steps graceful and confident, she moved toward him along the well-worn path as if crossing a marble-tiled hall.

Leo bowed as they approached. "Mrs. Mayes, ladies."

"Captain Archambault," their chaperone allowed. "Always a pleasure."

Lady Abelona leaned to one side as if looking beyond him. "Where is His Royal Highness?"

"Detained, alas," Leo said. "Matters of state." Which wasn't far from the truth, as his brother was drilling with the Imperial Guard. They all needed to be ready.

"A shame," Mrs. Mayes said as Lady Abelona pouted. "But I believe Lady Larissa would like to report our findings. If you'd join us?"

He fell into step beside Lady Larissa as the others continued forward, Lady Abelona and Mrs. Mayes in front, and Lady Calantha and Miss Bateman behind.

"Any progress?" she murmured as her sister and chaperone nodded to this acquaintance and that.

"No," he admitted. "You?"

She kept her gaze on the way ahead, as if she could see into the future. "I have it on good authority that a group of financiers are determined to keep King Frederick from approaching our king."

He stopped on the path, and Lady Calantha bumped into them.

"Forgive me," he told her as she detoured around him, face pinking under the shadow of her hat.

She hurried to catch up with her sister and Mrs. Mayes. Miss Bateman paused to eye him, but she made no move to leave him alone with Lady Larissa.

"Please, Captain," Lady Larissa said. "Do not make a scene. You cannot know who's watching."

How did she know about the spies that studied their every move? He began walking, and she and Miss Bateman joined him.

"Your reputation should be fine," Miss Bateman assured her. "Mrs. Mayes is just ahead. And half the time the *ton* thinks I'm your maid anyway."

Oh, *that's* who she feared. The gossips. Those who adored to find the least fault and magnify it. He'd lived under such pressure his entire life. Troubling to think she had the same problem.

"Forgive me," he repeated. "I would not see you harmed for the world."

She shot him a relieved smile. "Thank you. To answer your question, I have only one name: Lord Wellmanton. He is somewhat connected with the Envoy to England from Württemberg." She looked to her friend.

"But I have additional information," Miss Bateman said. "My brother invests in the Exchange. He talks to all kinds of people about what companies will do well and which will fail. Seems there's a good deal of talk about the silver mines in Württemberg."

Leo tensed, but he made himself keep walking this time. "Württemberg has in the past pressured us to expand the mines, but we refused anything that might pose a danger to our people or our land."

"Which may be why some would prefer the king not to regain control," Lady Larissa put in.

It made sense. But enough to send someone after his father? Why? Their enemies were already succeeding in keeping him from seeing King George while they poisoned the British monarch's mind against him.

Lady Larissa and her friend were both watching him avidly, waiting for his response to their revelations. Leo clapped his fist to his chest in salute. "Well done, ladies. You have been most helpful."

Lady Larissa nodded with a pleased smile.

Her friend went one further. "And you'll be sure to tell Prince Otto?"

"Everything I know the prince knows," he assured her.

"Good," she said. "He'll want to thank Lady Larissa especially."

"Petunia," Lady Larissa warned, eyes flashing.

She seemed the only one among them with no interest in pursuing the prince. The thought was oddly both encouraging and disappointing.

"Your friend is correct," he told her. "The prince will certainly want to thank you personally."

"He can do that when you join us tomorrow," Miss Bateman said, "for a tour of the Tower of London."

One of the passengers on the ship that had carried them to England had pointed out the fortress on the banks of the Thames as they came upriver. Leo was quite accustomed to having to tour installations with his father, issuing platitudes about ingenuity and might. But to tour it with Lady Larissa, or a set of young ladies with no Imperial Guards hovering about, no diplomats to impress and please? Now, that might actually be enjoyable.

"We will look forward to it," he promised them both.

CHAPTER FIVE

"THE TOWER OF London?" Larissa asked after she and her friend had bid farewell to the captain. She tried not to be obvious in watching him move through the crowds, but it was difficult not to admire that confident stride.

"Everyone goes there, don't they?" Tuny answered. "And, if you're done gawking, we should tell the others."

"I'm sure I never gawk," Larissa said, chin coming up, but her traitor gaze would linger to the south, as if hoping for one last glimpse of him.

Meredith smiled as they rejoined her and Callie. They had stopped farther along the Serpentine, where several gentlemen had surrounded Belle and were laughing at her quips.

"She makes all this seem simple," Callie said wistfully from a short distance away.

"Your sister has an enviable presence," Meredith agreed. "But you have a quiet strength others find appealing." As Callie blinked as if surprised by the praise, their chaperone turned to Larissa. "And was Captain Archambault sufficiently pleased with your news?"

"He seemed glad to know the truth, for all it wasn't what he hoped," Larissa said, gaze on her youngest sister. One of the men was standing entirely too close to Belle. Perhaps she should interrupt that discussion.

Tuny must have seen the problem too, for she stepped

forward. "I'll fetch her. She needs to hear what we have planned." She crossed to Belle. One whisper in her ear, and Belle was waving away her admirers to return to their sides.

"So we're going to take Prince Otto and the captain to the Tower to see the animals," she said.

Callie rounded on her. "We most certainly are not. They live in tiny cages and must submit to the unkind attentions of anyone who visits. The price of admittance can be a pet to be fed to the lions! Not the most auspicious way to welcome King Frederick and his sons to England."

Belle looked abashed. "You're right. Sorry." She brightened. "But there's always the Jewel Office."

"And several armories gentlemen generally find fascinating," Meredith put in, turning away from the water.

Larissa had to own the Tower was a fine suggestion. It was a popular destination in London, so they were bound to be seen with the prince and the captain, and she'd always appreciated the history of the place. Now, she just had to convince Callie to come along.

She positioned herself next to her middle sister as they started toward the gate closest to Clarendon Square. "I'm quite willing to forego the menagerie if you'll accompany me to see the other attractions," Larissa bargained.

Callie shook her head. "I should prepare for the next meeting of the Society. We have been debating which atrocity to protest first, bear-baiting or the use of ponies in mines. I want to make a case for the ponies."

"I can prepare some notes for you," Tuny offered with a look to Larissa. "Belle can stay and help. You go and have fun."

Callie smiled, but she didn't make any promises.

"Wear your gown with the tassels," Larissa encouraged. "You know you love it. I'm sure the prince will find it delightful."

"But will I find the prince delightful?" Callie countered. Larissa wasn't sure either. Belle had claimed the prince could be charming, but Larissa had seen little sign of it. She wasn't sure what to expect when he and the captain arrived at Weyfarer House the next day. Seeing the two of them side by side only reinforced the differences Callie had noticed. Prince Otto was an inch or two shorter and an inch or two broader about the shoulders, or perhaps it was the cut of his coat. He and the captain were both dressed in clothing of a British gentleman today—navy coats and fawn trousers—but His Royal Highness had a waistcoat shot with gold and his fitted coat boasted gold buttons impressed with the royal seal Callie had found in the book on monarchies. The captain's simpler silk-striped creamy white waistcoat was far more subtle and elegant, to her mind.

"Your Highness," Meredith said with a curtsey as she and Larissa met them in the withdrawing room, Fortune having been placed in the library with Tuny to keep her from attempting to escape out the door as it opened and closed. "We are honored to have you join us today. And Captain Archambault, you are always welcome. I believe we are only waiting for Lady Calantha."

She glanced to the doorway. As if on cue at the Theatre Royal, Belle traipsed into the room. Like Larissa, she had donned her green plaid gown, but while Larissa's had rows of green fringe along the hem and across the bodice, Belle's featured a triple row of lace at the hem and all over the puffed tops of her long sleeves. She was just tying on a white straw hat covered in ostrich plumes, the jaunty white satin bow sitting to one side of her chin.

"Your Highness," she said, curtseying. "Captain. Welcome."

Larissa returned her gaze to the doorway and wasn't surprised to find her foot tapping under her skirts. But no one else followed Belle into the room.

"I was under the impression your sister would be joining us," Meredith said.

Belle smiled prettily. "She was unavailable. I'm afraid you'll have to make do with me."

"I am certain that will be no imposition," Prince Otto said, offering her his arm.

Larissa gritted her teeth but kept her smile in place. Callie may have won this battle, but Larissa wasn't about to admit defeat in the war to see her sister happily settled.

"May I?" the captain asked, holding out his arm.

Larissa took it gladly. "Of course. Thank you, Captain."

He offered his other arm to Meredith, and the three of them followed Belle and the prince out of the house.

The captain and the prince had come in the royal carriage, which was a large, low-slung affair with sides lacquered in green and shiny brass appointments, pulled by four matched chestnut horses. A footman in livery handed her in after Belle and Meredith. She thought to sit beside them on the tan leather seats, but her littlest sister stuck out her toes and wiggled, forcing Larissa to a spot across from her, next to Prince Otto.

Of course.

At least the captain sat on her other side. His smile made the squeeze worthwhile.

"Will your coachman know the way?" Meredith asked as the vehicle turned out of Clarendon Square and the captain's body brushed Larissa. Did a lady enjoy the sensation of strength beside her? A shame neither her mother nor grandmother had thought to cover that protocol.

"We hired a local fellow when we arrived," Prince Otto answered. "You might say he came with the carriage. He appears sufficiently versed in the ways of your city."

As if to prove as much, a shout sounded from outside. "Get out of the way, cabbage brain! Where'd you learn to drive?"

Belle bit her lip as if to keep from laughing, but her eyes danced with merriment.

"It can be challenging moving coaches and horses across countries," the captain said as if to excuse the fellow. "Some of our staff have been with us for years. Others come and go as we change locations."

"It can make security more difficult," the prince said with a look out the window as if assessing his surroundings. She was reminded of the stranger they'd encountered at the reception. Funny that it had been the prince and not the captain who had first mentioned security today.

"Well, security is no challenge where we are going," Belle said. "The Tower of London has stood for centuries, protecting people and priceless objects alike." She beamed at the prince. "I thought you might like to see the Royal Menagerie, Your Highness, though my sister, Callie, advises against it."

Larissa thought he might protest, but, to her surprise, a shudder went through him. "I agree with her. I cannot abide seeing anything in a cage."

"Which is why we will be touring the Horse Armory and the Jewel Office today," Meredith put in smoothly.

The prince cocked a smile. "You British armor your horses? I must tell the king. He has fallen behind times."

The captain looked around Larissa at his brother. "What His Highness means is that we have had little call for cavalry in Batavaria. The mountains do not allow it."

The prince snorted. "*Tradition* will not allow it. I suggested it often enough."

"We would be wiser to invest in things all of our citizens could enjoy," his brother countered. "Churches, schools, festivals."

"Those will surely keep us safe," the prince muttered, gaze going out the window again.

A lady should not interfere in an argument between

two gentlemen but steer the conversation into more congenial subjects. But she could not help taking Captain Archambault's side.

"Surely safety cannot be the sole purpose of life," she put in. "Protection and security have their place, but so does the provision of knowledge and the appreciation of beauty."

"I can understand why you might think so," the prince said. "But I suspect you have never had to fight to protect yourself." He looked to his brother. "Explain to Lady Larissa how hard you have had to work to see the king and his crown prince safe, *Captain*."

Captain Archambault's firm cheeks were reddening. "It is my duty. I never considered it a burden."

"No," the prince allowed. "You wouldn't." He turned to her sister, who was watching him with wide eyes. "I wager your favorite sight in the Tower is this Jewel Office, Lady Abelona. What will we see there?"

Belle rallied and chattered on about the English Crown Jewels, but Larissa felt the tension in the captain and could only wonder at it.

What was wrong with his brother? Leo couldn't recall the last time Fritz had argued with him that way. They each had a role in keeping them all safe while they worked to see their lands returned. True, Leo's role was more often to battle with words on the field of diplomacy, while Fritz excelled on a more physical plane. But diplomatic matches could have the same deadly consequences as a battle if not dealt with skillfully.

Look at the issue of this Lord Wellmanton Lady Larissa had mentioned in the park yesterday. He had spoken with the king about the fellow, who had been at the reception.

"Portly and portentous," his father had proclaimed. "I saw nothing that would concern me. He even offered to escort us on a tour of their Royal Gardens." The offer might have been well meant, or it might have been the opening move in a chess match that would pit kingdom against kingdom. Leo would have to be watchful there.

At least his brother allowed Lady Abelona to carry the conversation now until the carriage came to a stop and the footman handed them down in front of the Tower of London. The impressive stone edifice crouched beside the dark waters of the Thames, the massive center block surrounded by shorter towers, other buildings, and both an outer and inner stone wall. The British certainly knew how to protect their rulers! Fritz too looked appropriately impressed.

A guard wearing a stout black hat and a navy coat with scarlet trim took them on the tour after Mrs. Mayes had paid for their admittance.

"They are Yeoman Warders," Lady Abelona explained to Fritz as if she had seen him sizing up the fellow. "Part of His Majesty's personal guard."

"Seems a poor use of a perfectly good guard," Fritz said, offering her his arm.

Leo's face felt hot again. "Not at all. Who could get into trouble when properly escorted?"

"Who indeed?" Fritz drawled.

Walking on his arm, Lady Larissa inhaled the air, as if she enjoyed the faint scent of brine from the Thames. Many of the other visitors they passed glanced at his brother and whispered behind their hands, but more gazed at her, nodding as if impressed. Who wouldn't be? That elegant glide, the tilt of her chin under her wide-brimmed straw hat, the interest that sparked on her pretty face. Her sister might be all bubble and boast, but Lady Larissa was made of something stronger, something finer.

"This is the Horse Armory," the warder explained as he ushered them into a long room with dark stones embedded in the ceiling and walls. Lining one side, figures in armor sat upon life-sized carved wooden horses. Many of the beasts had a leg raised, as if ready to step forth into battle. Swords gleamed in upraised arms. Pikes and spears stood in racks to be seized as needed. As he and Lady Larissa moved down the line, he saw a wooden face peering out of each helm.

"Every monarch of the realm is represented," the warder told them, his deep voice echoing against all the stone, wood, and metal. "From William the Conqueror to His Royal Majesty George II."

Lady Abelona shivered and pressed closer to Fritz. "They look ready to bite."

He tucked her arm in his. "I won't let them snap."

She giggled.

That would hardly do. What would Lady Larissa's sister think when Leo took up his true role? He could well find himself betrothed if Fritz didn't behave.

Lady Larissa did not so much as stiffen beside him, her gaze on the horse they were passing.

"What did Father tell us about armor, Belle?"

Lady Abelona straightened, which moved her ever-so-slightly away from Fritz. "That it is only as good as the man who wears it. If you do not tend to your armor, it will fail you."

Fritz cocked a brow. "Battle in armor regularly, does His Grace?"

Leo sent his brother a warning look.

"Our father must do battle of a different sort today," Lady Larissa said, turning away from him and continuing down the aisle in front of the carvings. "He fights for justice with words. I assure you, they can be every bit as sharp as a sword and as pointed as a pike."

Fritz shuffled his feet. Leo grinned at him before following her.

"Perhaps we could see the Jewel Office now," her sister

put in plaintively.

"This way," the yeoman warder replied.

That tight look was back on Lady Larissa's face as they followed.

"You must excuse His Highness," Leo felt compelled to say as they started up a set of curving stone stairs side by side. "He remembers when both French and Russian armies warred over our lands during the time of the Seventh Coalition and Napoleon."

She thawed a little, cheeks softening, lips relaxing. "Did you both have to fight?"

Leo nodded, memories threatening. "We each led a company of soldiers in an attempt to safeguard our citizens. We were seventeen."

"Seventeen?" she marveled. "You two must have been very skilled."

"We had been trained in the art of war, but we were in no way ready to lead men. Still, the men of Batavaria followed us. And many died."

Her hand slipped into his. "I'm so sorry."

Her touch warmed him even as it pushed back those dark days. He curled his fingers around hers.

"It was a difficult time for us all. Fear for the prince's life forced the king to confine him to the capital, but he learned to plan campaigns. Many of our men were taken prisoner by the French, and some of those never returned. Batavaria fought through. We sent a regiment to support your Iron Duke at Waterloo. Half came home to tell the tale that Napoleon was defeated at last. You should have seen the rejoicing. Horns rang from the mountains, and voices sang in the cities."

"It must have been glorious," she said, as if she could imagine it.

"It was," he said before the warder opened a door to admit them to another room, temporarily halting their conversation.

This room was small and dark, the stone walls pressing in on all sides. In the center, surrounded by a stout iron fence reaching nearly to the high ceiling, stood a display of shelves tapering in a pyramid. Even in the dim light, silver and gold gleamed, and jewels glittered.

"You see here a variety of items used by the Royal Family for centuries," the warder intoned. "The silver font is for baptisms."

Leo eyed the ornately carved pillar with its wider bath at the top. Near it sat a long golden scepter and a golden orb with a cross on top.

"And that's St. Edward's Crown," Lady Abelona supplied, nose nearly touching the cold iron of the fence as she gazed up to the top of the pyramid.

"Used to crown our gracious monarchs," the warder agreed.

Fritz sidled closer to Leo. "Very like the *Couronne des Montagnes*, the crown of Batavaria."

It was indeed. Trimmed in ermine, with gemstones encircling the base, four bands of gold arched up to hold another cross above purple velvet. His family's crown had six bands, one for each of the mountains that rimmed their beloved valley, and the velvet was white for the snow that usually covered them.

Leo lay a hand on the iron bars. "At least ours is locked up tighter."

The warder must have heard him, for he went so far as to chuckle. "Oh, you wouldn't get far with that crown, even if you could break through the fence. It weighs close to five pounds, and every Yeoman Warder would be on you the moment you set foot on the green."

"Well done," Fritz said. "Your monarch should be proud."

"He is," the warder assured him and Leo. "Only the best military men are chosen for this post. It's an honor to serve among them. And perhaps you could step back from the fence, milady. I wouldn't want to have to imprison you in the Tower for theft."

Lady Abelona backed away from the fence only to simper at him. "I would never be so bold, sir, I promise you."

Still, as soon as he looked to the others, her gaze latched onto the crown and refused to leave.

"Have you all seen enough?" Mrs. Mayes asked.

"Who does not enjoy surveying such treasure?" Fritz said, but he turned toward the door. With a sigh, Lady Abelona joined him.

Lady Larissa fell into step beside Leo as they started down the stairs again.

"You have a set of Crown Jewels as well, then," she said, gaze on the stone of the treads.

"A crown, a tiara, an orb, and a set of gold cuffs," Leo confirmed. "Like yours, they are only brought out on state occasions. And we do not put them on display."

"Certainly not," she said. "Not with all your traveling about. But perhaps you could display them here. I'm sure a number of people would enjoy seeing them."

And Fritz would go mad trying to make sure none of them stole the things. Besides him, Fritz, and the king, the Crown Jewels were all they had left of Batavaria. They had been locked in a sturdy iron safe in his father's suite, and only the king and the Lord Chamberlain had a key. If Leo had any say in the matter, they would remain in the safe until it was time to return them to Batavaria.

The warder led them out of the building, away from the tower, and to the gate in the stone wall, shutting it firmly behind them as soon as all five of them were through.

"A delightful diversion," Fritz told them, glancing around. "Now, where could our coachman have gone?"

Leo glanced around as well. Just down the street, carriages waited at the Customs House, where their ship had docked when they'd first reached London. Nearby, warehouses and shipping offices did a brisk business. He caught no sign of the green-lacquered coach with four perfectly matched chestnuts in the traces.

Only a gentleman slipping down an alleyway between buildings. He knew that face, that form. He'd seen them often enough across a room in Italy, up a street in the German states, and following behind them in France. He should not be surprised to find Mercutio, King William of Württemberg's favorite informant, here in England.

Another time, Fritz would have gone in chase, leaving Leo waiting impotently for some unknown danger. But today, *he* was the captain of the guard. It was his role to pursue, and it felt good.

"Your Highness," he said to Fritz, keeping his gaze on the alley entrance, "watch over our friends. I'll be back shortly."

He dashed after the fellow.

CHAPTER SIX

"WHAT'S HE DOING?" Belle asked. Baffled, Larissa shook her head.

Prince Otto did more than that. He stepped forward, gaze following his brother. "This is my job. Stay here, ladies."

Meredith moved to block him. "That would be unwise, Your Highness," she said sternly. "We require your escort, and you must allow the captain to do his duty."

His jaw was as hard as a rock as he glanced from her to the alley where Leo had disappeared. But he snapped a nod and made no more effort to leave them.

Larissa found it difficult not to stare at the alleyway herself. What had Leo seen? Was he in danger? Were they all in danger?

And when had she started thinking of him as Leo, as if she was a member of his family?

She glanced around at the tall stone buildings, the carriages and wagons coming and going from the Customs House down the street. Through the melee, the green coach of the House of Archambault came trundling toward them.

The prince remained frozen, lost in some kind of introspection, so Larissa held up her hand to signal his coachman. The carriage pulled in beside them, and still the prince did not move.

Larissa huffed and stepped forward. "Captain

Archambault requires your assistance," she told the coachman as the footman jumped down. "He's gone into that alley, there, and we don't know how many are awaiting him."

The coachman jerked his head, and the footman pulled a saber from a special case behind the bench and strode off toward the alley.

"Many thanks, your ladyship," the coachman said as Prince Otto stirred himself and opened the door for Meredith and Belle to climb in.

"Thank me after the captain has been rescued," Larissa informed him. "I suggest you block the alley so none can escape."

He hesitated, glancing at the prince. Prince Otto nodded, and the coachman touched the handle of his whip to the brim of his hat. Larissa climbed into the coach, and the prince followed, shutting the door and pounding on the roof to let the coachman know it was safe to drive.

"Forgive me," the prince said with a look to her as the carriage began swinging in a wide arch to take them back to the alley. "I am unused to waiting while others act."

Leo had mentioned they'd both led companies of men during the war. Perhaps it was hard for him to step away from leadership now.

"You are the crown prince," she told him. "The heir to your king. Your life must be protected."

For some reason, that did not seem to comfort him.

"Perhaps we should have sent for the constable," Belle put in, face puckered. "Or a guard from the Custom House."

"We may find the captain has things well in hand," Meredith reasoned.

Everyone rocked as the coach pulled to a stop, leaving the windows closest to Larissa and Meredith with a clear view down the alley. The buildings towering on either side left the space in perpetual twilight, but Larissa spotted the captain coming toward them, shoving a tall, slender man with a bristling black mustache before him. For a moment, she thought he'd discovered Beau Villers, but as soon as they moved into the sunlight, she saw her mistake. This man had swarthy skin and coal-black hair that fell onto his forehead.

Though the footman was there to assist, Prince Otto poked his arm through the window, opened the door, and jumped down. "Mercutio."

"Indeed," Leo said, giving the man a shake. "And so far from home." He glanced up to meet Larissa's gaze. "I refuse to tarnish your reputation by associating you with this fellow. Please, take the carriage home, ladies. Send it back to the palace when you are finished."

"I'll fetch you a coach, Your Highness," the footman said, edging around the three men.

She ought to thank the captain and go as he suggested. Mr. Mercutio was shifting in Leo's grip as if intent on escaping at any moment. But she couldn't abide the idea of simply leaving Leo behind.

"You'll be all right?" she asked him, hating the hitch in her voice.

He smiled at her. "Fine. I only regret ruining our outing."

Belle leaned closer to the window. "Perhaps we can take you on another outing, say Wednesday?"

He inclined his head. "I look forward to it."

"As do I," said the prince with a look to his brother, who colored. Then he turned to the coachman. "Drive on."

As the carriage rolled away, Larissa lost sight of them.

"Well," Meredith said, settling back against the squabs. "That was interesting."

"And exciting," Belle said with a little bounce. "Who

do you think they caught? Why was he following them? Mercutio—that's an Italian name, isn't it?"

"Shakespeare thought so," Meredith said. "And the king originally lived in Italy after he left Batavaria, if memory serves."

Had someone followed him here? For what purpose? And why had the crown prince seemed determined to confront the fellow? Wasn't that Leo's role? For that matter, why was Leo ordering the prince and the servants about? Things must be done very differently in Batavaria than in England.

"Spies," Belle said, jade eyes gleaming. "How exciting!"

Larissa sat taller. "How troubling, rather. We would do well to leave the matter to the captain, who is clearly trained to deal with such things."

Belle made a face at her and turned her gaze out the window.

Callie wasn't much better when they returned home. Larissa made sure to thank the coachman for his trouble before sending him on his way and entering Weyfarer House. Meredith went to see to Fortune, whom Underhill reported was napping upstairs.

Larissa found her sister and Tuny in the library. Each had her nose in a book, the quiet broken only by the crackle as a page turned.

"You were supposed to go with us," Larissa said, pausing in the doorway.

Tuny glanced up with a smile. "You're back. Did you enjoy the tour?"

Belle sailed past Larissa into the library. "It was great fun, especially when the captain went chasing off after a spy."

That brought both books down in a hurry.

"We don't know he was a spy," Larissa said, following her sister into the room. "But yes, someone was apparently watching us, and the captain took him into custody, after we'd had a lovely tour of the Tower."

"And we didn't see the animals," Belle said, fringe fluttering as she dropped into one of the upholstered chairs. "The prince said he didn't like seeing creatures in cages."

"Good for him," Callie said.

"Better for you if you had come," Larissa scolded her. "Belle's company is always delightful…"

"Thank you," Belle said, beaming.

"But I arranged this outing to give you an opportunity to shine," Larissa finished.

Callie sighed, fingers curling around the edges of her book. "Crowds of people, forced conversation in a carriage. Those aren't conducive to showing off my character."

"What is?" Tuny asked with interest.

Callie shifted on the chair as if she couldn't like being the center of attention. "Something quiet, instructive."

"The British Museum," Belle suggested, and Tuny nodded.

Callie wrinkled her nose. "Still crowded."

"Mr. Soane's museum, then," Larissa said.

Tuny brightened. "Oh, that's a good one. I've heard it's a fascinating place, full of art and sculptures and everything the architect managed to pick up along his way."

"It would likely be a private tour," Larissa said when her sister still hesitated. "We'd be the only ones there. And he has a sarcophagus."

"Belle and I can stay home to mind Fortune," Tuny volunteered. "Two less to cram in the coach."

Belle's foot swung under her skirts, but she didn't argue.

"Well," Callie said, shifting again, "I suppose his museum might be interesting."

"I'll ask Meredith to write to Mr. Soane to fix a time," Larissa said, "and let the staff at the palace know. And I will not accept anything less than your company this time, Callie. Be warned."

"What are you doing in England, Mercutio?" Leo demanded as soon as they were in a hack.

The courtier-turned spy cringed against the squabs. "You know it is my pleasure to always serve the Royal House."

"Of course," Fritz said. "The question is, which Royal House."

"Yours, surely yours," Mercutio warbled. "Such kind benevolence, such presence."

"Such nonsense," Fritz drawled. "Out with it. Why were you following us?"

"For your protection only, Your Most Royal Highness," he whined. "There are always those who wish to see you harmed."

"So you say," Leo put in, amused that their enemy's favorite informant had failed to notice that he and Fritz had changed places. "But I find it interesting that the person I see most often in the shadows is you. Who hired you?"

Mercutio raised his chin. "My loyalty is not for sale."

"Not cheaply," Fritz guessed. He glanced at Leo. "Pay him. I want this over with."

So did Leo, but it galled him to have to give money to the very person most likely to extort it from them. Indeed, at the mention of payment, Mercutio had straightened, smile slipping into place.

Leo crossed his arms over his chest. "I may be willing to pay for information, the right information," he hastened to add as Mercutio leaned forward.

"Of course," the courtier said slyly. "What would you want to know that I may be privy to in my lowly state?"

Lowly? The fellow had entrance to most of the courts of Europe, as far as Leo could tell.

"Who hired you most recently?" Leo asked.

"A personage connected to the legislature in Württemberg. But he wishes only to ensure your happiness and safety."

"So long as we stay far away from Batavaria," Fritz said.

"Just so, Your Highness." Mercutio smiled as if it were all so simple.

"And if we pursue our claims for the return of our lands?" Leo challenged.

The man shook his head, mustache drooping. "Then many will lament."

Fritz stilled. "Is that a threat?"

Mercutio held up his hands. "No, no! Never! I am your most fervent ally."

That's what Leo was afraid of. "So fervent you sent someone to spy on the king in the palace."

"The palace?" He frowned, glancing between the two of them. "Someone entered the palace?"

Fritz met Leo's gaze. It was said twins sometimes could sense what the other was thinking, feeling. Perhaps that was why Leo thought he knew what was on his brother's mind now. Mercutio might whine and flatter about matters he refused to divulge, but the fact that someone had entered the palace had thrown him off guard.

"It came to nothing," Leo told him, reaching into his coat to pull out a handful of gold coins from his purse. He thrust them at the courtier. "Here. And remember, if you hear anything about us or our cause, you will bring it to me first."

Mercutio's dark head bobbed. "Of course, of course. I am a loyal supporter of Batavaria."

And anyone who would pay his price. They dropped him off at the edge of the city.

"I believe him," Fritz said as the carriage set out for Chelsea. "He did not send the stranger to the reception the other night."

"Agreed," Leo said, leaning back with a sigh.

His brother eyed him. "Why do I sense that means I must continue playing your part?"

"A little longer," Leo said. "Until I know we are safe here."

Fritz shook his head. "Ensuring your safety should be my role. What were you thinking to run off like that? You could not know who was waiting."

"But I knew you would come to my rescue if I shouted for help," Leo reasoned. "And I could not take the chance of destroying our fiction. Though, I must say, you aren't helping matters. At moments, you were almost rude."

Fritz snorted. "A little arrogance is only to be expected from the crown prince."

"Is that how I seem to you?" Leo asked with a frown.

"On occasion," Fritz allowed. "But you cannot expect me to remain silent while others talk blithely of protection when their lives have been wrapped in fine silk."

"Our lives have hardly been difficult," Leo reminded him.

Fritz's eyes, so like his own, drilled into him. "Do you forget the men who were imprisoned or the ones who died in the war? They haunt me. I will live my life to honor their sacrifices."

Leo inclined his head, stung. "As is your right."

"And your duty," Fritz insisted. He drew in a breath. "But I will admit to nearly failing you just now. I attempted to follow you. The ladies noticed."

Leo stiffened. "Enough to realize the truth?"

"Doubtful, but Lady Larissa and her chaperone had to remind me that, as crown prince, I must allow you to protect me."

Leo winced. "Sorry about that. They could not know."

"They *should* not know," Fritz corrected him. "But I know. Do you think so little of my skills that you would avoid using them?"

NEVER PURSUE A PRINCE   75

"Never," Leo promised him.

Fritz shook his head again. "You sound like Mercutio."

"You will have your due soon," Leo promised.

His brother did not look convinced.

At least they had no appointments on Tuesday, so neither had to pretend. They spent the day being fitted by an English tailor for new riding coats and dress tunics and practicing with the Imperial Guard, which seemed to ease some of Fritz's tension. The guardsmen were always respectful of Leo, but it was clear their loyalty lay with his brother. Leo and Fritz returned to Mayfair and the Duke of Wey's town residence on Wednesday as requested in the note that had come from Lady Larissa.

His brother had recovered his spirits sufficiently that he could tease Leo as the carriage pulled up to the door. "She beckons, and you come at a run."

"As the king pointed out, she and her father may be our entrance into London Society," Leo responded. "Try to remember that you are Crown Prince Otto and behave accordingly."

He couldn't like the light that came to his brother's eyes, but Fritz inclined his head and made sure to exit first from the carriage.

"So kind of you to allow us to join you, Lady Larissa," Fritz said as soon as the butler had ushered them into the withdrawing room. Today, Mrs. Mayes, Lady Larissa, and her sister, Lady Calantha, were in evidence, though Fortune was once again missing. Leo could only wonder whether they thought it best to keep her out of sight of the prince.

As it was, the chaperone was in lavender; she must prefer the color, for Leo had never seen her wear any other. Lady Calantha was in a butter-colored gown with scallops of gathered material along the hem and neck. Lady Larissa was in spruce green, with a prim white collar and a shawl bordered in daisies. Both had on hats with a profusion of plumes.

"We are delighted to have you," Lady Larissa said to his brother, though her gaze strayed to Leo's. "We have a rare treat for you today. Mr. John Soane, one of our best architects, has invited us to view his collection. His sarcophagus of Seti I is renowned."

"Excellent," Fritz said, offering her his arm. "Shall we?" He cast Leo a smirking glance as he led her out of the room.

Leo bowed to Mrs. Mayes and Lady Calantha. "Ladies."

Mrs. Mayes latched on, but Lady Calantha walked beside him, head tipped down as if she thought she might trip if she didn't watch each step.

He was a little disappointed to find that all three women took the forward-facing seat, leaving him to sit beside his brother this time. To make matters worse, Fritz kept up a steady stream of stories as the coach wound through Mayfair and east. Leo had no opportunity for a word. Neither did anyone else. By the way Lady Larissa's pretty face was tightening, she wasn't any more amused.

"Lincoln's Inn Fields," Mrs. Mayes offered as the carriage drew up beside a tall townhouse faced with white stone. "Mr. Soane purchased three adjoining houses over the years and demolished them to build what you see."

"Impressive," Fritz said as the footman opened the door to hand them down.

Lady Larissa moved next to Leo, at last. "Wait until you see the inside," she said, hazel eyes shining.

He could have stayed where he was, basking in that light, but he offered her his arm before Fritz could and escorted her up the steps to the door.

An older woman with dark hair curled around a pleasant face opened to their knock.

"I am Mrs. Mayes," the chaperone told her. "And I have the honor of chaperoning Lady Larissa and Lady Calantha, daughters of the Duke of Wey. With us today is His Royal Highness, Prince Otto of Batavaria, and Captain Archambault of the Batavarian Imperial Guard. Mr. Soane agreed to allow us to view his collection."

"We have been expecting you," she said, stepping aside to let them into a high-ceilinged entryway. "I'm Mrs. Conduitt, his housekeeper. I understand you were most interested in the sarcophagus."

"Yes, please," Lady Calantha piped up.

"This way."

She led them to a doorway in the wall, then down a flight of stairs. Leo could only stare. The architect had opened the floors from the basement to a glass dome in the ceiling three stories above. On every landing, covering every wall, and filling every niche were vases, busts, reliefs, and carvings of marble, alabaster, and jade. He spotted statues that could have come from Greece, pottery that had to be Roman, and a mask that must be Egyptian.

"Mr. Soane loves to travel," his housekeeper confided as they descended through a treasure richer than any Leo had seen. "He won the Royal Academy Gold Medal for Architecture when he was a young man and spent two years in Italy. He's only expanded his collection since."

"Small wonder he had to keep purchasing more space," Fritz said.

"It wasn't just the space, Your Highness," she said, voice turning prim. "Many people look at these rooms and see clutter. Mr. Soane assigned them a certain order for study, according to his own mind."

Looking about, Leo could almost see it, a form, a function. The juxtaposition of a painting with a sheath of music might unearth new insights into both.

"Brilliant," Lady Larissa breathed as if she'd noticed as well. Her shawl was slipping from one shoulder. Leo pulled it up, fingers brushing her neck. She blushed. He fancied he could feel the warmth of her skin through his gloves.

They came out at the bottom, where a long, thick vessel of solid alabaster held pride of place. Tiny figures had been carved into the sides, marching loyally about their king for all eternity.

"Mr. Soane held a party when he first brought home the sarcophagus," the housekeeper said, smiling. "He had to demolish my sitting room to allow it through the wall. Nearly nine hundred of London's finest came over three nights to see this illuminated." She nodded to Lady Larissa and her sister. "Your father and mother were among them."

Lady Calantha smiled. "I remember. They said the light glowed through the alabaster and made the figures appear to be moving."

Fritz glanced up at the sunlight spearing down through the domed ceiling. "It must have been magnificent."

Not nearly as magnificent as the lady beside Leo. A shame he could not say that aloud, but a prince must be careful where he praised to avoid raising expectations.

Fritz didn't seem to realize the dangers. As they moved through the rooms, he gallantly shared his attentions with Lady Calantha and Mrs. Mayes. Still, Leo couldn't be displeased with the performance.

"Doesn't it just beg to be played?" Lady Larissa asked beside him.

He glanced at the golden lyre perched against the polished black of a Grecian urn. "Do you play the harp, Lady Larissa?"

She shook her head. "We all play the pianoforte, except Petunia."

"And what does she play?" Leo asked politely as they moved on to a wall crowded with paintings of various vintages.

"She doesn't play at all," she said. "Or sing for that matter. She was raised with different expectations. But a more loyal friend you will never find."

He smiled. "I think you must be a loyal friend as well."

"I certainly try." She moved along the row, head back as if to see the paintings closer to the ceiling. Such a graceful column of a neck.

"And do you consider me a friend?" The words popped out before he could think better of them.

She dropped her gaze to meet his, the hazel warmer than the colors of the art. "Of course, Captain."

Why did friendship seem suddenly too small?

CHAPTER SEVEN

HE DID NOT seem as pleased as Larissa had hoped to be called her friend. Yet what else could she call him? Much as she admired him, he was not what her mother or grandmother would have required in a suitor. The thought had never been more frustrating. Still, nothing said she could not enjoy his company.

So, they spent the next hour meandering through Mr. Soane's marvelous collection. How could one person have gathered so much and such a variety of objects? Callie must have stood for a full quarter hour reading the titles on the books behind the glass doors of a case. Prince Otto did not leave her side.

"The prince is being very thoughtful," she told Leo as they studied an elegant cork model of a Grecian temple.

"Indeed." The single word betrayed his surprise.

Larissa glanced to where His Highness had bent closer to listen to something Callie was saying while Meredith hovered nearby. "He is not what I would have thought of a prince."

"What did you expect?" Leo asked, moving on to another model of some ancient building, this one of sandstone.

Larissa studied the curves of the graceful building. "Poise. Calm. Power. An appreciation of his position and the weight of his responsibilities."

She looked up to find that he was standing taller. "He

was trained to carry that weight from birth."

"As is the daughter of a duke," she assured him.

He frowned. "I understood only the firstborn son in England inherits the title."

"Some titles can be inherited along the female line," she explained. "Even a few dukedoms. Not ours. We rely on my younger brother, Thalston, to be duke someday."

"Then what responsibilities does a daughter have?" he asked, clearly puzzled.

Larissa sighed as they moved on to the next model around the massive table in the center of the room. "The responsibility to be a credit to her family in Society and to marry well."

He coughed and stepped back from the models. "Dust," he said when she glanced his way.

"Ready to go?" the prince called.

Larissa made herself take Leo's arm, and they proceeded from the room.

"An excellent diversion," the prince pronounced as they stepped out the door at last. "How can I ever repay such kindness?"

Leo had been studying the stairs as if he thought they might crumble like one of the ancient temples they'd seen. Now he looked up, brightening.

"I believe I know." He turned to Larissa. "We will be holding a ball at the palace Friday night. Would you care to attend?"

The prince answered before she could. "Nonsense. Our guests will be even older than some of Mr. Soane's artifacts. Lady Larissa and her sisters have better ways to spend their evening."

Leo's jaw hardened, and, for a moment, Larissa thought he might argue with his princely brother. Then he put on a smile and inclined his head in acknowledgment. But when he spoke, he spoke to her.

"I fear His Highness is correct, Lady Larissa. Few of

our guests will be worthy of your attentions. But perhaps you and your sisters and Miss Bateman would consider attending anyway, as a personal favor to His Highness, and me."

He was putting his brother in a difficult position, and she was in complete charity with the notion. "Why, of course, Captain," she said, fluttering her lashes. "We would be happy to accept your invitation."

"Delightful," the prince drawled.

Fritz remained on his best behavior as he and Leo returned Lady Larissa and the others home. He waited only until they were on their way to the palace before speaking his mind.

"She is pursuing you."

Leo started. "Lady Larissa?" He couldn't fight his grin. "Do you think so?"

Fritz shook his head. "She must have seen through our performance. No one prefers the captain to the prince."

Sobering thought, but Leo couldn't believe it. "She has given me no indication she suspects."

"Yet you were quick to set aside your suspicions of her," Fritz pointed out. "Perhaps you were right then, and her beauty now blinds you. She may be a pawn of the enemy, intended to hinder our investigation."

"Her actions speak for themselves," Leo insisted. "She has done everything to aid our cause."

"Perhaps," Fritz said, but he did not sound convinced. "But I will leave you to explain to the king why Lady Larissa and the others will be attending the ball planned to wiggle his way into the good graces of King George's advisors."

And that was an even more sobering prospect. Few argued with the Lion of the Alps for long.

But when he broached the subject over dinner that

night, his father nodded thoughtfully. "They should come," he said, pausing to point his fork at Leo. "You can show them you are the crown prince."

Fritz looked away, as if he were swallowing a laugh.

"I had thought to remain as Captain Archambault," Leo explained to their father. "It would give me more opportunity to interact with them. You know the prince will be expected to dance attendance on King George's ministers. Besides, discovering our subterfuge in so public a way would only embarrass Lady Larissa and her family."

The king stabbed his fork into his veal. "Very well. But if you insist on playing the captain, you will play the role to its fullest."

Leo frowned. "And do what, exactly? Fritz knows the guards' routine far better than I do."

Fritz smacked his lips before attacking his dinner. "I can give the guards their assignments for the evening as I usually do. You can stand along the wall and watch for any sign of the enemy among these courtiers."

"And what will you be doing?" Leo asked, narrowing his eyes.

Fritz lifted a forkful of veal and examined it as if it were a rare jewel. "I'll be watching for the enemy as well. And I can assure you, if I find one, I will not be shy about calling her out."

Belle and Tuny were overjoyed to hear they would be attending a ball at the palace. They immediately started to plan dresses and hairstyles. Larissa made sure Callie was part of the conversation as well. This was the perfect opportunity to show her sister off. The other attendees might be old, but they might also have heirs looking to wed.

Friday evening, when they alighted from the carriage on the circular drive in front of Chelsea Palace, Larissa could not ask for a better presentation. Callie's cream-colored silk gown had a blue net overskirt that called attention to her eyes. Tuny and Belle were in white with blue satin ribbons in their hair. Their slippers positively danced up to the main entrance, the lanterns among the shrubs on either side of the stone walk reflecting on the satin of their gowns. The Imperial Guards at the front door inclined their heads as Larissa passed.

"They didn't do that for anyone else," Tuny whispered at her side.

"We probably just didn't notice," Larissa whispered back.

Inside, footmen in powdered wigs and an enormous amount of gilt on their uniforms ushered them down the same long, medallion-lined gallery to the reception hall.

Though she spotted several more guards around the walls, Leo wasn't among them. The prince and the king were in evidence, scarlet coats bright against the evening black of most of the men. This was clearly a more select crowd than at the reception. She recognized many families her father and Jane had entertained.

"That's Liverpool," she whispered to Tuny. "The prime minister."

Tuny ogled the slender fellow with the receding hair and bristling side whiskers. "Matthew doesn't like him much."

Her brother wasn't the only one. Larissa's father was more circumspect, as befitted a man of his station, but she'd heard him confide to Jane that the fellow tended to favor industry over the people. He could very well be part of the group wishing to keep the Batavarian mines operating and thus the king away from his kingdom.

It was, by and large, an older set, as the prince had predicted, but that didn't stop the gentlemen from seeking partners as the music started. Soon Belle, Callie, and Tuny were all dancing. Larissa partnered an earl in a fast-paced reel and a marquess in an old-fashioned sprightly gavotte. She was just catching her breath beside Belle and Meredith, waiting for Callie and Tuny to return to their group, when *he* approached.

Her heart set up a wild romp, until she took in the scarlet tunic and the bored expression on his handsome face. This wasn't Leo. This was his brother, the prince.

He inclined his head. "Lady Larissa, will you favor me?" He held out his hand.

Propriety demanded that she agree, for all she wished it were Leo offering. Belle apparently thought it a fine idea. She had her lips pressed together and her shoulders squeezed up, as if fighting a squeal of delight. Meredith tipped her head just the slightest, as if encouraging Larissa to move. Larissa put her hand on his and let him lead her out.

It was a waltz, of all things, still a bit scandalous in some circles. He put his hand on her waist and twirled her in time to the music. She'd learned the steps. She swirled around with him, gliding effortlessly, head high and gaze off to one side.

"You would have preferred to be dancing with my brother," he said.

Larissa did not miss a step, though her heart once more set up a fierce beat. "Captain Archambault was kind to invite us tonight, Your Highness. I would like to thank him."

"Perhaps you should thank me. I am the prince." He turned her into the middle of the room, and she caught a quick glimpse of Tuny standing along the wall with Callie, two thumbs up. It seemed Belle wasn't the only one who hoped for her to attract His Royal Highness.

"Well, certainly I thank you," she said. "This is a lovely ball. You and the king must be pleased."

He pulled her closer. "I would be more pleased if you gave me half the attention you give the captain."

Her grandmother had maintained that jealousy among suitors was a sign of a lady's popularity, but Larissa could not find it at all pleasant.

"A lady must be allowed to bestow her attentions where she sees fit, Your Highness," she told him.

Those diamond eyes were cold enough to send a shiver through her.

"Ah, but no one prefers a nobody to a prince without good reason. You want something from us. Position? Power? Payment?"

Larissa planted her feet, forcing him to jerk to a stop. Her mother would have been appalled, her grandmother bereft. She was breaking the rhythm of the dance, causing other couples to stumble and detour around them with open-mouthed shock. Such behavior was unthinkable.

His was worse.

"How dare you call your brother a nobody," she said. "I require no payment. I have position and power enough to satisfy that I have no need for yours. Do not approach me again. It would do no good to your hopes to win over our king if it were known that the daughter of the Duke of Wey had been forced to give you the cut direct, twice."

She turned on her heel and stalked to the nearest doorway, leaving him behind.

Leo started away from the shadows as Larissa left the room. Her head was as high as always, her steps as elegant, but something in the set of those shoulders told him she was hurting. What had his brother said to her?

If only his father hadn't set him to stand guard for enemies. He'd seen precious little. The prime minister had hesitated a moment before offering his bow. Not nerves, not Liverpool. He was famous for his circumspection. A few others had given similar indications that they either did not trust the king or feared he saw more than they intended.

And then Larissa had entered the room. Candlelight had picked out bronze in her dark blond hair, curled tightly around her face to spill over her forehead. The material of her blue-green skirts shimmered as she walked, like sunlight on a mountain stream. The ends of the satin ribbon around her waist skipped with each step. He had had to stiffen his spine to keep from joining her. It had been even more difficult to watch her dance with his brother. The moment Fritz's hand had clasped her waist, Leo's whole body had tightened. It seemed he wanted to be the one holding her. Well, if Fritz could behave out of character, so could he. He slipped from the room and followed her now.

She was standing in the corridor again, closer to the doors to the private apartments. His brother would have seen the location as suspicious, but Leo thought he knew why she favored it. She was making a strategic retreat, gathering herself before returning to the fray. He understood. He'd used the same tactic himself.

He didn't think he'd made a noise as he approached, but she wiped at an eye and turned toward him. Her lovely face was calm, composed. Most wouldn't have noticed the last tear tracking down her cheek.

The sight was sharper than a knife.

"What did he say to you?" he asked, closing the distance between them. "I will demand an apology."

Her brows went up. "From the crown prince?"

He'd played this game so many times, and few had ever caught on. Why was he so clumsy when it came to her? Of course the Batavarian second son would not reprimand the crown prince, at least, not in public. In private, Leo and his brother had overcome the forced differences in their positions years ago. At least, so he had thought until recently.

"It would be worth annoying my brother to see you smile again," he told her.

Her lips inched upward. "I believe I annoyed him quite enough for both of us. I made it plain I did not intend to speak to him again. Tonight may be the last time you see me."

More tears were gathering. He could have journeyed through the shadowed depths of her expressive eyes and never returned. Indeed, he found himself bending closer, inhaling the scent of orange blossoms. There were no orange trees in Batavaria outside the royal conservatory. What was it about this woman that reminded him of home? He could almost hear the breeze rustling the fir trees.

Rustling. Voices. His head snapped up.

"There you are," Lady Abelona said, smiling as she swept up to them. Lady Calantha and Miss Bateman were right behind. "Forgive us, Captain, but Mrs. Mayes is seeking our sister." She held out an imperious hand. "Larissa?"

He released her, and Larissa took a step away from him.

"Is anything wrong?" she asked, glancing from sister to sister.

"Everyone is talking," Lady Calantha confided, blue eyes wide and awed. "You walked away from the prince."

"Never knew you had it in you," Miss Bateman agreed, sounding impressed.

"He is obviously no gentleman to force you to such action," her youngest sister said, taking Larissa's arm. "I wouldn't think a moment on it. We'll find you another prince."

Her smile was tight. "I think we can dispense with princes altogether." She looked to Leo. "Thank you for coming to find me, Captain. If there is a way for you to visit us without the prince while you are in England, you would be most welcome."

At least she'd given him that opportunity. She could

not know how important she was to him…to their plans. Whatever Fritz had done, he could not allow her support to be lost.

"I would be delighted to visit," he said hurriedly before any of the others might pull her away. "But perhaps you could spare a few moments to walk with me now."

He couldn't help glancing at her youngest sister. Lady Abelona might look like a sugar-dipped confection in her white satin gown, but she seemed to have a will of iron. She was studying her sister now, little chin up and eyes narrowed. Then she nodded, as if making a decision. Miss Bateman must have realized it too, for she backed away. "I'll tell Meredith all is well."

Lady Abelona released her oldest sister. "Callie and I will be walking just behind. Take your time, Captain."

He would have sworn she winked at him.

Larissa drew in a breath as she accepted Leo's arm. Perhaps it was the mere act of walking that calmed her spirits after her upsetting conversation with Prince Otto, but she suspected the change was because of the man beside her. That black uniform, those sharp eyes, those confident steps all combined to give a girl comfort. He would allow nothing to harm her.

If only she hadn't harmed herself. Callie had said everyone at the ball was talking about her precipitous exit. Lady Larissa, walking out on a dance partner. She would be hearing about it for days, even weeks. Perhaps until the next scandal erupted.

What had she been thinking? Yes, his words had been insulting, to her and to Leo, but she knew better than to let harsh talk ruffle her feathers. She'd endured her share of waspish conversation over the years.

So superior, that Lady Larissa. As if she were more important than any other lady on the ton.

Just like her mother. They used to call her the Ice Maiden.
Small wonder no gentleman has offered for her.

She raised her chin now. No gentleman had offered because she had encouraged none of them. The important thing was to see Callie, Belle, and Tuny settled.

"The garden should be lovely in the moonlight," Leo said, stopping in front of the double glass doors, which gave back a reflection of his dark uniform next to her blue ballgown.

A moonlit stroll might add scandal to scandal, but surely not with her sisters behind them.

Belle must have thought Larissa hesitated too long, for she spoke up. "That sounds delightful, Captain. Lead on."

Larissa smiled an apology for the command, but he seemed to take no offense, for he held open one of the doors to allow the three ladies through.

A few stone steps led down onto a grassy path that wound through tall spikes of purple larkspur and white acanthus. The shrubs had been pruned into cones and hedges, lining the path. Moonlight touched on green and turned it silver.

Leo took Larissa's arm again, and they began to stroll down the path, the night air cool against her bare arms above her evening gloves. Belle and Callie trailed just far enough behind to be proper, but she knew her sisters would remain focused on what was happening. And Callie would be able to repeat the conversation word for word if Larissa needed help remembering.

"Your other guests seem pleased with the ball," she said, skirts brushing the grass.

"Only because the crown prince failed to insult them as yet," he said wryly. "Although your prime minister seems reticent. What do you know of him?"

"I have not been formally introduced to Lord Liverpool," Larissa admitted. "Father has mentioned him. They do not always see eye to eye, but they generally come to agreement."

"Perhaps I could speak to your father," he said. "Ask his advice."

Larissa shook her head. "He's not in London at the moment. Thalston fell ill shortly after Lenten term at Eton. Father thought it best to stay home until it was certain he would recover."

He glanced her way, eyes shadowed by the night. "Is the illness that serious?"

Larissa swallowed, remembering the tense nights, the worried conversations. "It was. Thalston had pneumonia when he was younger. The physician fears it damaged his lungs. Now the least cough can overset him. I've sat with him some nights. I never knew breath could be so harsh or so precious."

He lay his hand over hers where it rested on his arm. The touch spoke of concern, support.

"We all wanted to stay home and help," Larissa explained, "but the physician felt the less excitement, the better. And we were expected here for the Season. It is Belle's first."

A giggle behind her reminded her of her sisters' presence. She glanced back to offer them both a smile. She ought to shorten this conversation so they could return to the ball, but there hadn't been all that many eligibles, and she wasn't looking forward to facing the prince again. Besides, these might be the last moments she had with her dashing captain.

How could she simply walk away?

CHAPTER EIGHT

L EO COULD NOT seem to force himself from Larissa's
side. A need was building inside him, impossible to
ignore and equally impossible to meet. He couldn't very
well do as he wished and kiss her with her sisters a few
feet away, watching his every move. They were more
effective than the Imperial Guards!

Still, he might achieve something of his wishes. He
glanced her way again. The moonlight made hollows
under her cheekbones, deepened the pink of her lips.

"Perhaps I could ask one thing more," he murmured.

"Of course," she said, so quickly that he wondered
whether she had been hoping for a kiss too.

He settled for something less scandalous. "May I call
you by your first name?"

He did not think it his imagination that a shiver went
through her, as if the breeze from the Thames had brushed
the delicate flesh of her graceful neck. "That should be
permissible. What shall I call you?"

He hesitated only a moment. "Leo will do."

Her middle sister moved closer, pale hair shining in the
moonlight. "I'm Callie. And that's Belle. If you're going
to call Larissa by her first name, you should probably use
ours too."

Larissa smiled her approval.

"And do you have some shorter name I should use?"
Leo asked her.

She raised her chin. "No. I never saw the need to shorten my name."

"You might if you were named Abelona," her youngest sister put in. "But I agree that Princess Larissa has a certain ring to it."

She shook her head. "It was something I said, when I was a child," she told him, steps firm and face forward. "My mother was the most sought-after belle the year she came out. She married a duke. When I was seven, I promised her I would marry a prince. I have, however, realized that not all princes are worth pursuing."

They had reached the end of the garden. Beyond, the waters of the Thames tumbled past, black in the moonlight. She was a creature of silver and shadow, and he allowed his gaze to linger on her perfection.

Beyond her, something moved.

Leo froze, gaze raking the darkness. The night felt colder. Was someone watching them? Was she safe?

She must have seen the change in him, for she whispered, "What is it?"

The trees swayed in the breeze, heads nodding into the light. He shook himself. "Nothing. For a moment, I thought I saw someone, but likely it was a shadow. We should return."

They started back, her sisters closer now, as if they didn't like the idea of anyone hiding in the bushes either.

They came through the doors into the corridor to find three of the Imperial Guards thundering past. Leo put Larissa and her sisters protectively behind him before reaching out to snag the sleeve of the last man.

"What happened?" he demanded.

The guard stopped to salute him with his saber. Leo couldn't tell if he knew he was talking to the crown prince or thought Fritz stood before him.

"Trouble in the royal apartments," he reported. "The Lord Chamberlain fears the Crown Jewels have been stolen."

Larissa's sisters gasped.

Leo took a step forward, then stopped and glanced at Larissa. She stood with head high and bearing regal, every inch the daughter of a duke.

"Go," she told him. "We'll be fine."

His heart warned him to keep her safe, but he knew where his duty lay. He looked to the guardsman. "You will personally escort Lady Larissa and her sisters back inside and see them safely into the care of their chaperone, Mrs. Mayes. Then meet me in the royal apartments."

The man clapped his fist to his chest. "At once."

Leo looked to her, a dozen emotions chasing each other inside him. "I must trust your discretion. Please, say nothing about this matter until I give you leave."

"Of course," Larissa agreed with a glance at her middle sister, who cringed.

Leo pressed his fist to his heart, where he feared she had firmly lodged, and strode for the private side of the palace.

"Quickly, ladies," the guardsman said with a wave of his gloved hand. "This way."

Everything in her begged her to remain at Leo's side, but Larissa knew she could do little to help him this time. So she allowed the guardsman to escort her and her sisters down the corridor. His head kept swiveling, as if he expected an assassin to leap out from behind every statue. The thought made Larissa's breath catch. She reached out and pulled Callie closer on one side and Belle on the other. Both of her sisters were pale. Who could blame them? It wasn't as if they'd been raised for such intrigue.

And what of Leo? He had surely been trained for moments like this. Yet, who would dare steal the Crown Jewels of Batavaria? What was he facing—one man, two, a dozen? Did he have enough guards beside him to vanquish the villains?

Neither Belle nor Callie said anything until they reached the safety of the reception hall. Word of the incursion hadn't apparently touched that august space. The dancing had ended for the moment, and supper was being served in a room off one end of the hall. Through the open door, Larissa could see people seated at the long table, where crystal sparkled and silver gleamed. King Frederick sat at the head, but she could not catch sight of the prince.

Meredith and Tuny were waiting just outside the door. Their chaperone raised her brows as the guardsman marched up to her and bowed.

"Lady Larissa and her sisters have been delivered," he said as if they were a package. "I will take my leave." He smacked his fist to his chest, spun on his heels, and marched off.

"I thought you were talking with Captain Archambault," Meredith said. "What happened?"

Larissa didn't dare look to Belle and Callie, or one of the three of them might confess the story. "Captain Archambault had to leave us, on important business for the king," she explained. "I'm sorry if you were worried."

"When you three are together, I never worry," Meredith assured her. "I only became concerned when first the prince and then most of the guardsmen left."

Larissa frowned. "The prince left before the guardsmen?"

"At least a quarter hour before," Tuny put in.

"And any number of ladies were disappointed by the fact," Meredith added. "Petunia and I thought it best to wait for you instead of going in to dinner."

"And now we've missed it," Belle said with a sigh.

This time Larissa did give her a look, which made Belle drop her gaze.

"Perhaps," Meredith said, glancing between them,

"given all that has happened, it might be best if we were to leave."

Larissa stiffened. Leave? When she didn't know whether Leo was safe?

"If we were to leave early, it would be remarked upon," she temporized.

Callie rubbed one hand against her arm. "Well, they're already talking about you and the prince, and now all of us because we missed supper."

"Exactly," Larissa said before anyone could argue with her. "We've faced the worst. If we keep our heads high and stay until the end, we defeat them."

"I have ever believed in defeating one's bullies," Meredith said, mouth hinting of a smile. "If we must make our excuses for missing supper, we can say the excitement of the evening robbed us of an appetite."

That wasn't so far from the truth. Her stomach was knotting thinking about Leo and the danger he might be facing. "Perfect."

That settled, they found chairs along the wall and pretended to be in avid conversation until the rest of the guests began streaming from the supper room.

She didn't remember her dance partners the rest of the night. She kept looking toward the gallery, hoping to see a tall, curly haired man in a black uniform come striding in. But the quartet played their last. The king bid everyone a hearty good night as if his future hadn't been stolen out from under him. And they had no choice but to return to their carriage.

Everyone was silent as they drove back to Clarendon Square. Meredith watched them with a slight frown. Belle pressed her lips together as if she could not decide what to say. Callie hugged herself, holding her words inside. And Tuny glanced among them as if concerned for them all. It wasn't until they had retired for bed that her sisters and friend padded into Larissa's room and plopped themselves down on her bed.

"Tell us everything," Belle said.

Callie let her feet dangle over the edge of the four-poster bed, stockinged toes wiggling. "Starting with what really happened with Prince Otto."

Larissa rose from where she'd been seated at her dressing table. "He called his brother a nobody and made it clear I must have ulterior motives because I preferred the captain to him."

Belle wrinkled her nose. "How conceited."

"Quite," Larissa agreed, coming to join them. She cuddled next to Belle, who lay her head on Larissa's shoulder, golden curls tickling her neck.

"Good for you for walking out on him," Tuny said from her spot down the bed.

"There wasn't much else I could do," Larissa admitted. "But I can understand why that set the other guests to gossiping."

"Someone is always gossiping," Callie said. "But you could not allow him to think you a schemer."

"And then Leo came to find you," Belle said.

She said his name like a purr. Larissa chuckled. "And you know what happened then."

"I don't," Tuny reminded them, scooting closer.

"Leo asked her to walk with him," Callie reported. "He also asked her to allow him to use her first name, to which she agreed. Belle and I agreed too, though he didn't ask us. Larissa told him about Thal being sick and why she decided to pursue a prince years ago." She paused, lips turning down. "I didn't realize it was because of Mother."

"Our first mother," Belle clarified for Tuny.

Larissa shifted on the bed, but comfort eluded her. "Mother wanted the best for us. She expected us to strive for it the way she had. She married a duke. It stands to reason she would have wanted us to marry princes."

"Grandmother did too," Callie said. "I remember

all the times she talked about it over tea with Lady Quarrelsome."

"That's what we called the dowager Lady Carrolton," Belle explained.

Tuny cocked a grin. "Good name. She's been at a few of the parties I've attended. She never met a complaint she didn't like."

"She was grandmother's friend," Callie said with a shiver. "But I doubt she thought any of us would marry a prince, or anyone else for that matter."

Belle shook her head against Larissa's shoulder. "I don't need a prince. I just want a hero, someone who will love me and encourage me in all things."

"The way Mother does with Father," Callie agreed.

"Our second mother," Belle clarified again.

Tuny nodded.

But her friend couldn't appreciate the whole of it. Jane had been so good for their father. Until she'd come into their lives, he'd kept his distance from them, as if they were strange creatures who had invaded his castle and disordered his life. Only when Larissa was grown did she understand why.

He simply hadn't been sure how to deal with daughters, seeing them as fragile things that might disintegrate at the least wrong word or action. Jane had taught him otherwise.

Jane had taught them to be a family.

Something rose up inside her, a longing, a dream. That's what she should be seeking, not some prince from a legend but a husband who would help her make her own loving family. That sort of husband had never factored into her mother's instructions or her grandmother's hopes. Was such a thing truly beneath the daughter of a duke?

She shook herself as Callie paused in her recitation to eye Larissa expectantly.

"And then?" her sister asked.

"I also explained my regrets for not being able to associate with him because I cut out his brother, the prince," Larissa finished. "I'd like to continue helping him. I plan to write to Father and ask his advice."

Now Belle pushed off her shoulder to eye her too.

"What?" Tuny asked, glancing among them. "Is there more? Did he kiss you?"

Larissa pressed a hand to her chest as her heart tried to leap out of it. "No. He was a perfect gentleman." Though there had been a moment, in the garden, when he'd looked at her so tenderly, she'd thought, she'd feared, she'd hoped...

"But?" Belle prompted.

Larissa sighed, realizing what her sisters wanted her to do. "Tuny, you must promise not to breathe a word of this to anyone, not your brother, not Charlotte."

Her friend held up one hand. "I promise." She wiggled closer still. "What happened?"

"Captain Archambault ordered us back to the ball," Larissa said, "because someone may have stolen the Batavarian Crown Jewels."

Tuny's eyes widened.

"And he never returned," Callie put in. "I saw you watching for him, Larissa."

"He must have caught the thief," Belle reasoned, cuddling against her once more.

Larissa relished her warmth and her optimism. "I can only pray you're right. Now, we should get some rest."

Tuny climbed off the bed. "She's right. Come on, you lot. Good night, Larissa."

"Good night," Larissa said as her sisters slid off as well.

"Don't let the bedbugs bite," Callie called as she headed for the door.

Larissa smiled as they all exited. Jane had taught them that saying too, though no bed Larissa had ever slept in, here or in their home in Surrey, had ever had bugs.

As soon as they had left, she went to the table in the corner, which held her travel desk, and pulled out parchment. It took only a moment to sharpen the quill before she dipped it in ink and began writing.

Dear Father,

Belle, Callie, and I are all in good health and hope you, Jane, Thalston, and Peter are the same. We have been praying for Thal's swift recovery.

You may have heard the Batavarian court is visiting London this summer. We have had the...

She ought to write pleasure, but the only pleasing part of the matter had been meeting Leo.

...honor of meeting the king and his heir as well as Captain Archambault of the Imperial Guard, the king's second son and his most trusted advisor.

That might be overstating the circumstances. She hadn't ever seen Leo with the king. Of course, if he hadn't had King Frederick's confidence, they would hardly have been invited tonight.

He tells us that the king is most desirous of meeting His Royal Majesty so that he can request aid in recovering their kingdom, but some are attempting to keep the monarchs apart. I take it Lord Liverpool is one of those. I was hoping you could give me insight as to how the king might surmount this difficulty.

She paused again, fingers twisting the quill until she nearly pricked her chin. Nothing her mother or grandmother had taught her had said a lady couldn't ask for help. She set the quill to the parchment.

I would also like your advice on another matter. I find Captain Archambault to be a gentleman of the highest order. He continuously puts my well-being first, even against his duty. He has asked permission to use my first name, and I have given it. Do you think it unseemly for your daughter to find such a man fascinating?

Her throat tightened. She slipped the quill back into

the stand and picked up the parchment, ready to rip it to shreds. Her father would be concerned, perhaps even ashamed of her. Yet she longed to hear him say she had every right to let her heart lead her. That it was perfectly acceptable this once to think about her own feelings and not worry about how they might affect Callie and Belle.

She took a deep breath, lay the paper back down, sanded it to keep the ink from running, and sealed it. From the red wax, the image of the unicorn on the crest of the House of Dryden bowed to her.

Her dreams felt as unlikely as finding a unicorn in the stable.

Leo prowled around the royal apartments for another three hours before his father and Fritz returned. Was this how Fritz felt when Leo and the king stayed out late at some function? It was beginning to look as if he owed his brother an apology.

"We have had an incident," he told the king and Fritz as soon as they entered the salon. "The Crown Jewels of Batavaria have been stolen."

Fritz pulled up short to stare at him. "What! When?"

Their father merely frowned. "Are you certain?"

"Yes, Father," Leo insisted. "Your valet had gone to your chamber to prepare it for the evening and found the safe open. Everything in it was gone."

The king drew himself up. "Everything?" he thundered.

Fritz frowned at him, but Leo nodded. "The jewels, the gold we brought with us."

"The copies of your birth records?" his father pressed.

Fritz turned his gaze on the king. "Why would you bring those?"

Why indeed? And who would want them? Cold ran along Leo's spine.

"I always keep them with me," their father said. "If

something should happen to me, it must be clear who stands next in line." He looked to Leo. "Did anyone see anything?"

"I thought I saw someone in the garden, but it may have been the shadow of a tree. I had the guardsmen check with the servants, and I personally spoke to the guests who ventured close to the apartments. None of them saw anything."

"Let me guess," Fritz said, going to sprawl on the closest sofa. "The luscious Lady Larissa."

Their father dropped onto the other sofa and glanced between his sons. "What is this?"

"Nothing," Leo said with a look to his brother. "Fritz is right that I was with the daughters of the Duke of Wey. They are innocent, I assure you. Of more concern is what we lost."

The king leaned back. "We will survive the loss of your birth records. The originals are stored in the Royal Archives in Batavaria."

"They *were* stored," Fritz said gloomily. "Who knows what Württemberg did with the archives after we left?" He tapped a finger to his forehead as he glanced at Leo. "I may have to impersonate you for the rest of my life, Brother."

Leo refused to think about why that fact was the least troubling of everything that had happened.

"You will not impersonate your brother," the king growled. "The scar on his heel is attested to in my will, which is on file with a solicitor in Switzerland as well as in the archives. The line of ascension is clear."

"Then why were the copies taken?" Leo asked, moving closer.

The king's eyes narrowed. "Who knows? We must be doubly careful from here out. You will each have guardsmen attending you, day and night."

Fritz stiffened. "I am perfectly capable of taking care of myself."

"So am I," Leo told their father. He tried not to bristle when they both gave him a look. "That is not the issue. The loss of the jewels may make others think we are too weak to manage a kingdom."

The king grunted his agreement. "We must keep the matter quiet. Order the insurance agent to say nothing, Leo, when Lawrence files the claim tomorrow." He sighed as he heaved himself to his feet. "I am truly sorry you cannot give the tiara and cuffs to your bride. Diamonds, rubies, Batavarian sapphires? The pieces are being picked apart as we speak, the gold and silver melted. By tomorrow, they will be off to buyers. Another loss for us."

Leo felt it too, as if the last link to their homeland was fading. "I will do all I can to return them to you, Father."

His father put a hand on his shoulder. "Do not allow the matter to weigh on you. For now, I will bid you both good night." His steps from the room were heavy and slow.

Fritz shook his head. "They cannot leave him alone, like crows on a carcass."

Leo tasted bile. "We will find the jewels and convince the British king to help us."

"Always the optimist," Fritz said with a fond smile.

Leo turned on him. "And you, always the pessimist. How dare you speak to Lady Larissa as if she had malevolent intentions!"

Fritz reared back and held up his hands as if in surrender. "I told you my concerns. I only questioned her because I was protecting your interests. That, if you recall, is my duty."

"Nonsense," Leo said. "You have wronged an innocent. You will apologize."

"Very well," Fritz agreed. "But you are obviously much

taken with the lady. Will you propose to her, then?"

Leo snorted. "How? Until I have a kingdom, I have nothing to offer a bride. Apparently, not even the Crown Jewels."

CHAPTER NINE

L ARISSA HANDED HER letter to Davis, one of their footman, to deliver the next morning. Her other hand hovered at her side, as if it longed to pull back the note to her father and remove the last paragraph. Fortune seemed to know what the missive might cost her, for she rubbed herself against Larissa's skirts.

"We've a batch heading for the castle today, your ladyship," Davis told her, long face broadening in a smile. "I'll see this is included."

She nodded her thanks, then bent and picked up the cat as the footman went toward the kitchen door. Meredith was careful never to let her pet escape the house, but keeping Fortune safe was an easy excuse to hold the cat close. Her plumed tail swished against Larissa's skirts as she carried her into the withdrawing room off the entry hall.

Her sisters and Tuny had already come down and eaten breakfast. They were discussing plans for the day with Meredith. Their chaperone opened her arms, and Larissa surrendered Fortune into them. The cat stayed only a moment before wiggling to the floor and making the rounds to see which lap she preferred.

Meredith consulted the parchment in her own lap. "We have the Duchess's musicale tonight and church on Sunday. Yvette is hosting a soiree next Thursday, and Ivy and Kendall hope to be in town by the following week, so we may expect invitations from them as well."

Lord and Lady Kendall were neighbors of theirs in Surrey, and Ivy was Tuny's oldest sister.

"Ivy says she's planning on hosting a ball for Belle," Tuny offered.

Belle beamed. "How sweet of her!"

"Nothing for Wednesday?" Callie asked Meredith.

Everyone but Larissa looked to their chaperone. Larissa kept her gaze on her closest sister. Callie's lips were pressed tight, and her eyes were big and hopeful.

Meredith offered them all a smile. "Nothing, I'm sorry to say."

Larissa dropped her gaze to her hands in the lap of her blue cambric gown. Anything to keep from seeing the disappointment on Callie's face. Three years, and no invitation to Almack's, that treasured establishment for young ladies on the *ton*. The mighty patronesses were very select in their decisions about who might attend, and the daughters of the Duke of Wey had never been deemed suitable.

Belle tossed her head. "Well, who needs Almack's, anyway?"

"We might," Callie suggested. "It's where everyone goes to meet the most eligible gentlemen."

"Not everyone," Tuny reminded her. "You'll never see my brother there, and he married the daughter of a viscount."

"A viscount," Larissa felt compelled to put in. "Not a duke."

"Not every duke," Meredith said with a smile. "In earlier years, the patronesses even refused the Duke of Wellington when he arrived later than expected and wearing trousers instead of knee breeches."

Tuny made a rude noise. "I agree with Belle. None of us needs those nose-in-the-air types. Besides, we know a king."

NEVER PURSUE A PRINCE   107

"And a captain," Belle said with a wink to Larissa.

Her cheeks heated.

"We have any number of acquaintances," Meredith agreed diplomatically. "We have only to determine which of the many other invitations we've received to accept."

"Unless my behavior last night causes those invitations to stop coming," Larissa pointed out.

Tuny scooted forward on her chair. "Maybe we should answer them all now, before anyone has second thoughts."

Lowering prospect.

Still, they were having a lively debate over the merits of a boating regatta when Mr. Underhill stepped into the room. His nose was up, his voice deep with pride.

"Prince Otto and Captain Archambault are here, Madam. Are you willing to receive them?"

He was speaking to Meredith, as their chaperone, but his gaze veered to Larissa. Certainly she was willing to receive Leo, though she'd hoped she'd seen the last of his brother, the prince. But as Meredith looked her way as well, Larissa inclined her head. A lady knew when to use her power to most benefit.

"Please show them in, Mr. Underhill," Meredith said.

A moment later, and the two entered. How had she ever mistaken one for the other? The prince's eyes, as they met hers, were sharper, or perhaps it was the reflection of the dove grey morning coat he was wearing instead of his usual scarlet. And while Leo carried his head high and his steps easy in his black uniform, the prince walked more slowly, almost cautiously, as if he expected the Aubusson carpet to suddenly buck under his polished black shoes.

She was only disappointed when he chose the chair closest to hers, leaving Leo to sit near Belle and Callie. At least she could count on her middle sister to relay their conversation.

But, once again, the prince made himself the center of attention.

"I must apologize to you all and especially you, Lady Larissa," he said after Meredith had asked after the king's health. "The way you care for each other, you will understand why I find myself concerned for my brother and act to protect him."

Belle and Tuny frowned at him. Callie appeared to be examining the slipper sticking out from under her rose-colored skirts. Leo watched, waiting. Meredith nodded to Larissa to take the lead.

"I understand why you would wish to protect him," Larissa told the prince. "But I assure you we are no danger to the captain."

"Yes," the prince said, eyes glinting. "He vows that your desire to help us is motivated by a kind and generous heart."

Leo had said that about her? She glanced at him, and he inclined his head, smile edging into view. She smiled back before returning her attention to the prince. "He is very thoughtful to come to my defense."

"He should not have had to do so," the prince insisted. "I generally consider myself a good judge of character. I was mistaken in your case. Please forgive me."

"Of course," Larissa said.

Belle and Tuny nodded, as if they approved of Larissa's action. But Callie's wistful gaze was on the prince.

Had she finally found a gentleman she could admire? Her poor sister. Despite a few moments to the contrary, Prince Otto did not seem the sort to sit in a library with a good book. Unfortunately, nothing Larissa said would likely discourage her sister. Where Callie gave her loyalty, she would not be swayed.

Just then, Fortune stalked out from behind the curtains, where she'd disappeared when the two men had entered. Now she prowled up to the prince, stopping before him to regard him with her great copper eyes.

"Handsome animal," the prince said. He bent and held

out two fingers. "Here, kitty."

Fortune turned her back on him and strode from the room, tail lashing.

"Well, that's no surprise," Tuny said.

The prince frowned, hand falling. "Is there some significance to her response?"

"Nothing that need concern you, Your Highness," Meredith said smoothly. "We should not monopolize your time when all of London is eager to make your acquaintance. Thank you so much for calling."

He blinked as if he had never been shown the door before.

"If we might beg a moment more," Leo put in with a smile to Meredith. "You have all been so helpful in our work to uncover the culprit plaguing the king. I wonder if I might ask for your insights again."

Belle, Callie, and Tuny immediately agreed. Once more, Meredith looked to Larissa.

Larissa rose and moved across the room to take a seat closer to Leo. "Whatever you need, Leo."

His smile warmed her. "Thank you. I swore you to secrecy last night…"

"And I must ask you all to continue your silence," the prince insisted.

Meredith frowned, but the others nodded.

Leo drew an audible breath. "The Crown Jewels are indeed missing."

Belle gasped. Larissa reached out to lay her hand on his.

Meredith pressed her fingers to her chest. "How horrible! Have you alerted the magistrate?"

"No." The prince spoke first, rising from his chair and moving into their midst as well. "We cannot show ourselves weak, or your king will never agree to meet with us. This must be handled discretely."

Leo nodded, though he made no move to pull away from Larissa's touch, as if relishing it as much as she did.

"The king had the jewels insured the moment we reached your country. Our Lord Chamberlain, Lawrence, has sent word to the agency. They will no doubt want to conduct their own investigation into the matter. I was hoping His Grace, your father, might involve himself as well, to work on our behalf. We need someone well versed in the laws and protocols here."

"He is still in Surrey," Larissa said, mind whirling. "But when it comes to legal matters, I know who he'd recommend." She nodded to Meredith.

"I'm sure my husband, Julian, would be happy to help," Meredith said. "He is a solicitor of some renown, who has even done services for our king."

"Excellent," the prince said. "Engage him, Captain."

Leo's look to the prince was pointed and firm. "Of course, *Your Highness*."

What was that about? Larissa was too well bred to point out the edge to Leo's words, but she'd almost think them sarcasm.

"I will speak to my husband on your behalf," Meredith told them both as if she hadn't heard anything amiss in the exchange. "Come by Monday at eleven, and I will have him here to see you."

"There is more to that cat than meets the eye," Fritz observed as he and Leo left the duke's house.

Leo glanced back. Was that a twitch of the drawing room curtain? Surely not his Larissa. She would be a lady in all things. But it made him smile to think she might have been trying to catch one more glimpse of him.

"Fortune appears to be a uniquely discerning feline," he agreed as they reached the waiting carriage. "She clearly approved of me."

Fritz raised his chin. "Then it is only a matter of time before I win her trust."

His brother was by far the more practiced when it came to the ladies. Leo cast him a glance as they settled into their seats. "Thank you for apologizing."

Fritz shrugged as the carriage set out for Chelsea. "At least she was gracious about accepting."

Of course she had been. "And yet she moved to sit near me. Imagine that."

"Do not be insufferable," Fritz said.

Leo laughed.

"You have made an impression," his brother allowed, leaning back against the squabs as London passed by outside the window. "How, I cannot imagine. Perhaps Fortune is not the only female of discernment in that family."

Leo grinned at him. "Larissa has two sisters."

Fritz rolled his eyes. "I have no interest in following you down the road to matrimony. Nor is there any need. The bloodline runs through you. Your children are the ones who will rule one day."

Leo sobered. "If we have a kingdom to rule."

"Oh, must there be?" Fritz asked with an exaggerated sigh. "How much more fun to be a prince with no responsibilities. If we had the kingdom, you would be called into endless meetings about the size of the statue being erected in your honor and the need for carriage horses to wear plumes on their headdresses like aged doyens. And you would likely have to marry some princess you had barely met to cement a political alliance that would only dissolve two generations later."

There was that.

Leo rallied. "But what of the stories in the newspapers here and on the Continent? What of the letters written to Lawrence and Matterone by their families? By all accounts, Württemberg does little to help our people while forcing them to dig silver out of the mines."

"How do you know they are being forced?" Fritz

challenged as the city began to recede behind them. "Perhaps they like mining silver."

"Would you want to mine silver?" Leo retorted.

Fritz shuddered. "Don't be an idiot."

"At the very least, we should have the right to confirm their wellbeing," Leo said, fingers drumming on the wool of his trousers. "As it stands, we are cut off, with nothing but rumors to go on. If we could only gain the support of King George…"

"Everything would be grand," Fritz finished. "Angels would sing in chorus, unicorns would fly, and all would be well with the world."

"Pessimist," Leo jibed.

"Optimist," Fritz returned. "I only hope this Mayes fellow will be of some use to us."

So did Leo. But if meeting the solicitor gave him the opportunity to spend more time with Larissa, he would not protest.

He hadn't been sure what to expect of Julian Mayes, but Leo liked the solicitor at first sight when he returned to the duke's house on Monday. Fritz had remained behind to watch over the king. In the meantime, Leo, Fritz, and the Lord Chamberlain had met with the insurance agent, a Mr. Jenkins, who had gone over the royal apartments, looking behind every piece of furniture, pulling aside the drapes, and plucking at the edges of the carpet.

"What?" Fritz had whispered to Leo. "Does he think we dropped them and failed to notice?"

Jenkins, a tall fellow with dirt-brown hair and a sharp nose, had glanced up but did not otherwise show he had noticed.

"We will make inquiries," he had promised them before bowing himself out.

Julian Mayes seemed more suitable for making those

inquiries. His red-gold hair was sleek and smooth, with a dusting of silver at his temples, and his brown eyes held a light that could only be called savvy. He wore a neat beard and mustache and dressed in a tailored black morning coat and impeccable trousers. His bow was respectful, certainly not obsequious, and his tone was collegial.

"I thought perhaps we might avail ourselves of His Grace's library," he said after the introductions had been made in the withdrawing room. Leo couldn't help noticing that Fortune hadn't ceased prowling around the man's trousers, as if staking her claim on him.

"Perhaps Lady Larissa could join us," Leo suggested.

She rose perhaps a little too quickly, but she glided toward him with her usual grace. "Certainly, Captain. This way."

Her chaperone came to secure the cat, and they all watched them leave. Miss Bateman had her brows up as if skeptical, but Belle wiggled her fingers at him as if wishing him luck. Fortune regarded him solemnly.

The duke's library was a cozy place with upholstered chairs scattered along the tall oak bookcases that lined the walls. Larissa sat near the wood-wrapped hearth. Leo took a spot close to her, while the solicitor perched opposite.

"I understand there may have been a theft," Mayes said.

Leo nodded. "I count on your discretion, sir."

He inclined his head. "Of course."

Leo went on to explain the disappearance of the jewels. Both Mayes and Larissa listened, her gaze keen on him. She sent him an encouraging smile.

"And the only people who can open the safe are the king and your chamberlain?" Mayes asked when Leo had finished.

"Correct," Leo answered.

"I take it the chamberlain is above reproach?" Mayes pressed.

"He has ever been loyal," Leo assured him.

"What about the crown prince? Could he have gained access?"

Leo opened his mouth, then shut it. What, was he ready to suspect Fritz? His brother might pretend he no longer cared, but surely he wouldn't steal from the kingdom.

Larissa put a hand on his arm, but she directed her gaze at the solicitor. "I have been told the prince left the ball earlier than planned."

Had he? That was the first Leo had heard of it. Had Fritz grown bored playing his part, or did he know more about the theft than he'd indicated? Had it been Fritz he'd thought he'd glimpsed in the garden? It would have been just like his brother to keep silent watch over him.

"I will confirm that all were accounted for that night," Leo promised.

"Then, let us assume for the moment that the jewels were indeed stolen," Mayes said, steepling his fingers in front of his paisley waistcoat. "Who would know where they were kept?"

"Any thief might guess a safe held valuables," Leo hazarded.

"And any thief might guess a king would have jewels," Larissa added.

"True," Mayes allowed. "I was thinking more of someone who wanted to embarrass the king, perhaps see him suffer. I'm sure the number is small for so benevolent a monarch."

He would never have considered Leo's father benevolent if he'd seen one of the king's towering rages. "Alas, the king has made many enemies over the years," Leo told him. "One might have decided to trouble him. But I have not heard of any of them being in England. We are not on good terms with Württemberg, but it is my understanding that their Envoy to England is not in your country at this time."

Mayes nodded. "He must divert his time between England and Württemberg, but he keeps a staff, including a secretary, here in London. I believe the current gentleman to be named Gruber von Grub."

Leo refused to chuckle. He and Fritz had been tutored in English by a former major in the British army, so he knew enough of the English idioms to have made a joke about grubbing for gold. "We have not been introduced to Mr. von Grub."

"What about the man you caught near the Tower?" Larissa asked.

Mercutio? Possessing the jewels would have gladdened his avaricious little heart.

"A fellow followed us here from France," Leo explained to Mayes, who was watching him. "I cannot be certain where his loyalties lie. He claimed to be working for someone in the Württemberg legislature."

Mayes cocked his head. "Would this be Alonzo Mercutio?"

Leo stiffened. "Yes. How did you know?"

"We have had our eyes on Signore Mercutio for some time," Mayes acknowledged. "He sometimes aligns himself with the envoy. I'll ask if his whereabouts are known Friday evening. Is there anyone else in England who might wish you harm?"

Could he trust this man with the truth? He glanced at Larissa, who nodded as if she understood.

Leo drew in a breath. "We suspect Liverpool may be scheming against us."

Mayes leaned back and dropped his hands. "The prime minister? Well, that is concerning. Still, Lord Liverpool is an impressive enough power that he would be unlikely to send a thief. And Canning, the Foreign Secretary, has a strict non-intervention policy." He straightened. "I see several ways forward. First, we can wait until the insurance agency investigation is completed."

"We have already investigated," Leo pointed out. "I doubt Mr. Jenkins will be able to learn much more."

Mayes inclined his head. "Second, we could hire a Bow Street Runner to look into the matter."

"They are renowned for finding criminals and bringing them to justice," Larissa explained.

Leo grimaced. "I would prefer not to expand the circle of awareness of this particular crime any further."

"Very well," Mayes said. "Then I suggest we see what we can learn ourselves. London has establishments where one can go to buy jewels and jewelry without attracting undue attention."

"Really?" Larissa asked, obviously fascinated. "Where?"

He regarded her. "These are not places the daughter of a duke need go, your ladyship."

She dropped her gaze with a blush.

Something poked at Leo. She had been a staunch ally. She had named herself his friend, for all he was beginning to dream of more than friendship. If she wanted to continue helping, she had every right.

Leo put his hand over hers, and she raised her head, blinking. Now he offered her a smile in encouragement.

"Lady Larissa has helped us immensely already. So long as it is safe for her to be involved, I will insist on it."

She shot him a look of gratitude, eyes shining. He had to force himself to glance away.

"Very well, then," Mayes said. "It may be beneficial to have a lady involved, though I had thought to request my wife's help. Nevertheless, Lady Larissa is equally redoubtable."

"Thank you, Uncle Julian," she said, voice tinged with surprise.

Once more he inclined his head. "I've seen how tirelessly you nursed your brother, my dear, and the care you've shown for your sisters. If you've given your friendship to the Batavarian court, they are indeed fortunate."

"Yes," Leo said, "we are."

"Thank you," she said again.

Leo hadn't realized the room had gone silent until Mayes coughed. How long had he been gazing at Larissa? And did that warmth in his cheeks mean he was blushing of all things? How had his diplomacy failed him?

"Perhaps," Mayes said with an amused smile, "we should send you and Lady Larissa shopping."

She frowned. "Shopping?"

"For jewels," he clarified. "If we let it be known we're looking for something unique, it might be interesting to see what we are offered."

CHAPTER TEN

M EREDITH STRAIGHTENED JULIAN'S cravat the next morning. She and Fortune had moved into Weyfarer House while Jane and her duke were away, but she'd returned that morning to her home just down Clarendon Square for a few stolen moments. A lady could only be without her love for so long. The sunlight coming through the draperies now made the silver at his temples gleam. He had never looked more distinguished or more dear.

"And you're certain it's safe for Larissa at this jewelry shop?" she asked.

He caught one of her hands as she lowered them and pressed a kiss into her palm, sending a shiver through her. "Perfectly safe. Not only is Mortimer Hollingsworth related to the Earl of Danning, who married his daughter, but he's made a fortune finding the exact right gem for the exact right client. If the Batavarian Crown Jewels are for sale, he'll know."

"*If* they're for sale?" she asked, following him as he started for the door to their bedchamber.

As Julian opened the door, Fortune scampered inside. She cast him a glance as if letting him know she did not appreciate being left out. Julian inclined his head in apology.

"It's possible the jewels were stolen for their monetary value," he said, stepping out onto the landing. "It's equally possible they were stolen for their political value. In that case, they won't be sold. They'll be used for blackmail or worse."

The second shiver had nothing to do with pleasure. "This could be a nasty business, couldn't it?"

"Quite likely," he said, starting for the stairs. "But I've dealt with worse."

He had. Over the last thirteen years since they'd married, he'd untangled thorny problems for dukes, earls, marquesses, various ministers, and even the prince regent before he had become king. His work had yielded him accolades and rewards, but not the one he most craved.

A title.

"Be careful," she told him as they exited the house together, Fortune once more on the leash she abhorred. "If someone truly is out to stop King Frederick, they won't like anyone coming to his aid."

"You and your young ladies have provided him more aid than I ever will," Julian said with a smile. "Now, I'm off to fetch Captain Archambault. You have the clothing you need for Lady Larissa?"

"Petunia is bringing it," Meredith said. "We'll see you shortly."

He bent and pressed a kiss to her lips. The touch was as thrilling today as it had been the first time, under a kissing bough at her mother's annual Christmas Eve party, when Meredith had been only sixteen.

That's what she hoped for all her young ladies, as Julian called them. A gentleman who would love them more every day, for all their lives.

"We have work to do," she told Fortune, and they set out for Weyfarer House.

Larissa tugged down the sleeves on the plumb-colored gown Tuny had offered as part of the disguise, courtesy of her sister-in-law, Charlotte, who was about Larissa's size. Larissa was to look like a wealthy wife, not the daughter of one of the oldest families in England.

"Good English wool," Tuny said, stepping back to eye the outfit. "With just enough tucks and frills to impress."

"You look good, but not too good," Belle agreed, handing Larissa the wide-brimmed brown hat with its white ribbon, which Larissa tied at a jaunty angle on her curls.

Leo, on the other hand, was perfect.

He still wore black, from head to toe, but the long, tailored coat was cut away at his waist and emphasized broad shoulders and long legs. His cravat was simply but elegantly tied. Truly, no lady could have taken exception.

"You'll want to talk to Mr. Hollingsworth himself," Uncle Julian explained as his carriage set off down the street with him and Leo facing her on the leather seats. "Do not accept one of the clerks. They won't know what he knows."

Leo nodded. "We will make sure of it."

We. As if they were partners. Her mother's and grandmother's advice had also been lacking when it came to this sort of adventure. Very likely she should look serious, solemn. She couldn't seem to help her smile.

Mr. Hollingsworth had his establishment in a fashionable area of London, surrounded by the shops of famous dressmakers and haberdashers. Still, Uncle Julian had his coachman park around the block as if concerned someone might recognize it. Leo helped her alight, then walked with her onto the street, strolling along, arm in hers. Other shoppers in fine gowns and tailored coats moved past. She didn't recognize anyone, but she dropped her gaze just in case.

"Nervous?" he asked.

"No," Larissa admitted, keeping her voice low. "It's rather exciting, isn't it, this subterfuge? Who knows what we might learn?"

"Just be careful," Leo advised as they neared the shop. "We cannot know what we might face. I promise no harm will come to you."

Said that way, full of conviction and warmth, she believed him.

A bell tinkled as they entered. The shop was narrow and deep, with dark wood cases topped in glass running along one wall and a curtain closing off another room at the back. Inside the cases, gold, silver, and every manner of gemstone winked at her, calling her closer. Belle would have been in alt.

A young man in a brown wool coat, hair slick and face pale, came forward to greet them. "Good afternoon. May I be of assistance?"

Leo's face hardened into haughty lines, and he wrinkled his nose as if he'd smelled something foul. His voice lost all the lovely hints of another country, until she might have thought him the polished London gentleman he appeared. "I was told only to do business with the owner himself. Where is Mr. Hollingsworth?"

The clerk glanced toward the doorway at the back of the shop. A long-fingered hand swept aside the curtain, and an older man came through. Tall, thin, with white hair smoothed back from his wrinkled face, he moved up to them with a leisurely stride. Though his smile was welcoming, his gaze swept over her coolly.

Sizing her up. Taking her worth. Larissa did not so much as flinch.

"Were you looking for something special?" he asked.

Leo glanced at Larissa. "I would like my bride bedecked in splendor."

Though she knew he was playing a role, she found herself caught and held by his regard.

Mr. Hollingsworth rubbed his hands together. "Well, you've come to the right place. Should we start with a tiara? Perhaps a nice necklace and pin set."

Leo leaned closer and lowered his voice. "I was hoping for something a queen might wear. Or a king."

Hollingsworth's eyes narrowed. "Not sure I take your meaning, sir. I run an honest shop." He took a step back as if about to order them from the premises.

Larissa put out a hand. "I assure you, Mr. Hollingsworth, we value that honesty. That's precisely why we came to you with this important mission."

Leo frowned. Perhaps mission had been too strong a word, but taking it back would only make things worse. As it was, the jeweler was gazing into her eyes as unblinkingly as Fortune. Larissa kept her head up, her demeanor calm. A lady never surrendered in matters of commerce. Besides, he couldn't know that her heart pounded so hard she feared it might thrust through Charlotte's good English wool.

Whatever he saw must have allayed his concerns, for he stepped back and waved toward the doorway through which he had entered. "Right this way."

Leo put his hand on Larissa's elbow as they followed the jeweler into the other room. She'd thought it might hold a jumble of packing cases and sundry other supplies, but the space was neat and orderly, with tall shelves holding leather cases. Mr. Hollingsworth nodded them into leather-upholstered chairs in front of his clawfoot desk, took his seat behind the desk, then leaned toward them. His long nose pointed at Larissa. "Now, your ladyship, why don't you tell me why you're really here."

Leo stiffened, but Larissa lay a hand on his arm. She might have given away her identity, but that didn't mean he must do the same.

"You are very perceptive, Mr. Hollingsworth," she acknowledged.

The jeweler spread his hands. "When you deal with the aristocracy as often as I do, you learn to tell the pretenders from the authentic."

Larissa inclined her head. "Unfortunately, the story is not mine to tell. Suffice it to say that the family jewels of a good friend have gone missing, and we are trying to determine where they might reappear."

He leaned back and crossed his arms over his chest. "I don't deal in stolen goods."

"No," Leo put in. "Not a man of your standing. But you are known for being acutely aware of what is happening elsewhere in your profession."

Hollingsworth nodded slowly. "I do hear things on occasion. But nothing about any robberies of the magnitude I believe you're hinting. If I should become aware of such, how would I reach you?"

"Send word to Mr. Julian Mayes," Larissa said promptly. "He will know how to contact us."

Hollingsworth's thin lips twitched. "Very circumspect is Mr. Mayes. He could be representing anyone. Say the king of Batavaria?"

So, she hadn't been the only one to give away the game. To his credit, Leo offered no indication the jeweler had hit upon the truth.

"The visiting king must have his own emissaries to do his bidding," he said.

"No doubt," Hollingsworth allowed. He rose. "Thank you for coming to me. I'll see what can be done. In the meantime, I have some lovely betrothal rings. A sapphire would look very nice with the lady's coloring."

A coloring that was deepening by the moment, by the heat in her cheeks.

Leo stood and offered Larissa his hand to help her up as well. "We will take that into consideration should the time come."

They left Hollingsworth chuckling.

"We are terrible spies," Larissa said as they stepped out into the daylight of the busy street. "He recognized us before we'd said more than a few words."

"That is his business," Leo said, accent once more in place, as they started down the street to return to the carriage. "Though I suppose we could have left the coach closer for all the good hiding it did."

Larissa sighed. "I'm sorry. I'm not very good at dissembling."

He smiled at her. "No, you are not. And that is to your credit. You are who you are—the daughter of a noble house. Small wonder he noticed."

She had never blushed so much in her life before she'd met this man.

"And you are who you are," she countered. "That upright bearing and confident manner cannot be masked. You are a military man, a protector."

Something crossed his face, and he looked away as if he didn't want her to notice. "Even a soldier must pretend if it means preventing the enemy from gaining the advantage."

"Well, he does not appear an enemy," Larissa reasoned. "I believe him when he says he'll help. We have taken the first step in returning the Crown Jewels to their rightful place."

She glanced at Leo to find his smile had broadened, as if she had given him hope. She should be pleased to be his ally and friend, but something inside her protested. Was it not possible she might be more?

If only she knew what her father thought. Despite his reputation for reserve, he had convinced kings to decamp, barons to bow out. He would know what to do about the lost jewels, the king's quest to see his kingdom restored, and her growing feelings for a certain captain. He hadn't answered her note as yet, but she wouldn't have expected an answer to come until tonight or tomorrow. The castle was a good few hours from London, and the footman who had made the trip would have needed time to rest before returning. And her father might have been standing watch over Thal.

Which meant, for now, she was on her own.

Leo ought to have been disappointed in their progress, but he found it difficult to mope with Larissa at his side. They located the carriage and relayed the results of their mission to Mayes.

"Word will get around," the solicitor promised, tapping on the roof to signal the coachman to start for Weyfarer House. "The more people who talk about missing jewels, the more difficult it will be for the thief to find a willing buyer. I hope for more news soon, Captain."

Leo leaned back against the leather. "And were you able to establish the whereabouts of Alonzo Mercutio on Friday evening?"

Mayes' face darkened. "He was dining with Mr. von Grub at the home of the Envoy from Württemberg on Upper Brook Street that evening, and the entertainment ran late."

Leo shook his head. "Either could be vouching for the other."

"True," Mayes said. "But the gentleman who relayed the information noticed no one leave the house during that time, and he saw no coaches in the area."

It sounded as if the solicitor knew something of spying himself. A formidable ally indeed.

"Should you speak to this secretary to the Württemberg Envoy, Leo?" Larissa asked, glancing between them. "You would know better what questions to ask to determine his innocence or guilt."

Tempting. His father had deemed the man of little consequence, but it was possible von Grub might be privy to other information. "An excellent suggestion," Leo said. "Why not this afternoon?"

The solicitor stroked his short beard with one finger. "I would caution you against it, Captain. You would be entering the lair of your enemy, alone."

Across from them, Larissa raised her head. "Not alone. He may not have his guards at his back, but I doubt Mr. von Grub would dare try anything with the daughter of a duke in attendance."

Mayes frowned, but Leo could not help his grin. "Then let's pay a call on Herr von Grub and see what we can learn."

"Home first," Larissa insisted. "If we are to play a part, we must dress for the occasion."

Leo glanced at the plumb-colored wool gown that draped her curves. "I see nothing wrong in how you are dressed."

She smiled at him. "Thank you. But this is a gown for the wife of a prosperous merchant. I must look like a lady."

"You," Leo said, "could never look anything less than a lady."

She dimpled before directing her gaze at the solicitor. "Uncle Julian, I believe it would be wise to take our town carriage instead of yours. At the very least, the envoy's footman would see the crest and be more likely to allow us in."

Mayes quirked a smile. "You *are* intending to impress. But I'm afraid Meredith would chide me if I encouraged you and the captain to be alone in a closed carriage. Your finery should take no harm if you walked from Weyfarer House. The envoy's house is two doors down from the corner with Park Lane, on the south side of the street. I can await you with the carriage near Hyde Park to spare you the walk home."

The plan agreed upon, they returned to Weyfarer House, where Larissa hurried upstairs to change. The solicitor's wife had taken the other ladies out shopping, the butler reported when Mayes asked, so Leo and his companion waited in the withdrawing room.

"Lady Larissa seems much taken with you," the solicitor remarked from his chair by the hearth.

Leo smiled. "I assure you, I am much taken with her as well. She is the most elegant female of my acquaintance."

"I felt the same about Meredith," Mayes confided. "Even as a girl, she had a presence that could not be denied. So did Lady Larissa's mother."

Leo's gaze was drawn to the dark-haired woman in the painting over the hearth. "I see what you mean."

Mayes swiveled to look at the painting as well. "That is the duke's second wife. Lady Larissa's mother was an ethereal blonde who knew the power she wielded with every arch look. She was the daughter of a duke as well."

Small wonder she had expected her daughter to marry a prince. Yet he could not see Larissa wielding her beauty or position as a weapon. She had been generous with her time and her friendship. She even put his needs before her own.

"You set much store by position in England," Leo observed.

He nodded. "Position and duty. They are two sides to the same coin."

Leo had been raised under a similar belief. Something inside him, however, prodded him to argue. "And what of happiness? Fitness for the role?"

"There are those who hold that happiness is immaterial," Mayes allowed. "And that fitness is less important than lineage. I see it more as a matter of training and expectations. If you are trained to be fit for the role and know others depend on you to fulfill it, you are more likely to be happy in that role."

He wished he could believe that. He had been trained to be king one day, but, the more time he spent as the captain, the more he wondered about his fitness.

He was glad Mayes turned the topic to schooling in England. He was asking about the differences between Oxford and Cambridge when he heard the sound of a footfall on the stairs. Rising, he watched as Larissa swept into the room.

Her maid had crimped her warm blond hair around her face, with one curl hanging tantalizingly over her forehead inside a spring green, satin-lined bonnet. Her peach-colored gown was of a lustrous material that glinted as she approached them. The gathered sleeves and fitted bodice were embroidered with thread the exact shade of the dress. The skirts draped from a satin belt at the high waist down to more gathers at the hem. She was, as she had set out to be, every inch a lady of taste and breeding.

"Well done," Mayes told her with a proud smile.

Leo glanced down at his black coat and trousers. They too were of fine material, wool with jet buttons and tailored to his form, a far better costume for this enterprise than his uniform. Still, Larissa was right. This confrontation required his position to be as clear as hers. She deserved to be seen on the arm of a prince.

But how could he be the crown prince when she knew him as the captain?

CHAPTER ELEVEN

"SUITABLE FOR OUR meeting with the secretary?" Larissa asked, turning in a circle. She came around and faced Leo, only to find such a look of awe on his face that she knew herself admired and admirable.

Heady feeling.

"Suitable for meeting with your king," Leo assured her. He offered her his arm. "Shall we?"

"Be careful," Uncle Julian warned as Larissa put her hand on Leo's arm. "If von Grub is involved with the theft of the jewels, he could well be acting under orders from someone higher. We don't want to give away your intentions. And if he is innocent, you would not want to cause an incident that would come to the ears of our king."

Suitably chastened, they left the house and set off toward the north.

Leo cleared his throat before they had reached the edge of Clarendon Square. "I feel as if I must be more impressive as well, if only to do you justice."

Larissa smiled at him. "Surely, the Captain of the Imperial Guard is impressive enough."

"In some circles," he allowed, and she wondered if he was thinking about Liverpool and his set. "But if you can play a role with Hollingsworth, perhaps I should play a role with von Grub. I could pretend to be my brother for a time."

Larissa squeezed his arm. "Brilliant! You haven't met Mr. von Grub. Surely, he won't recognize the difference. And he might be more forthcoming thinking he faces the crown prince."

Leo shot her a glance as they started past the townhouses on Park Street. "You don't find it a cruel deception, pretending to be something you aren't?"

Larissa cocked her head, satin ribbon under her chin tightening. "If we were pretending as a way to defraud, we would certainly be in the wrong. But we pretended to be something we were not with Mr. Hollingsworth to protect your family. That would seem a noble cause."

For some reason, he did not seem content with that reasoning. "And what about von Grub? He may be an innocent."

"Then you will profusely beg his pardon next time you meet," she said. "Believe me, it is rare on the *ton* to find someone who isn't pretending to be more than they appear."

He frowned. "Even you?"

Larissa dropped her gaze to the pavement. "Perhaps not me, at least, not to putting on a different character. My mother and grandmother were very firm about how a lady should behave. I try never to go against their advice. But I can see how pretending allows you to do things you wouldn't have in your own guise. There is a freedom in that."

She glanced up as they turned onto Upper Brook Street to find that he had reddened.

"Yes," he murmured. "So I've noticed."

Before she could question him, he stopped in front of a white townhouse with black shutters on the multipaned windows and a black wrought iron fence separating it from the pavement. Two houses from the corner, south side. This must be the envoy's home. Her stomach fluttered as she climbed the steps to the black-lacquered door.

A middle-aged woman dressed in black with a white apron answered Leo's knock.

Larissa pulled a card from her reticule and handed it to her. "Lady Larissa, daughter of the Duke of Wey, and His Royal Highness, Prince Otto of Batavaria, to see Mr. von Grub, if you please."

The woman glanced from the card to Leo and stared. "*Der Prinz?*"

Leo inclined his head even more regally than his brother. "At your service, madam."

She dropped a deep curtsey, then straightened and pushed the door wider. "Please to come in. I will ask."

They stepped into a small, black-and-white marble-tiled entry hall. The pink plastered walls were mostly covered in oil paintings of various men and women who might have been famous citizens of Württemberg, but who did not appear particularly pleased by the fact. The woman shut the door behind them, then trotted down a corridor toward the back of the house.

"Her accent sounded German," Larissa whispered to Leo. The sound hissed about the space, as if the dour-faced portraits were whispering back.

"Württemberg is one of the German states," he explained, glancing around as if he expected to find the Crown Jewels on display like the spoils of war.

A slight man in a dark tailcoat and trousers hurried down the corridor toward them. His blond hair was carefully combed over the top of his head, and his smile was pleasant.

"Your Highness, Lady Larissa, I am Gruber von Grub, and I am at your service," he said with only a hint of an accent. "Please, join me." He gestured to a room off the entry hall.

They followed him into a sitting room no doubt used for diplomatic discussions. The walls were a cool blue, the chairs upholstered in a striped pattern of a darker shade, and the wood trim painted white. The set of chairs was spaced more like a circle than the square she was used to seeing, and there was no sofa. Not allowing anyone to take sides, it seemed.

He and Leo waited until she was seated before sitting as well. The secretary glanced between them. "How might I be of assistance?"

"I was hoping for news of the envoy," Leo said. "Does he intend to return to England soon?"

"The envoy remains, regrettably, out of the country," the secretary answered, grey eyes bright, "but I would be happy to help one of my fellow Württemberg citizens."

Leo stiffened. "I am not a citizen of Württemberg."

Mr. von Grub spread his hands. "No, of course not. You and your family were asked to leave."

How rude! A lady did not allow a friend to be treated so poorly. Larissa leveled her glare on the fellow. "I am shocked the envoy left you in charge, sirrah, if this is how you address those who call on you."

Immediately, he inclined his head. "My utmost apologies, your ladyship. I did not mean to offend. I was merely stating a fact. Prince Otto and his family, alas, are no longer allowed to set foot on Württemberg soil."

"On Batavarian soil," Leo corrected him, voice as icy as the mountaintops of his homeland. "I am pleased to say we have been welcomed by England's citizens."

"But not by its king," von Grub lamented, even though the glint in his eyes belied the sorrow in his tone. "Perhaps I could be of assistance there. I have frequently been a guest of His Royal Majesty, King George."

"As has my father," Larissa put in, unwilling to grant the fellow even this concession. "The opinion of His Grace, the Duke of Wey, carries much weight with our king."

"I am certain it does," the secretary said. "He is supporting the Batavarian's claim to the throne, then?"

Those eyes were far too eager. She could not answer yes, not when she hadn't seen a response to her note. "My father is an ardent supporter of just causes," she told the secretary.

His pleasant look did not falter, but he leaned back as if to distance himself from the idea. "How kind of him."

"And what of the Batavarian Crown Jewels?" Leo demanded.

Now, there was a bold statement. Those glittering eyes, that lift of his chin in challenge. Anyone looking at him now would not doubt that here was a prince among men.

The secretary was certainly no proof against the posturing, for his look finally melted into a frown. "The Crown Jewels? You took those with you. You cannot make a claim for them now."

"I have no need to claim what is mine," Leo said, pushing up from the chair. "Thank you for receiving us. Have the envoy contact Lawrence, our Lord Chamberlain, when he returns. There is much we should discuss." He held out his hand, and Larissa took it to rise.

The secretary popped to his feet, seized her other hand, and bent over it. "Your ladyship, a pleasure. Please give my regards to your illustrious father." He pressed a kiss against the back of her hand, the grip and pressure possessive.

Larissa barely hid her shudder as she retrieved her fingers. "Good day, Mr. von Grub."

She was relieved when the door closed behind them.

Leo had to force his steps to slow as he led Larissa away from the envoy's home. Part of him wanted nothing more than to put distance between him and the loathsome secretary. He could not remember a time when anyone had dared speak so disrespectfully to him.

But if von Grub happened to look out the window, Leo

would never have wanted to give him the impression he was running away.

"That did not seem helpful," Larissa said as they headed for Park Lane.

"Helpful enough," he told her. "He delighted in hinting of the power he and his king hold over us, even to the point of being familiar with your king. If he had known of the theft of the jewels, he would have hinted at that as well."

She was rubbing at her glove, where von Grub had dared to kiss her hand, as if she would remove every trace of his touch. "I suppose you're right. But that means we still have no idea what happened to the jewels. Mr. Hollingsworth would appear to be our only hope. I'm so sorry, Leo."

They had reached busy Park Lane. Beyond the passing carriages, lorries, and horses, the trees of Hyde Park stood like a green wall, protecting the lawns and ponds beyond.

He took her hand. "You have no reason to apologize. This situation was none of your making. I am only grateful you chose to involve yourself on our behalf. I should be the one to apologize if anything he said or did upset you."

Her gaze dropped to where his thumb was making circles on her glove. "I have no idea what possessed him to kiss my hand. I certainly did not give him leave."

They were in full view of every passing stranger, but Leo couldn't stop the words from coming out of his mouth. "Would you give me leave?"

She sucked in a breath, and, for a moment, he feared he'd overstepped. But then she nodded.

Humbled, honored, he raised her hand to his lips and pressed a kiss against her knuckles. Something inside him hitched. A similar tremor went through her arm. And he knew a kiss on the hand would never be enough.

He bent closer, gaze on her rosy lips. The scent of

orange blossoms swept away all other thoughts except
the need to kiss her. She raised her gaze to his, and he
was certain he saw a desire matching his own. When she
leaned toward him, he met her to caress her lips with his
own. So soft, so warm. Ah, but this was perfection.

She pulled back and opened her eyes to gaze at him in
wonder.

"You were right," he murmured, lifting a hand to touch
her cheek. "Playing a part does allow you to do things
you would not have dared otherwise."

"Yes," she murmured back. "So I've noticed."

With a rattle, the solicitor's carriage drew to a stop in
front of them. Leo could have wished her uncle to the
moon, but he forced his hand to fall. Her face flushed
crimson, she allowed him to hand her up into the coach.

"I hope you didn't have to wait long," Mayes said as
Leo and Larissa were seated next to each other on the
forward-facing bench. "Traffic. Were you successful in
your mission?"

For a moment, Leo thought the solicitor meant the
kiss, and he was hard-pressed to think of a suitable answer
besides a besotted grin.

Larissa saved him. "Mr. von Grub was not tremendously
helpful," she said. Her color was coming down, and
she held herself as properly as always. "But Captain
Archambault believes the secretary has no knowledge of
the theft of the Crown Jewels."

Mayes' look was commiserating. "A shame. We will
keep searching."

He did not ask any more questions as the carriage
trundled back toward Clarendon Square. Larissa seemed
determined to look everywhere but at Leo. Was she
regretting the kiss? He couldn't. Such fire, such joy. The
promise of a future, if he could only find a way to claim
it.

As the coachman turned the carriage onto Clarendon

Square, Leo caught a glimpse up the street toward Weyfarer House. Another carriage stood before the door, bearing a crest of a bowing unicorn.

Larissa must have seen it too, for she pressed both hands to the glass. "Father's here!"

Even Mayes grinned, as if he looked forward to greeting his old friend.

Leo knew he should be glad to meet Larissa's father, but all he could think about was having to lie about his identity to one more person.

Mrs. Mayes was coming out of the house as the carriage slowed, Fortune up in her arms.

"Perfect timing," she told her husband with a smile as he climbed out. "I wanted to give the family time to become reacquainted. We can send for my things later."

"I'm delighted to be of service, my love," Mayes said as Leo handed Larissa down. He nodded to Larissa. "Tell your father I'll see him after he's settled in."

"I should go as well," Leo said, feeling craven.

"Don't be silly," Larissa said. "You must meet His Grace. He can tell you what we should do about Liverpool and the other matters." She seized his arm and headed for the door with the briefest of nods to Mrs. Mayes, who opened her mouth as if she had more to say. Fortune looked at them chidingly.

Leo steeled himself as Larissa sailed into the entry hall and glanced up the stairs, then into the withdrawing room as if seeking her father.

A dark-haired woman turned from where she had been talking with Callie, Belle, and Miss Bateman. If the drape of that dusty redingote was any indication, she was sturdily built, like the maidens who worked on the Alpen ranches, and her large brown eyes took him in with a certain assessment.

"There you are, Larissa," she heralded, eyes crinkling in delight. "And who's this, then?"

Larissa froze, all color fleeing. "Your Grace," she said, normally serene voice strained. "Allow me to present Captain Archambault of the Batavarian Imperial Guard."

Your Grace? This was the Duchess of Wey? He glanced at the painting over the hearth for confirmation. When his gaze dropped, he found the duchess looking him up and down.

"No uniform?" she asked.

Leo offered her a bow. "Forgive my casual dress, Duchess. We were on private business for the king."

"But he usually wears a fine uniform, Mother," Belle put in with a smile. "Sharp black with plenty of gold lace."

"Rather dashing," Callie offered.

The duchess took a step closer, gaze now fixed on his face. "Never married?"

Leo blinked. "No."

"Opposed to the idea?"

"Certainly not." What was it about this woman? He, his brother, or his father were generally the ones demanding answers. He'd never felt such pressure to respond and respond to another's satisfaction.

"Sisters, brothers?" she pressed. "And what of your parents?"

Leo stood taller, ready to bear up under the scrutiny. "One brother. Mother deceased. Father alive."

"Planning to stay in England?" she asked, pouncing as effectively as Fortune.

"Your Grace," Larissa put in. "This is not an inquisition."

"That's a shame," the duchess said. "But you're right. Allow me to welcome you back to Weyfarer House, Captain Archambault."

Leo inclined his head, feeling a bit dizzy. "Thank you. And if I can answer any other questions, you have only to ask."

It was the diplomatic thing to say, but Larissa only paled

further.

"Good," the duchess said with a grin. "I have a lot of them. Let's get comfortable first. This way." She patted Callie on the shoulder. "We'll get caught up shortly, my loves."

Miss Bateman smiled hopefully, and Belle gave him two thumbs up as he followed the duchess and Larissa out of the room. Her Grace shucked off her redingote as she led them down the corridor to a library. The blue gown underneath was made of a fine material, with enough trim at the hem to be fashionable.

"At least we won't have to worry about Callie hiding in a corner," she said, tossing her coat to the hovering butler, who caught it with a worshipful look. She took a seat on one of the upholstered chairs in a flurry of fabric. "Would you care for anything to drink, Captain?"

A cup of thick coffee might be wise at the moment, but Leo shook his head. "No, thank you."

She waved him into a seat close to her, then nodded to the butler. "Thank you, Mr. Underhill. Perhaps tea for the girls?"

"At once, Your Grace," he said before marching himself out.

"You don't have to call me Your Grace," the duchess told Leo. "I never accustomed myself to it. Jane will do. I understand you're using Larissa's first name."

He glanced to Larissa to find her squirming on her chair.

"I thought Father was coming," she said.

Jane's face softened. "He'll be along shortly, with Thal and Peter. He thought perhaps another lady might be better to answer the questions you sent."

Larissa's sigh was audible.

The duchess transferred her gaze to Leo. "So, where were we? Ah, yes. How well can the second son of a king support himself?"

Well, that was plain-speaking. He wasn't accustomed to it, but he found he liked it. He would never have to guess what the duchess was thinking.

"Well enough to allow a wife and family," Leo said. "Although I had not thought about marrying, until recently." Unbidden, his gaze swung to Larissa.

She had her hands clasped in her lap, her body still and ready, as if she might leap up and run from the room any second. If his mention of marriage had affected her, she gave no sign. His spirits dipped.

The duchess was nodding. "And what about my question on location? Are you planning to stay in England, or will you follow your king when he returns to his country?"

"Our country, at the moment, is in doubt," Leo explained, trying not to let the statement depress him further. "But I am pledged to follow the king wherever he goes."

"Makes for a questionable future," she said.

"Jane," Larissa warned.

Jane, not Mother as her sisters had called their stepmother. Why would that be?

The duchess tsked. "You mustn't mind me, Captain. This is the first chance I've had to interview a suitor. It's much more fun than I expected."

Laughter forced its way up despite his best efforts. "It must be like when I negotiate with a minister from another country," Leo said. "Anything he says might lead me to a better solution."

"Exactly," Jane said with another nod. "And I like what I'm hearing from you, Captain. I think you'll do nicely." She stuck out her hand.

He'd passed the test. He wasn't sure what that meant, but he couldn't help grinning, especially when he saw that Larissa was smiling at last. He shook the duchess's hand, and that made Larissa smile all the more.

CHAPTER TWELVE

H E LIKED JANE.
Larissa felt as if the sun had come out for the first
time after a month of steady rain. She was never certain
how others would take her irrepressible stepmother, but
she refused to allow anyone to treat her ill. Jane had been
the best friend any girl could have wanted. She simply
couldn't be the duchess others expected. Larissa had long
ago resigned herself to the fact.

Sitting in the library, chatting with Leo as if he were an
old friend, she found herself smiling more than she had
in days. When it was time for him to go, she walked him
to the front door herself, leaving Jane giving instructions
to Underhill in the library.

"Her Grace is a unique woman," he mused as he paused
in the entry hall. "But then, so are you. I look forward to
meeting your father."

"I can't wait," Larissa assured him. "I'm sorry I'll never
have the opportunity to meet the queen, your mother."

"So am I," he said, voice deepening. "She died when I
was a lad. She would not approve of the kingdom's loss.
She spent much of her time making sure no one lagged
behind. She arranged schooling for the young, training
for those ready to take on work. And she made sure no
widow was left alone or penniless."

Now, there was a queen. "She must have been much
loved."

"She was," he said. "By her people and our family. The king never considered remarrying, though there were offers from other ruling houses. She set a high standard for us all."

She understood something of standards. At times, she wondered whether she might ever measure up to the expectations her mother and grandmother had set. Would it even be possible to find a gentleman to please them, for her, Callie, and Belle?

"I can only commend your father, the king, for continuing to take such an interest in his people," she said.

Leo sighed. "In truth, we have faced so many obstacles over the years that sometimes I think he has resigned himself to letting the past go. I am the one who keeps pushing to see the kingdom restored."

"As is your right," Larissa said. "But I can understand. Sometimes, we have to lead when others need help."

"As you helped with nursing your brother," he said.

Larissa nodded. "And I must help Callie and Belle navigate Society. I adore Jane, but, as she said, she's never accustomed herself to being a duchess." She steeled herself. "She was our governess first, you see."

She waited for the censure, the arch look of contempt. Instead, he stuck out his lower lip. "Your father knew a duchess when he saw one."

Larissa beamed. "Yes, he did. And I know a prince when I see one."

He stiffened.

Larissa held up one hand. "I realize your custom only allows the firstborn to be given the title of prince. I just want you to know, Leo, you will always be a prince to me. I find you in all ways the very best of men."

Tuny would applaud her for such a statement. Belle would approve. Callie would be amazed. Her mother and grandmother would be appalled. But she couldn't regret it, particularly when he took a step closer. As before when he'd kissed her, he waited as if to ensure she was as willing. She should have refused when they'd stood on Park Lane. A lady did not kiss a gentleman in public.

But she'd wanted to kiss him, and she wanted it even more now. She raised her chin, and he lowered his head to hers. The kiss robbed her of breath, of thought.

As he pulled back, his diamond eyes glowed with warmth. "I really must meet your father. Until then, I remain your devoted servant." He bowed and left her.

She wanted to spin around the entry hall, run to the top of the stairs and slide down the banister. Surely a lady was allowed some show of elation when she knew herself cherished and admired.

"How well does he ride?" Jane asked, coming down the corridor.

Larissa swallowed her smile and focused her thoughts. "I haven't seen him ride yet. I imagine he does it well."

"We should test that. I think I fell in love with your father the moment I saw him on Belle's unicorn."

Larissa moved to join her as they started into the withdrawing room. "I remember that day. Belle vowed she wouldn't ride unless you located a unicorn for her. But the horse you found wasn't really a unicorn. You just arranged the mane to make it look that way."

"What did I tell you about unicorns?" Jane challenged, brows up.

Larissa laughed. "It's the quest that counts. I remember that too."

Jane linked arms with her and tugged her into the withdrawing room to join Callie, Belle, and Tuny.

"What did you think of Leo, Mother?" Belle asked, scooting over on the sofa to give Jane room between her and Callie.

"A fine young man," Jane said, squeezing between them. "And what's this I hear about you meeting a prince?"

Tuny rolled her eyes. "Not much of a prince. He's frequently rude."

"He knows how to charm as well," Callie put in. "We had a diverting conversation about the depiction of animals in art when we visited Mr. Soane's."

Larissa blinked. "You did?"

Callie's cheeks turned pink as all gazes swung her way. "I have some social skills, you know."

"We know," Jane assured her.

"At least he apologized for his behavior at the king's ball," Belle put in.

Jane rubbed her hands together. "Oh, this story I must hear. Come now, tell me all about what you've been up to."

They spent the next little while sharing everything that had happened since she had left them to tend to Thal.

"Thank the good Lord your brother is doing much better," she said when they had finished and asked after their brothers. "Both the boys and your father should be joining us soon, though how we'll keep Thal and Peter busy while you're gallivanting about, I'm sure I don't know."

"I'll stay with them," Callie offered.

Larissa frowned, but Belle rounded on their sister. "You are not escaping! This is our Season. We made a vow."

"A vow, is it?" Jane asked, glancing around. "And what would that be?"

"You might as well tell her the truth," Tuny said. "You know she'll have it out of you."

"We promised Belle we would do everything possible to see all four of us wed before harvest," Larissa explained.

Jane's dark eyes lit. "A campaign? I always was good at planning those, or at least critiquing the campaigns of others. Do you have gentlemen in mind? Larissa has her captain, of course."

"I'm still meeting people," Belle told their stepmother

as Larissa blushed. "So I cannot say."

"I haven't met anyone who would be suitable for me," Callie said, dropping her gaze.

Jane looked to their friend. "And what about you, Tuny?"

To Larissa's surprise, Tuny turned scarlet. "No one to speak of."

"No one you *want* to speak of," Jane guessed. "Very well. I won't press you. At the moment." She hugged Belle and Callie close. "Oh, it's so good to be back with my girls. How I've missed you."

It wasn't until they were heading upstairs to change for dinner that Jane took Larissa aside.

"Give me a moment," she said, watching as Belle, Callie, and Tuny climbed the stairs. "Tell me about your captain."

Larissa laughed. "You've already quizzed him thoroughly. What more is there to tell?"

"Tell me how you feel about him," Jane said, gaze coming back to hers. "What you like about him. Your father showed me your letter."

Of course he would. Larissa should have thought of that. "He's focused on his goal, to see his king back on the throne. He's very protective of his brother, the crown prince, even when the prince is unkind to him. He has a way of talking."

Jane nodded. "That accent. I noticed it right away. Gives a girl shivers."

"It's not just the accent," Larissa insisted. "There's an elegance to his manner, and he is far more eloquent than you might think for a military man."

"Oh, I've met a few military men who knew how to spin a tale," Jane said. "But go on."

"There's not much more to tell. I like who I am when I'm with him. I feel clever, useful, and admired."

"Nothing wrong with that," Jane said. "But think about

what you want for your future. Would you follow him if
he goes back to his kingdom? Would you be willing to
help him rebuild?"

It was certainly not the vision her mother or
grandmother had had for Larissa's future. They had made
it seem as if the prince she'd marry would be right here
in England, so Larissa would always be surrounded by
those she loved. And when she'd thought about being a
princess, she'd imagined beautiful dresses, lovely soirees,
and serene waves from balconies far above the noise.
She certainly hadn't imagined being the kind of selfless
person his mother had been, though she found that trait
highly commendable.

Still, Leo wasn't a prince the way his country viewed
such matters. He served at the king's pleasure. What if
spending the rest of her life with him meant following
him from one assignment to another?

Jane reached out and squeezed her hand. "I followed
the drum for many years with my first husband. I can't
regret it. However, I will own having a permanent home,
a family, is every bit as wonderful and more."

Larissa nodded, and Jane pulled back her hand. With
a glance up the stairs, she leaned closer. "Callie doesn't
seem happy. Is this prince giving her trouble?"

"A little," Larissa murmured. "I thought at first she
didn't like him, but now I fear she likes him too well.
Still, he's only the beginning of my concerns. She's always
tended to hang back a bit. Now she positively hides."

"Well, we'll have to see what can be done," Jane said.
"What do we have planned for the next little while?"

"Aunt Meredith mentioned a soiree at Lady Carrolton's.
Let's see what else has come in." Larissa went to the silver
tray on the hall table, where a stack of vellum invitations
waited. She cracked the seal on the first. "Caroline
Netherbough is following through on her threat to hold
a ball for the prince. She writes the Batavarian waltz will

be featured."

"Never heard of it," Jane said, wandering closer. "Do you know it?"

"No," Larissa told her. She lowered the invitation. "Trust Caroline to find a way to put the rest of us in the shade."

"Not having it," Jane said. "Not my girls. We'll get ourselves a dancing master."

Larissa frowned. "You know a dancing master who is fluent in the Batavarian waltz?"

Jane grinned. "Indeed I do. I was just introduced to him."

By the next morning, Leo's pleasure in meeting the Duchess of Wey had faded into frustration, and the only thing keeping him sane was the memory of Larissa's lips against his.

He'd shared with Fritz and the king about what he'd learned from Hollingsworth and von Grub. His brother had been none too pleased with Leo confronting the envoy's secretary with only Larissa at his side, but even worse was the report of who had called on the king in Leo's absence. Mr. Canning, the Foreign Secretary, had advised against approaching King George. Apparently, he felt England could not embroil itself in the affairs of other nations, despite the fact that England's plans at the Congress of Vienna had cost them the kingdom to begin with.

And then there was Fritz. Leo hadn't forgotten Larissa's story that Fritz had left the ball earlier than planned the night of the theft. He finally had a moment to corner his brother alone in the salon and ask.

Fritz hesitated to answer, and Leo's heart sank.

"Tell me you aren't involved with the theft of the jewels," he commanded his brother.

Fritz, who had been lounging on the sofa, pulled in his limbs, face darkening. "I shouldn't have to tell you, Your Highness. You should know. But you were too busy acting the part of the dashing captain that I had to take both roles. I left early to check on each of the guards to make sure all was well. If you doubt me, ask them."

His conscience shriveled. "Forgive me, Fritz. I should have thought of that."

"Yes," his brother said. "You should. But I begin to see your role is not as easy as I thought. How do you manage the droning conversation? If I have to comment on the English weather one more time, someone is going to regret it."

Leo smiled. "Wait until they ask you if you find their daughter or sister lovely."

Fritz made a gagging noise. "Spare me. I always thought being the center of attention would be gratifying, but there is something to be said for anonymity."

Leo nodded to the pile of invitations on the desk in the corner of the room. "Neither of us appears to be anonymous at the moment."

His brother rose to go leaf through the invitations that had been coming in at an alarming rate. "And what onerous duties await the crown prince now? Another ball in his honor, another dinner with aged Parliamentarians determined to thwart our cause. Ah, and a note for Captain Archambault."

Leo held out his hand. "Give it to me."

Fritz clutched it tight. "For all you know, this is to me."

"No one in England knows you are you," Leo reminded him, striding toward him.

Fritz backed away. "You cannot be certain of that. Perhaps I was indiscreet."

He wasn't about to let his brother's teases stop him. "You are frequently indiscreet, but not about that. Now, give me that note."

A light came to Fritz's silver-blue eyes, and he slid over the back of a chair to put the upholstered furniture between them. "How does it feel to be merely the captain? As crown prince, I may do as I please. Perhaps I will open this for you."

Of all the arrogant... Leo dove over the top of the chair and came up on his feet, but Fritz was already across the room. The sound of tearing parchment split the air.

"Dear Captain Archambault," he began reading.

Leo veered around the sofa and closed in on him. Fritz dodged and continued reading. "We have been invited to a ball in the prince's honor, and we would like your assistance in learning the Batavarian waltz."

He froze, and Leo was able to yank the parchment from his hand.

"Please wait on us at your earliest convenience," Leo finished. He glanced up to find Fritz still standing there, a frown on his face.

"You see something nefarious in the duchess's request?" he asked.

Fritz shook his head. "I continue to be amazed that your captain is preferred to my prince."

"Perhaps it is not the role but the man playing it," Leo teased.

"Perhaps you are right," Fritz said.

Something in his tone made Leo lower the note. "You could come too. *Noblesse oblige* and all that."

Fritz dropped his gaze. "The Duchess of Wey hardly needs me to condescend to her."

"Perhaps not," Leo agreed, marveling at the change in his brother, "but you would like her. She used to be their governess."

Fritz's head came up. "Really?"

"I have it on good authority." Leo took a step closer. "Come with me. Larissa and her sisters are always up for fun. So is their friend Miss Bateman. Besides, if we train them in the Batavarian waltz, we will always have partners when we must dance it here."

"As if that were a good thing," Fritz countered, but he was at Leo's side and pretending to be the crown prince when they met Larissa, her sisters, their friend, and the duchess at Weyfarer House the next day.

The long room to which they led him and his brother must have been a gallery, for pictures lined the pink-papered walls, but all the furniture had been removed and the carpet rolled up to leave a wide space down the middle. The dark, polished wood floor reflected the green of Larissa's skirts, the blue of Belle's and Miss Bateman's, and the pink of Callie's, like patches of flowers in a mountain meadow.

Mrs. Mayes and Fortune were also in evidence, the former once again in lavender and seated at the piano at the far end of the room, and the latter padding about from lady to lady as if soliciting donations for the poor.

The duchess, gowned in a practical blue cotton dress, scooped Fortune up into her arms. "You best stay with me," she told the cat. "I wouldn't want you to get stepped on."

"She's more likely to bat at our skirts," Miss Bateman said, but she stepped forward before anyone else could. "Why don't you start with me, Captain? The others can watch."

Larissa looked to her friend, brows up as if in surprise, and Leo curbed his impatience and bowed politely to the blonde.

Fritz held out his hand to Belle. "If you would favor me, Lady Abelona."

"Only if you agree to call me Belle," she said, putting her hand on his.

Callie and Larissa backed away, but not before Leo caught a frown from his proper beauty. She didn't like him dancing with her friend, it seemed. Why did that please him?

"I have some traditional music," Mrs. Mayes offered. She played a trill and looked to him.

Leo nodded. "Perfect, but perhaps I should explain first."

They were all watching him now, even Fortune with her unblinking stare.

"The Batavarian waltz grew out of the dances of our people," he explained. "We are, first and foremost, mountaineers, able to scale mighty peaks in search of adventure."

"What he means is the dance has a great deal of hopping about," Fritz said *sotto voce* to Belle, who giggled.

Leo tried to ignore him. "The man is supposed to preen, the lady to command. First, we offer the usual salutations." He bowed, and Miss Bateman curtsied.

Mrs. Mayes began playing. He'd always thought his country's traditional songs had a military air to them, as if his people defied even Nature to stop them from achieving their dreams.

"Twelve counts of the usual waltz steps. One two three, two two three." He swirled Miss Bateman around. "Then we lift." He seized his partner around the waist with both hands and boosted her into the air.

"Oh, my," she breathed as he let her down. She moved out of reach and fanned herself with one hand. "Give me a moment."

He stepped closer. "Are you all right, Miss Bateman?"

She met his gaze and dropped her hand. "Fine," she murmured. "That was just an excuse to speak to you privately. See that you treat Larissa well. My brother used to be a pugilist. He could still take you."

Leo blinked, but she curtsied and went to stand along the wall.

"Perhaps you should continue, Larissa," she said.

Larissa stepped forward eagerly.

Leo put his hand on her waist. The memory of the last time he'd held her nearly swamped him. Her gaze met his, unwavering, confident he would never let her down. And he would never disappoint her.

"The pattern repeats," he made himself say for their audience, "but each time the lift is longer, and the gentleman may add flourishes."

"Like this," Fritz offered, and he lifted Belle high in the air and twirled around with her before lowering her.

"I love it!" she cried. She pulled back. "Come, Callie. You must try."

"I'd rather watch," Callie said, edging closer to the duchess.

"Nonsense," her stepmother said, moving away. "Let's see you give it a go."

As if she agreed, Fortune bumped Callie's arm with her head, pushing her forward.

Callie drew in a stuttering breath and went to join Fritz.

Mrs. Mayes started the piece from the beginning.

Around and around they went, dancing, lifting. His world narrowed to Larissa's lovely face, the sparkle in her eyes, the rose blooming in her cheeks. The first lift, he caught the scent of orange blossoms. The second, he held her up and twirled her around, watching the delight spread across her fine features. When he lowered her, she clung to his arm. He could only praise whoever had invented the Batavarian waltz.

"That's quite enough!"

Larissa stumbled at the cry from her sister, and Leo caught her, only to find Callie yanking out of Fritz's hold, her face flaming. She gathered her skirts and ran from the room.

Now what had his brother done?

CHAPTER THIRTEEN

"EXCUSE ME," LARISSA said, stepping away from one of the loveliest moments of her life. Leo nodded, though she liked to think he looked disappointed that their time had ended so quickly. She followed Callie from the room.

Her sister had only ventured as far as the stairway. Larissa found her on the first landing, arms wrapped around her waist as if giving herself a hug.

"If he was rude again, we can send him on his way," Larissa told her. "He may be a prince, but this is our home."

Callie offered her a ghost of a smile. "He wasn't rude. I'm sure others would have enjoyed the conversation."

Larissa frowned. "But you didn't. Why?"

Callie's arms fell against her pink skirts. "He was flirting with me, Larissa, saying outrageous things about my beauty. We both know he doesn't mean it."

Larissa pulled her into a hug. "Well, you don't have to dance with him any more if you prefer. Tuny or Belle may be willing to oblige him, though, after the way you left, they may prefer to chuck him out on his ear, as Tuny would say."

Callie shook her head as Larissa released her. "I wouldn't want them to take him in dislike. I'm sure few do."

"Very likely," Larissa said. "Which is why he has an overinflated opinion of himself. I'm glad you realized it."

"I have," she promised, but the fact did not seem to cheer her.

"You could dance with Leo if you'd like," Larissa offered.

Her sister would never know the sacrifice she'd made. The feel of Leo's arms about her, his strength as he lifted her, the wonder on his face as his gaze met hers—she could have dined on those feelings and been thoroughly satisfied.

"No, thank you," Callie said, and Larissa forced herself not to smile in relief. "I think I understand the steps. Besides, it isn't as if anyone is going to ask me to dance."

"That's quite enough of that," Larissa said, taking her arm. "If you stopped hiding behind potted palms, the gentlemen would be only too happy to partner you. Jane and I are determined to help."

Callie heaved a sigh. "Oh, not Mother too."

"Yes, Jane too," Larissa said with a laugh. "Between her and Belle, you might as well surrender now."

Callie allowed herself a smile. "Very well. I yield. Let's go back to the others."

Tuny was partnering the prince, and giving him an earful by the look on his face, and Jane was with Leo when they returned. Meredith broke off the melody, and the prince came to bow to Callie.

"Please forgive my wayward tongue, Lady Calantha," he said. "Sometimes I find English a trial. I will endeavor to be a gentleman in your presence."

Tuny eyed him, clearly skeptical, but Callie accepted his apology, and they were able to continue practicing with some semblance of congeniality.

They switched places a few more times until Jane announced that they were all splendid.

"You'll outshine everyone else at the ball Saturday night," she predicted.

The prince bowed to her. "I quite agree, Your Grace. I

look forward to seeing you all there. Come, Captain." He strode from the room. With an apologetic smile, aimed at Larissa, Leo did the same.

Tuny turned to her. "If I can pry you away for a moment, I'd love to take a trip home. I believe I've left a pair of gloves and slippers there I'll want for Saturday."

When Tuny had moved in with them this Season, she'd marveled that she'd brought every stitch of clothing she owned, and it still hadn't been enough to fill the wardrobes in the room she'd been given. But Larissa thought she understood the request now. This trip might be their only chance for a quiet moment, without her sisters, Jane, or Meredith.

"I'd be delighted to help," Larissa said. "If you'll excuse us."

Fortune wandered closer, as if she wanted to go too. Larissa refused to look too deeply in those knowing eyes.

Jane scooped the cat back into her arms. "Fortune and I are watching you two. But off you go, and give my love to your family, Tuny."

It took only a little while for their coachman to bring around the smaller carriage they used in town. As soon as Larissa and Tuny were safely inside, her friend leaned back against the squabs and sighed.

"So it really is to be Captain Archambault, then?"

Larissa smoothed out the wrinkles in her green skirts. "I haven't decided. And he certainly hasn't asked. Why? Do you see something amiss in the connection?"

"Not at all," her friend said. "He's a fine fellow. I just never thought I'd see you falling for someone who didn't have a title and a dozen properties scattered around the world."

Guilt tugged at her. She could almost see her grandmother's frown. "Perhaps titles aren't as important as I thought."

Tuny grinned. "Took you long enough."

"And what about you?" Larissa challenged. "Jane asked whether you had someone in mind, and you blushed."

"Well, it's a nosey question, isn't it?" Tuny answered, but her gaze veered to the window.

"And it's Jane," Larissa said. "She only wants what's best for you."

"It's possible what's best for me doesn't want me," Tuny muttered.

Larissa straightened. "You sound like Callie. What's wrong with you two? You'd think every eligible bachelor on the *ton* had thrown rocks at you!"

Tuny sighed, gaze returning to hers. "You know what they say about you and me, Larissa. We're on the shelf, bound to be spinsters, despite our family's best efforts."

"They are quite ignorant," Larissa said. "We've merely been focused on assisting Callie and now Belle, and I will say again how much I appreciate your help."

"Not much help," her friend protested. "I don't have the connections your family does."

Larissa raised a brow. "Sister-in-law the daughter of a viscount, sister a marchioness?"

"And still only accepted in certain circles," Tuny reminded her. "I'm only saying that I'm glad you found someone you can care about who cares about you in return, but that doesn't mean it will happen the same way for the rest of us."

"And that doesn't mean it won't," Larissa countered. "We promised Belle we would give it our all, and that's what I intend to do. Now, was there really anything you needed at home?"

"Most likely not," Tuny said with a laugh. "But it will be good to see Matthew and Charlotte all the same."

It was. Tuny's family always welcomed Larissa into their home off Covent Garden. Sir Matthew Bateman, Tuny's older brother, still looked as if he could go a round with the country's champion pugilists, especially in the tailored brown coat that fit his rugged frame.

His wife, Charlotte, was always gracious, as if the red in her russet hair mirrored the warmth of her heart. She helped her brother on occasion with the scientific matters he pursued. Otherwise, she kept busy raising her two daughters or investigating mysteries with Sir Matthew. The two had distinguished themselves in that area. A shame they were entirely too obvious to suit the Batavarian's need for secrecy, or Larissa might have recommended them for the investigation into the loss of the Batavarian Crown Jewels instead of Uncle Julian.

"I trust your family and Meredith are well," Charlotte said as they sat in the white and green withdrawing room of the little house.

Larissa assured her they were, with the possible exception of Thal, and asked after her brother and sister-in-law; Daisy, Tuny's other sister, who had married a barrister and was currently expecting her second child; and Ivy and her marquess. Not for the first time did Larissa marvel that Mrs. Mayes and Fortune had had a hand in so many couples finding true love.

True love.

Was that what she and Leo felt for each other? Sometimes, when he looked at her, she knew she was right where she belonged. Had that been the case for Charlotte and Matthew? Tuny's sister-in-law had married below her in some people's eyes, and look how happy she was. She might not be welcome in certain circles, but then, neither was Jane.

"Mum," one of the Bateman daughters, Rose, said from her place on the sofa next to Tuny. Her hair was as red as her mother's, and her eyes were as wide and brown as her father's. "We were going to go to the market. Can Aunt Tuny and Lady Larissa come too?"

"There are sweets," Daphne, their youngest, agreed with a nod of her sable head. She offered a hopeful, gap-toothed smile.

"The market can wait," Charlotte promised them both, but she glanced to Tuny and Larissa. "Unless you'd truly like to visit Covent Garden."

"You don't have to ask me twice," Tuny said.

Larissa laughed. "I would never want to disappoint such charming young ladies."

Charlotte popped to her feet only a moment after her daughters.

Larissa had first met Tuny when her friend had come to Surrey to visit her sister, Ivy, the Marchioness of Kendall, one summer. Since then, they'd visited whenever Tuny was in Surrey or Larissa was in London. So, she knew how much Tuny and Charlotte loved Covent Garden.

The scene always seemed like so much noisy, fragrant, colorful chaos to her. Wooden stalls ran along the edges of the square, with more hastily erected tents, wagons, and wheelbarrows clogging the middle. The air was scented with ripening fruit, smoked meat, and fresh flowers. Sellers shouted the benefits of their wares, sometimes over the top of each other, and children darted among the shoppers. Tuny had taught Larissa to keep her reticule close.

Today, basket over one arm, Charlotte wended her way through the masses. She had a cook who could shop for her, but she still stopped here for carrots, there for a spool of ribbon. She held Rose's hand, while Tuny attempted to keep Daphne out of trouble.

"Those are rather nice," Tuny called to Larissa, tipping her chin toward a seller who had carved-wood hair combs laid out on his table. "Callie's birthday's coming soon, isn't it?"

"Perfect present for a pretty lady," the seller said with a grin that showed his yellowed teeth. His gnarled hand swept over his wares as if beckoning Larissa closer.

The sunlight winked off something bright, sending

rainbows across the crowds. Larissa blinked, then turned to find the source. She caught herself stopping and staring. Just across the narrow aisle, spread out on crimson velvet on a wooden crate, jewels in gold settings glittered in the sunlight.

Daphne must have seen them too, for she towed Tuny past Larissa. "Look, Aunt Tuny! Sparkles!"

Larissa followed them.

"Fancy a crown, missy?" asked the vendor, a wizened woman dressed in black. She plucked up an ermine-edged bit of gold and held it out toward Larissa. "Prettiest ones you'll find short of a jeweler's." She cackled.

Gold arched up from the jeweled base in six bands to form a cross over a massive crown that glowed with rubies and sapphires. The gold orb next to it was studded with diamonds. The gold of the two cuffs was nearly hidden by the number of stones clinging to their sides. And the tiara—silver entwined with sapphires and a diamond at the peak. She could imagine it resting on her head as she stepped down from the dais on her prince's arm.

"Where did you get these?" Larissa asked, not entirely surprised she sounded breathless.

"A lady never tells, does she?" the vendor asked with a sly wink. "But I hear they look just like what that visiting king brought with him, him and his son with the mark on his heel."

She had no idea what the woman meant by a mark, but Larissa met Tuny's gaze. Her friend's eyes were wider than those of the little girl at her side.

"Is it possible?" she asked Larissa.

Larissa would not take that chance. She stepped forward. "I'll buy them all."

The woman reared back. "All?" She scowled. "That will cost you."

"Whatever it costs," Larissa promised. "I'll send my coachman for the funds. Wrap them up in that velvet as soon as the money arrives, and we'll take the jewels with us."

The next morning, Leo strode up the walk to the duke's home, Mr. Jenkins, the insurance agent, scurrying behind. Hope marched with them. Larissa had a clue as to the whereabouts of the jewels, she'd said in her note. He could not be sure if his steps were fueled by that comment or the chance to see her again.

She must have been watching for him, for she met him in the entryway before the footman could do more than take Jenkins' hat.

"They're in the library," she said. "I know it's too much to hope they're what you're seeking given the price I paid for them, but perhaps the thief didn't know what he'd stolen." She reached out and took Leo's hand. "Oh, I hope I'm right."

"Whatever you've done is more than anyone else has accomplished," Leo assured her, her touch more buoying than a squadron of guards.

Jenkins humphed.

Mayes was in the library when they entered. He straightened from where he'd been bent over a small side table draped in crimson velvet. "Captain Archambault, Jenkins. I'm glad you could come so quickly. See what you think."

Leo joined Larissa beside the table. On it reposed a crown, a tiara, on orb of state, and a set of gold cuffs. The ruby at the center of the crown winked at him. His breath stuttered.

"Yes, these look exactly like the Crown Jewels," he managed.

Larissa grinned, then schooled her face to its usual serenity to look toward the insurance agent.

Jenkins edged forward, pulling a jeweler's loupe from

his pocket and affixing it to his eye. "If I may?"

Larissa inclined her head.

He picked up the crown, turning it so the diamonds flashed as well, and studied it through the magnifying glass. He then went on to the tiara and each of the other pieces.

"Well?" Leo asked when he showed no sign of releasing the tiara.

Jenkins set it down at last. "The metal is brass with gilding, and I'm sorry to say the jewels are copies. Good paste copies to be sure, but not the actual stones."

Leo bit back his disappointment. "Thank you."

Larissa deflated. "Only copies, then. The seller said as much."

Leo took her hand and gave it a squeeze. "Thank you for trying."

Her smile was sad. "But you are no closer to finding the real Crown Jewels."

"No," Mayes put in. "But we haven't given up hope. We will see you compensated, Lady Larissa."

She pulled out of Leo's grip. "There's no need. I was glad to be of help."

She didn't sound glad. She sounded as dejected as he felt. Mayes might not have given up, but Leo was finding it hard to continue hoping. His father was no doubt right—the jewels had been pried from their settings and sold to unscrupulous buyers.

Yet if they had been stolen solely for their monetary value, why take the birth records as well? Did the thief intend to hold the loss of the jewels over the king's head, as Mayes had suggested? When could Leo expect the ax of blackmail to fall? And what would be demanded in payment?

"We appreciate that help," Mayes was assuring Larissa. "Mr. Hollingsworth is still on the case as well. We may know more shortly. Perhaps the captain will be able to give you news at the ball on Saturday."

Her smile turned shy. "Yes, of course, the ball. I look forward to it."

So did he, until he returned to the palace and learned his father had a different idea for the future.

The king and Fritz had come back from a visit to Regent's Park and were looking over the invitations for the next few days when Leo entered the salon. He had confided his hopes to his brother, so he wasn't surprised when Fritz looked up eagerly.

"And?" his brother asked.

"Paste," Leo said, joining them. "Mayes, Jenkins, and Hollingsworth are still looking."

His father glanced up at him as well. "And you are worried. I can see those lines across the bridge of your nose. Let it go, Leopold. The insurance agency will pay for the loss, and we will continue as we have."

Leo went to sit near his father. "And continuing as we have is sufficient for you?"

The king spread his hands. "Why not? We have everything we could want with none of the responsibilities that put that frown on your face."

"You sound like Fritz," Leo complained.

"Perhaps your brother and I have learned to be content in all things," the king said, leaning back. "A sound practice, recorded in the Holy Book. I recommend it."

If only it were that easy. "What about our people?" Leo pressed. "They have no advocates."

His father's face hardened. "Württemberg wanted to rule them. Let them be the advocates."

Leo resorted to something he knew his father cared about. "And what happens when the treasury grows emptier? How will we pay for your courtiers and ceremonies?"

"You and Fritz will simply marry heiresses," his father said blithely before picking up another invitation to peruse.

Leo stared at him.

"That should be easy," Fritz said with a look to Leo. "Many women dream of becoming princesses. Even the daughter of a duke, I hear."

Leo stilled. "She told me that in the garden that night. You were supposedly with Father."

Fritz's frown gathered, nearly as stormy as their father's. "I *was* with Father, until I went to see to the guards because you could not be bothered. Lady Calantha imparted the tale to me."

"Enough," the king said. "We should look to the future and the brides you will bring to the family."

"As Fritz has pointed out," Leo countered, "the one good thing about losing the kingdom is that neither of us will be required to make a match for political reasons. We ought to be able to marry for love."

Fritz unbent enough to nod, but their father snorted.

"Idealistic notion," he said, lowering the invitation. "Marriage is always an exchange—beauty for title, position for wealth. You are a fine fellow, Leo, and you have a brain in your head. You are the crown prince! That title alone should win you an heiress." He returned to studying the invitation.

"I have no plans to marry until we have settled the disposition of the kingdom," Leo informed him.

The king looked up, and Leo willed himself not to flinch. The man might be his father, but he was also his liege, and Leo was duty-bound to do as commanded.

"There was a wealthy, ambitious banker at the ball," the king said. "He has two daughters. One of them should do nicely. I will have Lawrence speak to the father."

"No!" Despite his best intentions, the word came out entirely too much like a yelp. Fritz raised his brows, and their father cocked his head.

"I would prefer to arrange my own marriage," Leo said.

"In this day and age, surely both the father and the lady in question will expect it."

His father nodded. "At your earliest convenience, then. But do not try me in this, Leopold. You want to make sure we have a future? Find a wife who will bring wealth to the family."

"I wonder how big a dowry a duke's daughter might have," Fritz mused. "Particularly when she has two younger sisters, and her father is considered a hermit."

"I said I would see to the matter," Leo gritted out.

"That you did," his brother said. "Let me know if you need any help."

CHAPTER FOURTEEN

CAROLINE NETHERBOUGH RENTED Almack's for her ball.

"Of course," Belle said.

Larissa shook her head as she lifted her skirts to follow Jane up the stairs from the King Street entrance to the ballroom proper. It was her first Society event since she'd snubbed the prince at the ball, and she wasn't sure what she would face. But once through the doors, and she wasn't the only one craning her neck to see the hallowed halls they were not otherwise allowed to enter.

"It's smaller than I imagined," Callie murmured as they made their way into the main room, which was paneled in pale colors as if the designer had been determined to call attention to the attendees instead. There were certainly a number tonight. The candlelight from the sconces along the walls glowed on bright satins and gleamed on dark tailcoats. Jewels, more real than the ones she and Tuny had found, sent rainbows here and there.

"This place is legendary," Tuny whispered to Larissa as they moved deeper into the room. "All we need is one of Belle's unicorns to complete the picture."

There might not be any unicorns about, but Caroline had made sure to include a number of presentable gentlemen on her guest list. In fact, so many thronged the space that none of the ladies had to wait for a turn to dance. Soon, everyone was on the floor, even Callie.

Julian had Meredith, and Jane was partnered by an elderly admiral with a spring in his step.

Larissa kept glancing around for Leo, though it was nearly impossible to spot acquaintances among the crowd. She managed to make out Caroline near the entrance. The way their hostess' foot was tapping as it peeked out below her cream-colored satin skirts, the prince and his set had not yet arrived, for all the ball was supposed to be in his honor.

"I don't think he likes her any better than the rest of the *ton* does," Belle observed when they had regathered near the door to the supper room.

"I'm surprised to see you here, Lady Larissa," Lady Wellmanton said, pausing as she and one of her daughters promenaded past. In shades of silvery grey, they might have been two cats prowling the premises.

"Indeed," her daughter said, peering closer. "I heard you'd taken His Highness in dislike."

"A tempest in a teapot," Larissa assured them, careful to keep her smile in place.

"His Highness is ever so friendly," Belle agreed. "If you'd like, we could introduce you."

They both brightened at that. Still, Larissa breathed easier once they had moved on.

Belle patted her arm. "See? That wasn't so bad."

"Everyone's too busy talking about the prince to even think of us," Callie added. The fact seemed to please her by the smile on her face.

Just then, a ripple went through the crowd, as every head turned toward the entrance. People stopped, shifted, stared. Whispers sounded louder than a rising wind. Callie clutched Larissa's arm, and Belle stood on tiptoe.

Larissa had a clear line of sight to the doorway, so she saw when Prince Otto entered, his step elegant and his face solemn. Resplendent in his usual crimson, medals spanning his chest, he inclined his head to this one, tipped his chin to another. Ladies curtsied, and gentlemen bowed low. Callie sighed.

A moment more, and the black uniform came into sight, dour among all the bright silks. His curly hair caught the light as his gaze swept the room. Likely he was checking for any possible danger so he could protect the prince. But a little shiver went through her when his gaze met hers, and his smile blossomed.

Caroline hurried forward and planted herself in the prince's path. "Your Highness," she said, collapsing in a curtsey nearly to the floor, "you honor us with your presence."

He offered her his hand to help her rise.

"Probably couldn't have stood up on her own," Tuny whispered to Larissa.

"My dear Mrs. Netherbough," the prince said. "You are the one to honor me with such a marvelous event. Will you partner me in a dance?"

Her smile broad enough to cross the Thames, she allowed him to lead her onto the floor. Her husband looked on, chest puffed out as if he couldn't have been prouder of her.

She waved a hand, and the string quartet she had hired began playing martial music.

Belle stiffened. "It's the Batavarian waltz! Quick, find a partner!"

Everyone else was scrambling as well. Larissa leaned left, right, but she couldn't see Leo. Was he expected to dance with some high-ranking lady as well? Another man approached, and she gave him such a glower he hurriedly offered for Tuny. She wasn't helping her reputation any at this rate, but she found it difficult to care.

A broad shoulder wedged its way through the other couples, and Leo bowed before her. "Lady Larissa, would you favor me?"

"Of course," she said. Funny. The dance hadn't even

started yet, and she was breathless.

They took their places on the floor. Prince Otto and Caroline started the dancing, and soon everyone was swirling around, skirts brushing trousers, hands holding waists. Larissa tried to focus on the steps. A lady was always graceful and poised on the dance floor. But one glance up and she was slipping into that diamond gaze.

"You are so beautiful," he murmured.

That was the praise she'd been taught to expect, but she'd never thought to hear it said in such a husky voice, as if she left him breathless too. The hands at her waist held her tenderly, until it was time to lift her, and then she was all too aware of the strength in those arms and the power of his body.

What had he said? The man was supposed to preen and the woman to command? He was certainly preening. That grin held a challenge. Larissa lifted her chin and raised her hands over her head, striking a pose. Leo's smile broadened, and he circled her, hands sliding around her waist. Then he seized her, lifted her high, and twirled her about.

Beyond him, she was dimly aware of others stopping, watching. She focused on Leo, moving through the dance, bodies and hearts attuned. When he stomped his feet, she followed suit. When she raised her arms, he raised his. They were joy, they were light. There was nothing they couldn't do.

Then he slowed to a stop, and she realized the music had ended. The last of the couples parted. When he released her, she nearly cried out at the parting. She curtseyed to his bow and made her legs move to accompany him back to where Jane and Meredith were standing beside one of the tall columns that edged the room.

"Very nice," Jane said. "I knew we were right to have you come tutor us, Captain."

He inclined his head. "Thank you, Your Grace." He

turned to Larissa. "I must be a gentleman and partner others. Will you hold the supper dance for me?"

"Of course," she promised.

He bowed to her again, then took himself off.

Larissa caught herself fanning her face with one hand and hastily dropped her arm.

"The supper dance, eh?" Jane asked with a smile. "So he can take you in to supper, no doubt. Figure a military man to think strategically."

"And two dances?" Meredith mused, tapping her chin with her lace-edged fan. "The fellow must be smitten."

So was Larissa, truth be told.

Immediately, other thoughts rushed at her. Despite her vow to Belle, she had not intended to fall in love this Season. She had a duty to Callie. And falling in love with Leo was hardly the act of the daughter of a duke. She could imagine her mother's and grandmother's disdain at the very idea. Loving Leo might also mean she must leave England and her family behind.

"Oh, hush!" she muttered as Jane and Meredith greeted new partners. One of the gentlemen looked at her as if she was quite mad. Perhaps she was.

"Phew!" Tuny collapsed against the wall beside her as she left her most recent partner. "That waltz is more fun than anything except the Sir Roger de Coverly, but it leaves me parched."

"Me too," Callie said, joining them. "Shall I go for ratafia?"

Tuny made a face. "Oh, not that insipid stuff. Surely Caroline can do better." Suddenly, she stood upright, and one hand touched the curls on the top if her head as if to make sure they were still in place.

Lord Ashforde moved up beside them, face betraying no emotion. Larissa had met the ascetic young baron on her first Season. Any number of ladies had set their caps for him over the years, but Lord Ashforde had proven immune. She wasn't sure why.

He was certainly of an age to marry. Debrett's showed him as the last of a distinguished family, which included admirals, statesmen, and cabinet members among its number. Jane had discovered he was rich as the legendary Croesus. Callie had reported no unkind rumors of the fellow, although some claimed him entirely too devoted to his library of classical literature. Still, he was certainly handsome enough with his ink-black hair and emerald-green eyes to illicit a few sighs.

"Lady Larissa," he greeted her. "Might you be willing to partner me?"

This was what she had been born to—polite conversation, cool partnership. Though it felt suddenly foreign, lacking, she offered him her hand.

"Of course, my lord," she said. As he led her out onto the floor, she thought she heard a sigh behind her. Callie? Or Tuny?

It was a country dance, with a great deal of stepping and skipping, which spared her any attempt at conversation at first. Indeed, conversation would have proven difficult in any regard, as her gaze and attention kept swinging down the set to where Leo was partnering a dowager countess. The lady seemed appropriately impressed with him by the fatuous look on her pale, powdered face.

When it came time for Larissa and Lord Ashforde to stand out at the end of the line, she forced herself to put on a smile and talk of commonplaces. "And how are you enjoying the Season, my lord?"

"As well as usual," he said. "And you?"

"It's been delightful becoming acquainted with the Batavarian court," she offered.

His gaze drifted to where Prince Otto was mincing down the line with Lady Bellamy, wife of a prominent Parliamentarian.

"They do appear rather popular," he said. "A shame we

know so little about them."

She would not take umbrage. "They are the scions of a mighty house, here to petition King George for assistance in retaking their kingdom. What else is there to know?"

"Why do they want to retake their kingdom?" he asked, green gaze coming back to hers and holding more curiosity than censure. "It is by all reports well supported by Württemberg. Is it merely prestige that beckons them?"

Her loyalty to Leo won out. "You, my lord, sound decidedly cynical."

His mouth twitched. "So I have been told. But I find it a position all too often supported, alas."

She was glad the dance required their attention, then, so she did not have to continue the conversation. Otherwise, she might have allowed herself to show more than a momentary pique.

Unfortunately, as the evening progressed, her other partners proved just as lacking. Most were tolerable dancers. Some were handsome and charming. A few were engaging conversationalists.

But none of them was Leo.

For three Seasons, she'd smiled and chatted and danced her way through event after event, always looking for someone Callie or Tuny would find interesting. Always hoping she might find someone interested in her. Not one of the many young men she'd met had stirred her heart. Now it seemed Leo had spoiled her for anyone else.

Why wasn't that fact more troubling?

Leo watched as Larissa danced her way down the set on the hand of a dashing lord. The moment she'd lifted her chin in the Batavarian waltz, she had captured him heart and soul. None of the other ladies had her poise, her elegance. None brought a smile to his lips merely by looking his way. None made him want to hold them close, cherish and protect them all the days of his life.

Oh, but he was lost.

He couldn't claim her hand again until the supper dance, which turned out to be a traditional waltz. If he held her a little too close, it was only because the room was so crowded. And so he would tell any who dared comment on the fact.

He joined her and her family and friends in the supper room afterward. Though the duchess was with them, they had been given a table near the back of the room. Perhaps Mrs. Netherbough was less than impressed with Mr. Mayes and his wife. He could not credit she would dare slight the duchess herself.

Fritz, meanwhile, was taking every advantage of his role at the top of the room. Their hostess and her husband devoured every word he uttered more quickly than the thinly sliced ham, and her friends tittered at his wit. If Leo ever resumed the role, he would have to remake a lot of impressions.

If he resumed the role?

He nearly dropped the piece of lobster patty he had on his fork. Of course he would resume the role. He was the crown prince, the firstborn of the king of Batavaria. Playing Captain Archambault was merely a way to ensure they met their goal to restore the monarchy. As Larissa had said, pretending gave him a certain freedom. He should not become attached to it.

Across the table, Mayes leaned closer. "I wonder, Captain, might I have a private word with you on Monday?"

"You have news?" Leo asked eagerly, as the ladies at the table all perked up as well.

Mayes offered him a crisp smile. "Nothing tangible, but I would like your opinion on the matter. Could you come to my offices in Whitehall, say eleven?"

"I will be there," Leo promised.

"And what else does His Highness have planned for the rest of your visit to London?" Mrs. Mayes asked.

The question was casual, the usual conversation over supper at a ball, but there was a light in her lavender eyes. The other ladies were regarding him as avidly.

"I believe we have been invited to meet with a number of noteworthy organizations," he said. "The Royal Botanic Gardens at Kew; the Royal Foundling Home; the Annual Meeting of the Royal Society for Arts, Manufactures, and Commerce; and a new society for the prevention of cruelty to animals."

Callie choked and dropped her fork, then hastened to cover her mouth with her napkin.

"Callie and I support that society," Miss Bateman informed him as if daring him to criticize.

"A worthy endeavor," he assured her. "We too often take advantage of our animals when in fact they are partners in every area of our lives."

As a lady, they beamed at him.

Even Mayes grinned. "Well said, Captain."

"A man after my own heart," Larissa agreed.

Another smile like that from her, and he'd pop the gilt braid right off his swelling chest.

Unfortunately, he'd already danced with Larissa twice, and taken her in to supper, so he wouldn't be allowed another dance that evening without setting expectations he wasn't prepared to confirm. He wasn't sure whether to be glad or annoyed when Fritz rose from the supper table to announce to all and sundry that he must take his leave.

"Important business for the crown tomorrow," he said, nodding around at his doting acolytes. "Best wishes to all."

"And what business do you have tomorrow?" Leo asked as he followed him out of the assembly rooms.

"Nothing whatsoever," Fritz said. "I leave all matters of

business to you. I must have some recompense for taking on the burden of the crown, even if it is only leaving events when I like."

Leo shook his head. "You are making it difficult for me."

Fritz shot him a grin. "Then you should not have asked me to assume your role."

"I will need you to do so on Monday as well," Leo told him as they came out onto the street, where the lights from the assembly rooms made an uneven patchwork on the pavement. "Mayes wants to talk to me. Something to do with the jewels, I assume."

"Wonderful," Fritz drawled, raising a hand to summon their coachman, who was waiting down the block. "That means I will be consigned to chucking orphans under their chins and promising the future will be brighter."

"You will manage," Leo promised.

Suddenly, Fritz's eyes widened, and he thrust Leo behind him. Leo caught a glimpse of a man darting out of the shadows. Light glittered on a blade.

Even as Leo tensed, Fritz was moving. He stepped to one side and let the fellow's momentum carry him past them. Then he caught the man's wrist and twisted. The knife clattered to the pavement, but their attacker righted himself and slammed his other fist into Fritz's nose. His brother stumbled back, bumping into Leo, who steadied him, trying to keep his own footing.

"Ho, there!" their coachman yelled as he pulled the carriage into position and the footman jumped down. "What do you think you're about?"

In answer, their attacker fled.

Leo darted around Fritz. "After him!"

Fritz caught his arm and held him in place even as their footman hesitated. "Get in the coach, Leo."

Leo yanked away. "Are you mad? He's escaping!"

"Or going for reinforcements," Fritz said. He stripped

off one glove and wiped at his nose with his bare hand. Dark blood marred his fingers. "Let me do my job for once, Your Highness. I can only fight so many." He lifted his elbow. The crimson sleeve was slashed, showing the white of his shirt.

"Want me to send Marcel for the constable?" their coachman asked.

Tempting. The way his heart was pounding, Leo could have run down the villain himself. Yet he had to think of his brother. Once again, Fritz had stepped in to protect. Leo could only be thankful for it, and humbled.

"No," he said. "Thank you. Return us to the palace."

He clambered in. Fritz picked up the knife and followed.

"How badly are you hurt?" Leo asked, perching on the seat.

Fritz had pulled a handkerchief from his coat and was applying it to his nose as he sat opposite him. "It's only the nose. He was aiming too low if he hoped to hit something vital with the knife." He glanced at the slim dagger on the seat beside him. "Which makes me wonder. Was he attempting to kill?"

"A warning only, then," Leo surmised, taking a deep breath. "Against attempting to retake our lands."

Fritz nodded. "He thought I was you. What better way to stop a man than to threaten his heir?"

Leo chuckled, though there was nothing humorous about the situation. "They cannot know Father well."

"Or perhaps they do. You saw him, Leo. The fire has gone out of him. If something happened to you, he might give up."

Much as Leo hated to admit it, he'd seen the signs himself. The Lion of the Alps had all but lost his roar.

"We must petition Liverpool again," Leo said as the coachman drove them out of the city. "Between our entertainments and this ball tonight, we have public sentiment on our side. He and Canning cannot keep refusing to allow us to see King George."

"Agreed," Fritz said. "But you must let me resume my position, Leo. I cannot protect you if you send me touring orphanages while you put yourself in danger."

"No one knows you are me," Leo reminded him. "I will stay in the palace tomorrow aside from attending services, if that comforts you. Surely no one will attack us there. But I must see Mayes on Monday."

Fritz sighed. "Go as the captain, then. I will take your place with Father, but you can be sure I will watch for any treachery."

So would Leo.

CHAPTER FIFTEEN

INSIDE ALMACK'S, CAROLINE Netherbough attempted to continue the ball after Leo and the prince had taken their leave, but the event had lost its luster. Larissa didn't protest when Jane suggested they go. Neither did Callie, Belle, or Tuny. They trooped down the stairs with far less animation than when they'd arrived.

"I need new dancing slippers," Belle said as they waited for their coach. She lifted a dainty foot from the ground. "These are nearly worn through."

"Small wonder when you are on the floor for every set," Jane said with a smile. "We'll go shopping Monday if your father hasn't arrived by then."

"Pardon, lady."

Larissa stared at the man who had appeared beside her, for all the world as if melting out of the brick of the building. Covered as he was in a hooded black evening cloak, she could only tell that he was tall and had a long black mustache.

On the other side of her, Belle brought her foot down with a slap. "I know you! You're the man Captain Archambault caught."

Larissa took a step back, keeping herself between Belle and the man. "What do you want?"

He reached a hand into his cloak, and Jane darted in front of them both. "Here, now! What do you think you're doing?"

"Jane!" Larissa caught her shoulder and pulled her away from the fellow. "He's dangerous."

"Watch!" Tuny shouted. "Ho, the watch!"

The fellow winced, but he whipped out a folded note and thrust it at Larissa. "For the prince. Very important. See that he listens."

As the sharp clack of the watchman's rattle sounded down the block, he turned on his heel and dashed off.

Jane puffed out a sigh, shoulders slumping. "Well, that was an adventure."

"It certainly was." Belle hopped from foot to foot. "What do you think it says? Why didn't he give it to the prince himself?"

The watchman and their coachman arrived in the same moment.

"What's all this about then?" the weathered watchman asked, gripping his wooden rattle. "Who called for me?"

"I did," Tuny admitted. "We were set upon."

"Were you?" He peered closer. "Gentleman not willing to dance, eh?" He chuckled at his own wit.

Larissa drew herself up, but so did Jane.

"See here," Jane said in ringing tones that bounced off the building behind them. "I am the Duchess of Wey, but I shouldn't have had to tell you that. Your job is to prevent the sort of mischief my girls and I just endured. We were accosted by a fellow with an impressive mustache and an accent, Italian, if I don't miss my guess. He ran off that way. I expect you should follow."

He glanced at the crest on the carriage, then bobbed his grey head as he edged around them. "Yes, Your Grace. At once, Your Grace." He toddled away.

"Oh, Mother, that was well done," Belle crowed.

Jane smiled. "Never hurts to throw out your title. I suppose that's what they're for." She held up a hand. "No need to come off the bench, Mr. Thomas. We'll be leaving now."

Their coachman nodded, and Davis jumped down to hand them in. Larissa could not seem to catch her breath as she settled next to Callie and Jane. Belle and Tuny sat across from them.

"Well," Jane said, arranging her skirts. "Let's see it."

Larissa unclenched her fingers from around the piece of paper. It was folded shut, but it hadn't been sealed. "He said it was for the prince." A lady surely didn't read a message intended for another. Worse luck.

"And he appeared out of nowhere and scared us half out of our wits," Jane countered. "Let's see what all the fuss is about."

Belle was right. There was no use arguing with their stepmother. Still, Larissa's fingers fumbled with the note as if just as hesitant as her heart as she opened the paper.

"A friend advises that a plot is forming against you," she read aloud. Her mouth felt suddenly dry, and she swallowed before continuing. "Do not approach the English king, or it will go badly for you."

Her hand was shaking as she lowered the note. She managed to keep her voice calm. "There's no signature."

"There wouldn't be," Jane said. "Cowards use any excuse to hide."

"We must tell King Frederick," Belle put in, glancing between Jane and Larissa. "He must protect the prince."

"They must all be protected," Larissa said. She turned to Jane. "Can we send a footman tonight?"

"Of course," Jane said. "I'll send Mr. Thomas and young Davis as soon as we're home. Now, what's this about you knowing our mysterious postman?"

Belle and Callie told the story between them. Larissa kept turning the letter in her hands. In the dim light of the coach's lantern, she couldn't make out any tell-tale marks. But likely Leo would know better.

She handed the note to Davis after Jane had explained his mission.

"Please give this to Captain Archambault," Larissa said. "He'll know what to do. And tell him if he should be walking in Hyde Park tomorrow at three, we would enjoy his company."

Davis nodded, and Thomas, waiting on the coachman's bench of the carriage, touched his whip handle to the brim of his hat. "Yes, your ladyship. Count on us."

The footman hopped back up beside him, and they were off.

A shame her fears lingered behind.

Larissa barely attended to services the next morning. If her lips moved, it was only to mutter prayers for Leo's safety. The odious note may have threatened the crown prince, but that didn't mean he was the only one in danger. What if Leo was hurt trying to prevent his brother's injury? It would be just like him to stand in the breach.

"Is there a sale at Hatchard's?" Tuny teased as they promenaded in Hyde Park that afternoon. "Getting the best prices at your favorite bookseller might explain why you're walking so fast."

Larissa glanced behind them and was surprised to see Jane, Callie, and Belle far in the distance, having stopped to speak to some gentlemen.

"Sorry," she told her friend, slowing her steps. "I'm worried about Leo."

Tuny smiled. "Then it's a good thing he's headed our way."

Larissa had to stop herself from running to him. A lady did not chase after a gentleman. She beckoned a fellow closer with her welcoming smile and lustrous gaze.

Neither of which felt at all useful at the moment.

He met them near where the chimney pots of the Keeper's Lodge rose above the trees. "Lady Larissa, Miss

Bateman. I must thank you for sending that note."

Larissa stared at him. That voice, those eyes! "You! What are you doing!"

Tuny frowned at her as if she couldn't see the difference.

Prince Otto, in Leo's dark uniform, gold braid glinting in the sunlight, took Larissa's arm and drew her off the path and under the shade of the trees. Tuny followed.

"Forgive me," he told them both. "I came instead of Leo because I wanted to thank you personally and to make sure you and your family had come to no harm. Believe me, my brother protested. He finally relented when I reminded him this might be the only way to keep the crown prince safe."

What a bucket of humbug! He'd come because it pleased him. "You would have been perfectly safe if you had allowed him to meet us in your place," Larissa informed him.

"But I had questions," he said, as if that was all that mattered. "Who gave you the note? Where?"

"I don't see why Captain Archambault couldn't have asked those questions," Tuny put in. "And much more nicely, if you take my point."

He drew in an audible breath through his nose, as if gathering his patience, then curved up his lips in a smile that did nothing to brighten his eyes. "My apologies. You will understand why that note left me more than a little concerned."

"Then perhaps you can understand why we are *all* concerned," Larissa told him. "And why we are more than happy to assist. To answer your questions, the fellow whom Captain Archambault subdued near the Tower handed me that note last night as my family and Miss Bateman were leaving the ball."

He narrowed his eyes. "Time?"

Larissa glanced at Tuny.

"Just after one," her friend said. "About a half hour after

you'd left."

He nodded as if that made some sort of sense to him. "Did he say anything else?"

"Only that I was to see that the note reached you," Larissa supplied.

He stilled, diamond eyes drilling into her. "Me?"

"The crown prince," she clarified.

"Ah," he said, muscular body relaxing. "And where did he go when he left you?"

"Away," Tuny said. "With the watchman on his tail. You might check with Newgate to see if he was caught."

"Newgate?" he asked, glancing from one to the other.

"Prison," Tuny said. "It's where we put folks that break the law." Her tone was terse, and Larissa couldn't blame her. Gentlemen should not corner ladies and pepper them with questions. She could only hope Jane and her sisters would catch up shortly. Let him try this sort of thing with the duchess!

But it was plain the prince wasn't ready to release her and Tuny just yet. "And you can tell me nothing more?" he pressed.

"No," Larissa snapped. "I don't know why you persist with these questions, Your Highness, but I don't intend to play your game."

He leaned closer. "Perhaps you should ask my brother what game he insists on playing, then, for it is the most likely to see someone hurt."

He struck a fist to his chest and strode off through the crowds, once more leaving her staring.

Leo prowled the palace until Fritz returned that afternoon. It had taken the combined insistence of his father and brother to convince him to remain behind. He was waiting in the gallery when Fritz came in.

"What did you learn?" he demanded. "Is she safe?"

Fritz held up one hand as if to forestall other questions. "Lady Larissa and her family and friend are fine. She is, however, annoyed with me."

"You?" Leo asked, following him as he started toward the private side of the palace. "You-you or you-me?"

"The very fact that you must ask the question should tell you something," Fritz said, stride lengthening.

Leo had no trouble pacing him. "Answer the question."

Fritz cast him a look out of the corner of his eyes before doing so. "The me she assumes is the crown prince. She made it quite clear she would have preferred to speak to her gallant captain."

Leo couldn't help his grin as they entered the salon. "Once again, she prefers the captain to the prince."

"There is no accounting for taste," Fritz said. "Unfortunately, she could tell me little more. She confirmed the note came from Mercutio, as I suspected."

"And we have no idea where he is?" Leo asked.

Fritz went to close the draperies against the tall windows overlooking the grounds, as if concerned someone might be watching. "No. And the more you have me play the noble prince, the less opportunity I have to find our enemies."

Leo winced, then rallied. "But you were Captain Archambault today."

His brother turned from the window. "I was. At Miss Bateman's suggestion, I checked with the local authorities. No one of Mercutio's description was apprehended. Most likely he slithered into the shadows until he is ready to send the next dire warning."

"Then we have nothing," Leo said, hands fisting.

"There was that request from the solicitor to meet with him," Fritz said, clasping his hands behind his back. "I believe you said he was looking into Mercutio's whereabouts as well. I can meet with him tomorrow."

"No, I'll go," Leo argued.

Fritz raised his brows as if surprised by his vehemence. Leo was a little surprised by the outburst as well. Was he becoming that fond of the freedom enjoyed by Captain Archambault? Or was it merely that he hoped for an opportunity to see Larissa?

"You were not privy to the discussions," Leo temporized. "You could misspeak and tip him off to the game."

"And you could be killed if Mercutio or this enemy he mentions is on to the game as well," Fritz pointed out.

"I know."

"Do you?" His brother closed the distance between them. "Do you really understand the stakes of this game, Leo? Father's right. We are no longer children. If anything happens to you, I am not ready to lead a nation."

"Neither am I."

Fritz reared back, but Leo couldn't stop the words coming out of him. "Yes, I was trained to take Father's place. Yes, I am willing to lay down my life for my country. But you and Father and his courtiers have worked my entire life to shelter me from anything that might harm me. I did not see that before coming here. Now I can only wonder whether I have the experience to deal with the challenges we face."

"Yet you would ask me to step aside, stop taking the role I was born to," Fritz said.

"No," Leo said. "I want you at my side, always. But this is my future. Should I not have a more active role in securing it?"

Fritz looked to the ceiling a moment as if invoking Heaven's aid before dropping his gaze to meet Leo's. "You will go to see Mayes as the captain, and you will take three of the Imperial Guards with you."

"Agreed," Leo said, relief surging through him. "They can wait in the carriage."

Fritz bristled.

"They have no need to be privy to what Mayes has to

tell me," Leo reasoned.

Fritz nodded. "Very well. See that you stick with your itinerary."

Leo inclined his head, but he made no promises. If he happened to stop by Clarendon Square on the way back, his brother need not be concerned.

Several clerks were toiling away at desks behind a railed divider when Leo arrived at Julian Mayes' offices at precisely eleven on Monday, leaving three of Fritz's guards waiting impatiently beside the carriage. One of the clerks was happy to escort Leo back to a private office overlooking London. Surrounded by bookcases groaning with thick-spined legal tomes, Mayes nodded him into the chair in front of his desk and resumed his seat behind it.

"Thank you for coming, Captain," he said. "Let me state at the outset that I have found no evidence of the Crown Jewels, a fact that is both baffling and bothersome."

"A shame," Leo agreed, hands on the arms of the wooden chair. "Yet if someone is intent on blackmail or ransom, they are strangely reticent to put their plan into action."

"My thoughts exactly," the solicitor said. "In the course of my investigation, however, I unearthed some unsettling facts." He hesitated a moment, and Leo tensed.

"Were you aware, Captain, that the House of Archambault has not been paying its debts?"

Leo frowned. "No. I have on occasion seen reports from the royal treasury, such as it is in exile. Everything seemed appropriate."

"Your steward allowed me a look at his account books as well," he confirmed. "But additional conversations around town proved that nothing has been paid outside the initial deposit on the palace. The food, the entertainments, the new clothing—all are awaiting payment."

"The merchants need only submit their invoices, and they will be swiftly paid," Leo assured him.

"Alas, the merchants have submitted invoices, sometimes more than once, and nothing is forthcoming." He leaned closer. "Is it possible, Captain, that His Majesty and the crown prince are in more dire straits than the loss of the jewels would suppose?"

Once he would have denied the possibility. The House of Archambault prided itself on its honor. But he had cautioned his father that they could not continue living so lavish a lifestyle forever. Surely they hadn't reached the point at which they could no longer pay what they owed!

"I will look into the matter," Leo said.

Mayes inclined his head. "I would advise it. And, if I may add one more item to consider, a payment of insurance for something as valuable as the Crown Jewels would go a long way toward settling those debts."

Something snapped inside him, and Leo surged to his feet. "Take that back, or name your second. As crown prince, I…"

The look on the solicitor's face warned him a moment before he realized what he'd said.

"Ah," Mayes said, leaning back. "I had wondered why your brother was a bit mercurial for the role of head of state. Do I have the pleasure of addressing the real crown prince?"

Leo sank onto the chair. He'd done exactly what he'd warned Fritz against. How his brother would laugh.

"Yes," he admitted. "The prince you have been seeing is my twin, Frederick Leopold. We both hold the title of captain in the Imperial Guard."

He nodded as if it all made sense. But Leo was struggling to make sense of any of what he'd learned. Was it possible his father had arranged the theft of the jewels? He hadn't protested their loss as much as might be expected. The money a claim would bring in would go much farther than gold and diamonds stuffed in a safe. But if his father was responsible, then the theft could not be connected with the attack Mercutio had warned about.

"Does Lady Larissa understand?" Mayes asked quietly.

Leo shook his head, pulling his mind back to the moment. "No. As far as I know, you are the only one to discover the truth."

Mayes lay his hands on the desktop. "You must tell her. She deserves to know."

"I will," Leo said. "But not until we have settled things, with the lost jewels, and with those who would stop us from approaching your king."

He raised his brow. "That could take a great deal of time, Your Highness. Lady Larissa and her sisters are like daughters to my wife and me. I do not like the idea of anyone lying to them."

His father would have berated the man for daring to speak that way. Leo might have once as well. Now he could only applaud Mayes for caring.

He rose. "I promise you I will reveal all to Lady Larissa at the first opportunity. Thank you for telling me what you learned and surmised, Mr. Mayes. You have given me a great deal to think about."

So much so, in fact, that the matters weighed heavily on his mind. He didn't stop at Weyfarer House after all but told the coachman to take him and the guards directly back to the palace. Time to put these endless rumors to rest.

CHAPTER SIXTEEN

L EO STALKED DOWN the corridors until he located their Lord Chamberlain. Lawrence was consulting with an older fellow in a tailored coat that did nothing to broaden his narrow shoulders. Normally, their chamberlain would have stopped all conversation to tend to Leo's requests, but he kept Leo standing for some time before motioning the fellow off and striding closer.

"Yes, Captain?" he asked. "I have important work for the king. Is there something you need?"

Leo narrowed his eyes. "Is that how you address my brother?"

Lawrence blinked, then peered closer. Whatever he saw made him snap upright. "No, Your Highness. Certainly not. Had I known it was you…"

"I expect you to extend the same courtesy to Captain Archambault," Leo informed him. "And I expect you to bring any concerns about our finances to me."

Lawrence licked his thin lips. "Finances, Your Highness? Surely such matters are best left to Lord Matterone, the Royal Steward."

"You hire the staff," Leo reasoned. "You see to the care of the palace and all entertainments. Who was that with you?"

Lawrence glanced after the man. "An architect, Your Highness. His Royal Majesty felt the chandeliers did not impart sufficient light at his events. I was trying to determine the best way to improve the conditions."

Leo drew in a breath. "Tell the architect we changed our minds. Are you aware that invoices for our previous entertainments have yet to be paid?"

Lawrence waved a hand. "A momentary lapse. His Royal Majesty was clear in his instructions. We are to be slow in responding to such matters." He leaned closer and lowered his voice as if he suspected the gilded paneling of hiding spies. "I take it this is a ploy to convince the English to let him see their king."

"An interesting strategy," Leo said as he straightened. "I will be sure to discuss the matter with the king. Until then, make no more plans for anything outside the usual household expenses."

He inclined his head. "Of course, Your Highness."

Leo strode from the room to find the Lord Steward, and then his father.

The king was reclining on the couch in his bedchamber, coat slung on the arm and feet up on a tasseled cushion, when Leo located him.

"Where have you been?" his father demanded. "I thought we agreed you would remain in the palace until we had resolved this issue of the threat. Fritz went off on some tour of something. The home for indigent sheep? The museum of sewing thimbles? These English and their causes."

"We had a cause," Leo reminded him, coming to stop in front of him and holding his temper by a thin thread. "A noble cause. I thought we agreed we would do nothing to hinder it."

His father saluted him with the crystal glass. "Batavaria Prorsus."

"Batavaria Entirely," Leo translated. "The family motto. I always understood it to mean our first devotion must be to the kingdom. Apparently, I was mistaken." From his uniform, he pulled the invoices the steward had

NEVER PURSUE A PRINCE 189

reluctantly released and held them out to his father. "Are we truly at the point where we cannot pay our way?"

The king stiffened, mustache bristling. "Who told you that?"

Leo lay the invoices on the couch beside him. "These speak for themselves."

"Trivia." The king swept them off the upholstery, sending them fluttering to the thick carpet. "Are we merchants, that we haggle? Bankers, that we calculate? We are the rulers of Batavaria! Let them grovel before our might."

His father's bluster had once set courtiers and servants to quaking. Now Leo could only shake his head. "Our might consists of a handful of loyal guardsmen, royal staff, and servants, and they will not stand by us long if we fail to pay them too."

"Then they are not true sons of Batavaria," his father said scornfully, clutching his goblet closer. "It is an honor to serve such a noble house."

"I once thought so." He made himself take the other chair in the room, across from the king. "And what of the Crown Jewels? It seems they may not have been stolen after all."

His father slammed his goblet down so hard on the arm of the couch Leo thought the crystal would shatter. "Lies! Who is filling your ear with such things? I will have that insurance agent's head." He narrowed his eyes, as if he could see inside Leo. "No, not the agent. That solicitor, Julian Mayes. He is discharged. I do not want him working on our behalf another moment."

"Mr. Mayes has done exemplary work," Leo started.

The king heaved himself to his feet. "Do you argue with your king?"

Leo rose, as propriety demanded. "No, Your Majesty. But I will remind the king that his reputation and the reputation of his house have direct bearing on the conversation he hopes to have with the king of England. That monarch may take a dim view of us if we fail to pay his subjects what they are owed."

"Bah." His father sank back onto the couch, the sneer on his upper lip only half hidden by his mustache. "You should have heard the stories of him when he was Prince Regent. He had to give Parliament all manner of concessions to have his debts paid. He will understand if I have other things on my mind than his nation of shopkeepers."

Leo bent to collect the invoices. "Will he? It seems to me King George has changed since he was crowned. He has aligned himself with the conservative Tories rather than his once-beloved liberal Whigs. He has attempted to unite his kingdom by visiting Scotland and Ireland. He may very well take exception to a king who cannot pay his debts."

"If you are so worried, where is your heiress?" the king retorted. "You promised me you would find one to marry."

"Circumstances have prevented that," Leo said. "You asked me to stay close."

"And you disobeyed me there too," his father complained. "Remember your duty, Leopold. And convince that insurance company to pay me what I am owed. They are the ones holding up our money."

Leo could not help siding with the insurance agency. Something was very wrong, even if his father refused to acknowledge it.

And as for marrying an heiress, the king had claimed marrying a prince would be enough for some women to hand over their dowries. The bargain seemed even more unfair if the king intended to spend the money as fast as it came in. A wife had a right to expect her husband to provide for her.

How could he do that when it appeared he could not

even provide for himself?

Meredith looked up from their dinner of jacketed potatoes and mutton to find Julian staring off in the middle distance again. Her husband had been strangely quiet since returning from his office that afternoon, and he'd sat with Fortune for a full quarter hour, running his hand down the silky grey fur. Fortune had tolerated the touch for as long as she could, before jumping to the floor and offering him a berating glance. She had retreated to the upper floors and had only come down for dinner in the kitchen.

"What is it, dearest?" Meredith asked Julian now, setting aside her fork. "A problem with one of your clients?"

He sighed so hard the candle flames stuttered. "We continue to have trouble with the matter of the Batavarian Crown Jewels."

Meredith made a moue. "You can't solve every case brought to you."

Julian chuckled, but there was no joy to the sound. "That's just it. I believe I have solved the case, and the answer doesn't please anyone." He pushed back his plate. "Besides, the captain sent word the king would like me to cease my services on his behalf."

Meredith stared at him. "He had the poor judgment to sack you?"

"Without pay," Julian confirmed. "It seems the king and both his crown princes are punting on the River Tick until the insurance claim is paid."

"It doesn't surprise me the way they throw out largess." Meredith shook herself. "Wait a moment. Did you say there are two crown princes?"

His mouth turned up for the first time. "Only one, but as the two are nearly identical twins, it seems they on occasion play each other's part."

"Then Captain Archambault..." she started.

"Is actually the crown prince," Julian finished. "I informed him he must tell Larissa."

"He ought to tell all of London," Meredith scolded. "What was his reasoning for such a subterfuge?"

Julian cocked his head. "Do you know, he never said."

She drew a breath. "That man, at the Tower. Both the prince and the captain suspected him of nefarious deeds, and Jane told me he accosted her and the girls outside Caroline Netherbough's ball. Is His Royal Highness in danger?"

"Possibly," Julian said. "There are those who do not want him to retake the kingdom. I'm sure it isn't always easy being the crown prince of a country that no longer exists."

"Especially with a father determined to pretend they still reign," Meredith agreed, "with all the pomp and circumstance associated with the role. Our own gracious Majesty will not be amused when he learns of their game."

"If he learns of it," Julian said, straightening. "That was another matter that came up this afternoon before I was discharged. I managed to speak with Liverpool about their cause. He claims that was the first he'd heard of it."

Meredith frowned. "How could that be? Speculation was in all the papers. The king invited him to a ball. Do you mean to tell me he never broached the subject?"

"According to Liverpool, the king spoke mostly in generalities," Julian told her. "The prime minister received nothing formal, not even through Canning. Of course, it's possible the request was mislaid. Liverpool must receive hundreds of petitions every week. But I doubt the fervent request of a foreign court would be mislaid for long."

Meredith retrieved her fork. "Prince Otto Leopold must be told. Someone is working against them, and that person may be in their own household."

"Sadly true," Julian said. "But as I've been discharged, there's little I can do."

"But a great deal I can do," Meredith promised him. "I'll see that His Highness is apprised of the matter. And I will let him know that he must tell Larissa the truth, before I do it for him."

Larissa didn't see Leo the next couple of days. Very likely he was busy protecting his brother and the king. He would be thorough, not wanting harm to come to any of them. The thought should hold a certain satisfaction. She'd always been one to appreciate duty and constancy. But she missed him. She'd spot a statue in the Greek style and remember when they'd first met. She'd hear martial music and think of the Batavarian waltz and the tenderness in his eyes as he'd lifted her. And the memory of his kisses was never too far from her mind.

Then again, her time was busy too. Her father had arrived at last, with both her brothers in tow. Belle and Callie made much of them, especially Thal. Few remembered her oldest brother's name was Andrew. At his birth, as the heir of a duke, he'd been awarded her father's courtesy title of Lord Thalston, by which he would be known until that day when he must ascend to the title of the duke. As such an exalted personage, he might have been insufferable. But then again, his mother was Jane.

"I'm fine," he protested when Belle shooed everyone off the sofa so he might recline if needed. "It was only a momentary fever. I probably stayed out too long on the cricket pitch."

Larissa caught her father and Jane exchanging glances. So, there was more to that story. She was just glad both her brothers looked hale and hearty now. Unlike her and her sisters, who favored their mother, twelve-year-old Thal and eight-year-old Peter had their father's green eyes. They also had thick dark hair that defied neatness. That most likely came from Jane.

They were all seated at the dining table, finishing a game of commerce, with cards piling up, when her father rose and motioned to Larissa. "A word?"

Thal and Callie looked up. Larissa stood, offered them both a reassuring smile, and followed their father down the corridor to the library.

"I apologize for not coming sooner," he said after they were seated on two of the chairs. "Has anything resolved itself?"

He might have been asking about the king and Liverpool, but she was fairly sure by the way his elegant fingers twitched on the arm of the chair that he was trying to find an appropriate way to ask about her feelings for Leo.

"They may be on their way to becoming resolved," she hedged. "Thank you for sending Jane in your place. She is a dear, and it's been good to have her with us again. But I'm glad you're here."

He smiled. His smiles always transformed his face from a mask of hauteur and rank to one of warmth and caring. "I'm glad to be here too. All my girls, all my boys, together as they should be."

Larissa leaned closer. "And Thal? Do you still worry for his health?"

His smile faded. "The physician believes it a momentary aberration. But I prefer to remain vigilant."

She understood, at least a little. Her mother had been carrying his first son when she and the babe had died. Her father would not want to relive that moment.

"What of Liverpool?" she asked, hoping to change the topic. "Any advice for the prince and king there?"

He leaned back and crossed his arms over his chest.

"Find another ally. And not Canning."

Larissa raised her brows. "That bad?"

"Perhaps not impossible," he allowed, "but improbable. Liverpool was the architect behind the agreements reached at the Congress of Vienna, and Canning has made sure they are implemented following Castlereagh's untimely death. He will not want to see the peace he achieved undermined."

"Even by returning a small country its autonomy?"

"Batavaria's economy is now intertwined with Württemberg's," he pointed out, dropping his arms. "Separating the two may prove fatal to both."

"I see."

She must have sounded as disappointed as she felt, for her father reached out to pat her hand. "Very likely this is all posturing on the part of the king. It has been nearly ten years, after all. Once he has exhausted all avenues, he will have discharged his duty. He can then retire to a villa in sunny Italy and live out his life in comfort."

Somehow, she could not see Leo being content with so prosaic a lifestyle. Even the crown prince might balk in such a narrow sphere of influence.

She glanced up to find her father watching her, jade eyes so much like Belle's. Larissa offered him a smile. "Thank you, Father. I will tell Captain Archambault what you advise."

"If the prince or His Majesty would like additional input," he said, "I'd be happy to help."

"I'll write to him now," she said, rising.

It was the proper thing to do. She had promised to enlist her father's aid, and she should let Leo know the results. But writing for that purpose was only an excuse. She knew that as she sat at her travel desk in her bedchamber.

Normally a young lady did not summon a beau to her side. A gentleman liked to think he was the one doing the pursuing. A lady offered a smile in encouragement, deftly hinted at the appropriate outcome.

And either let her displeasure be known or fell into a decline if her wishes were not honored.

None of those stratagems her grandmother had taught her seemed appropriate at the moment. In fact, they seemed nothing short of manipulative. Tuny would have said what was on her mind. So would Jane.

Taking a breath, she gripped the quill.

Leo,

I hope you, the prince, and the king are safe and well. I know you must remain vigilant to protect them from this unknown threat, but my father has relayed some news you should hear. He has offered to provide additional insight as well. Would you wait on me at your earliest convenience?

She paused a moment before plunging in.

I hope you will not delay overly long. I miss you. The day seems less bright when you are not at my side.

Before she could regret the statements, she signed the letter, sanded it, and sealed it to carry to Davis for delivery.

Then she returned to the bosom of her family and tried not to think about how Leo would take the message.

CHAPTER SEVENTEEN

THE SPEED OF Leo's appearance was most gratifying. Likely it was because he wanted to hear what her father had to say, but still. He and the prince arrived so early the next morning that Larissa and Callie were still taking a constitutional, having joined Meredith and Fortune in the park at the center of the square. Larissa looked up from admiring a cluster of tall blue larkspur to find Leo and his brother striding toward her down the graveled path.

Prince Otto's black boots were as shiny as the silver buttons on his tailored navy coat. Leo, in his black uniform, looked more like a shadow, and she couldn't help noticing the dark circles under his eyes as he reached her side.

"Good morning, Larissa, Callie, Mrs. Mayes," he greeted with a half bow. The prince inclined his head as well.

"Captain," Meredith replied. "Your Highness."

Fortune stopped her prowling long enough to glance from gentleman to gentleman, then rubbed her fur along Leo's boot, bringing the leash taut against the leather.

"We saw you through the trees," Leo began explaining.

"And of course the captain had to pay his respects before we met with your father," the prince finished.

"Unfortunately, my father and brothers have gone riding," Larissa told them both. "We expect them back shortly."

"I'm sure the duchess would be happy to entertain you while you wait," Meredith said, tugging on the leash to bring Fortune back to her side. The cat cast her a reproachful glance.

Larissa was hard-pressed not to do the same. Oh, for a moment alone with Leo! A lady, however, saw to the needs of her guests first. Both her guests, however much she favored one over the other.

Prince Otto took a step closer to Leo, as if he knew Larissa had designs on his brother. "I would never impose on Her Grace. We will wait in the park, with you."

Leo eyed him. "No need to deprive yourself of the pleasure of the duchess' company, Your Highness. You and Callie can retire to the house. I will escort Mrs. Mayes and Larissa."

He wanted time with her too? Warmth pulsed through her.

"Would you abandon your prince, Captain?" his brother asked, brow up in challenge.

Oh, but he was full of himself today!

Callie edged away from them, green skirts blending with the bushes. "I'll just let Mother know you're here."

Larissa couldn't blame her for wanting to escape this time. Leo and the prince were looking daggers at each other.

"Thank you, Callie," she said, making sure none of her disappointment crept into her voice. "Aunt Meredith and I will stay here with our guests."

Callie glanced between Leo and the prince. To Larissa's surprise, she squared her shoulders and put on her best smile.

"I wish I could persuade you to come with me, Your Highness," she said as brightly as Belle. "You always have such interesting things to say." She fluttered her pale lashes.

The prince stared at her as if she'd smacked him over

the head with one of her beloved books. Then he strode forward and offered her his arm. "I would be honored, Lady Calantha." He shot Leo a glance. "But do not tarry, Captain. You should not leave your prince unprotected." He escorted Callie toward the gate.

Leo shook his head as if he couldn't believe what he'd just seen any more than Larissa did, then he grinned at her, and all was right with the world.

"Shall we?" Meredith asked, and she set out along the path.

Larissa accepted Leo's arm, and they fell into step behind Meredith and Fortune.

The park featured patches of grass shaded by tall elms and dotted by evergreen shrubs with beds of flowers here and there. Paths wound from side to side and one end to the other, with the occasional stone bench to invite contemplation. Larissa's former chaperone set out at a leisurely stroll while Fortune took every opportunity to rub up against the shrubs as if hoping to dislodge the hated collar. Leo and Larissa moved at the same sedate pace, a few steps behind.

"Thank you for the note," he murmured. "It offered the first hope in days."

"No news on the jewels then?" she asked.

"Alas, no," he said. "But I look forward to hearing what your father thinks."

"I can share a little of that." She went on to explain what her father had told her about Liverpool and Canning. She left out the part about the king being better off retiring to Italy. No sense putting ideas in anyone's head.

"Then we will never see your king," Leo said, voice grim. "Liverpool and Canning have been preventing it, just as we thought."

Meredith glided back as Fortune darted across their path to slip under a hedge. "Not necessarily, sir. A shame your king saw fit to discharge my husband, or he might have told you what he'd learned."

Larissa rounded on Leo. "The king sacked Uncle Julian?"

The shadows from the trees could not hide his wince. "Not before I argued against it, I assure you. I have found Mr. Mayes to be a savvy and thorough ally."

"Thorough enough that he discovered Liverpool has never received a request from your king," Meredith informed him.

Leo frowned as he halted near a shrub that had been trimmed in the shape of a vase. "What? I saw the notes leave the palace."

"Then perhaps you should ask where they were delivered," Meredith said, nose in the air.

"I will," Leo promised. "Thank you, and please thank Mr. Mayes. I will see that he is paid, somehow."

"Yes," she said, lavender gaze directed away from him. "He mentioned that you were having trouble in that area. And there was another matter he hoped you would disclose."

Color climbed in Leo's firm cheeks. "Please assure him I am working toward that end."

"See that you do."

Fortune must have tugged on the leash, for Meredith stalked off as if to retrieve her.

Larissa watched her chaperone go. "What other matter must you disclose?"

He commenced walking again, perhaps a little faster this time. "A personal matter I find difficult to discuss."

It was unlike him to be so close-mouthed. Perhaps it was something to do with the kingdom he was not allowed to confide. "I believe I understand. It is a matter between you and the crown prince."

His uniform must be growing hot in the sun, for he tugged at the collar. "Exactly."

"I am trying to appreciate your brother's position,"

Larissa said, lifting her skirts a little to match his pace. "But he has the oddest way of speaking. When he met us in Hyde Park, he advised me to ask you what game you are playing, as if you would be so dishonorable."

He coughed as if dust had lodged in his throat. "There are many ways to look at honor."

"I'm certain your brother thinks so," Larissa said. She squeezed Leo's arm. "Please understand that I am not upset with you in the least. It's merely troubling to know that the king discharged Uncle Julian. I've seldom heard Aunt Meredith speak so sharply."

"Her dedication is admirable," Leo murmured, pausing under the shade of an elm. "I could wish for such a wife."

This was the moment her grandmother had counseled her to watch for, the suggestion that a gentleman might be interested in seeking a bride. Her nerves skipped and bucked like a colt let free in the pasture. Not an ounce of it showed.

"Yes," she said calmly, "you mentioned to Jane you were thinking of marrying."

"I had not thought overly much about it," he said, taking her hand. "Until I met you."

Oh! Every rule she'd memorized, every piece of advice she'd held dear, fluttered away like butterflies before the warmth in his diamond eyes. She could not look away as he leaned closer.

The kiss was gentle, a mere brushing of lips, but the very earth seemed to tilt into place, as if this was where she had always belonged.

He pulled back, smile wistful, as if he had felt the same.

A cough let them know they were not alone. Turning, Larissa saw a footman in powdered wig and old-fashioned longtailed coat standing a short distance away.

"Begging your pardon, Captain," he said. "His Highness has spoken with His Grace and would like to leave now."

His brother probably hadn't phrased it so nicely. Leo

must have thought so too, for his smile evaporated.

"Inform His Highness I am on my way," he told the footman, who bowed and hurried toward the street.

Leo looked to Larissa. "I do not know when I can see you again, but I will do all in my power to make it soon."

"Please," Larissa murmured.

From the opposite direction, Meredith and Fortune were returning. If their chaperone had noticed their lapse in propriety with the kiss, she gave no indication. Indeed, she had picked up her pet and appeared to be whispering something. Fortune's ear twitched.

Leo bowed to them all. "I must take my leave. Good day, Mrs. Mayes, Fortune."

"Sir," Meredith said, inclining her head. She and Larissa watched as he headed for the gate of the park.

"I certainly hope he can convince his father to see reason," Meredith said, hand running absently down Fortune's fur.

Larissa gathered her wits, which seemed as scattered as leaves in autumn. "He must. Someone is poisoning their efforts to regain their lands. That person must be uncovered."

"Commendable for you to take such an interest in justice," Meredith said, nodding toward the gate. The two set out. Fortune wiggled as if she wanted to stay in the park, but Meredith would have none of it.

"It is only right," Larissa said.

"And does the captain share your views?" she asked as they neared the street.

"Of course," Larissa said. "This is his fight."

"Had he no other topic of conversation?" Meredith pressed.

The kiss rose up, as potent in memory as it had been in reality. Larissa swallowed. "Nothing of any import."

Across the street, Leo and the prince were climbing into the royal carriage. He waved a hand in farewell, and she raised hers in response when all she wanted to do was run to him, stay with him. But he had a duty, and so did she. Still, as the carriage pulled away, the breeze seemed somehow colder.

Larissa shook off the feeling as she and Meredith crossed the street and entered Weyfarer House. From the drawing room, her brothers' voices babbled about the horses they'd seen on their ride. Larissa was having trouble hearing anything but the memory of Leo's voice, promising he would do all he could to return to her soon.

Seeing her in the doorway, her father rose to join her, even as Meredith and Fortune went in to Jane and the others.

"I may have good news for you," her father said, standing near the stairs. "A young man came to request my permission to pay his respects to you."

Larissa clasped her hands in front of her with the insane idea she could keep her heart from bursting free. "Oh, Father!"

"Indeed. Prince Otto was adamant in his admiration of you. I told him he had my permission to ask you to marry him."

She felt as if someone had dropped a teapot on her head. "Prince Otto?"

"The crown prince himself," her father assured her. He must have noticed the change in her, for his smile evaporated. "What is it, Larissa? I was under the impression you wanted to marry a prince."

"No," Larissa said, choking. "Not in the slightest. I'm in love with someone else entirely."

"Why so glum?" Fritz asked as they settled into their seats on the way back to the palace.

Leo had never had such trouble tucking away his

feelings. Each time he left Larissa, it was harder to pull away. Each time, he wanted more.

No, not more. He wanted forever.

He forced himself to focus on the issues. "Mrs. Mayes told me Liverpool never received Father's requests for an audience."

Fritz frowned as the carriage turned out of Clarendon Square. "You strolled through a private park with your love, and the best you could think to do was talk to her chaperone?"

"Not only her chaperone," Leo said. Despite his best intentions, he felt his smile forming as he remembered the kiss he'd shared with Larissa.

"Apparently not," Fritz said, brow raised.

"It was merely a kiss," Leo said, schooling his face into submission.

"But you would like the lady's hand as well," Fritz guessed.

Leo nodded. "She is everything I could have dreamed of in a wife—gracious, clever, dedicated to those she loves. But she deserves a prince, and I am one in name only."

"Not even in name at the moment," Fritz pointed out. "Unless you unburdened yourself after that mere kiss."

"I had hoped to tell her somewhere private," Leo confessed. "But privacy is difficult to come by with the daughter of a duke."

Fritz leaned back with a grin. "Good thing I took matters into my own hands."

Leo frowned. "And what does that mean?"

"While you were in the park kissing your love, I asked the duke's permission for Prince Otto Leopold to marry his daughter."

Leo stared at him. "What!"

Fritz waved a hand. "No need to thank me. He agreed. So, all you have to do is go down on bended knee."

"Impossible," Leo protested. "Surely you see that. What do either of us have to offer a bride?"

Fritz's eyes turned hard. "Intelligence, devotion, a good family name. And I understand neither of us is considered hard to look upon."

"What of protection, provision?" Leo challenged. "Do you know how far in debt we are?"

His brother shook his head. "Father always made it sound as if we had wealth to sustain us for generations."

"About another fortnight, as far as I can tell," Leo countered. "Unless that claim comes through on the jewels, we are a pair of bankrupts."

Fritz washed white. "That cannot be right."

"It gets worse," Leo said. "Father may have arranged the theft of the jewels himself."

Fritz stared at him, and then he started laughing. "The crafty old man. He found a way to put his hands on the money we need."

"By fraud!" Leo protested. "What honor in tricking an insurance agency to pay your bills?"

"What honor living in poverty?" Fritz argued.

"Better poor than a liar and thief," Leo retorted.

Fritz drew in an audible breath. "Suppose you have it right. Suppose the king did seek to defraud the insurance agency. What will you do? Tell the insurance agent? That will go far in impressing King George."

"We are unlikely to see King George any time soon," Leo told him. "Either Father never sent those requests to Liverpool, or someone has been intercepting them."

Fritz shook his head. "Any other revelations I should know?"

"No," Leo told him. "But you must see why I would hesitate to offer marriage at this time."

"I see," Fritz said. "And I am truly sorry, Brother. Lady Larissa is a fine female. She would have made you a wonderful wife."

"I know," Leo said, heart tightening in his chest. "But until I can resolve the issues facing us, I cannot bring her into this."

"I will write to the duke as soon as we return," Fritz promised. "Tell him circumstances require me to withdraw my offer. I will apologize and promise him it has nothing to do with his delightful daughter."

"No," Leo said. "I must speak to him. He deserves to hear the truth from me, and so does Larissa."

But when they reached the palace, they discovered there was no need. A note was waiting from the Duke of Wey. Leo could only think the fellow must have dispatched a footman in a carriage moments after Leo and Fritz had left.

Your Highness, it read. *I regret my promise this morning to you regarding my eldest daughter, Larissa. After speaking with her, I must withdraw my permission for you to marry her. It might be wise for you to curtail your visits to our home for a time. Your devoted servant, Alaric, Duke of Wey*

Leo's hand fell, even as his chest hollowed. "He refused my suit." His voice sounded dull even to his own ears.

"Actually, he refused *my* suit," Fritz pointed out. "At least, the me who was you."

Leo shook his head. "Either way, the prince has been barred from visiting."

"What!" Fritz grabbed the note and scanned the contents. "Insupportable! I am a member of the Royal House of Archambault. No English duke is going to tell me where I can go, who I can see."

Had Leo sounded so arrogant once? Never again.

"We will honor their wishes," he said, head coming up. "She is smarter than either of us. She saw through our posturing. It's the only explanation."

Fritz shoved the parchment at him. "But you love her. Talk to her!"

"And tell her what?" Leo demanded. "That I am a

prince with no country, no income, no hope of a future? That I cared so much about her that I lied to her, for weeks? If her father doesn't throw me out, she should."

"Fool!" Fritz stormed. "Do you think love just happens? You have spent years arguing for your country and your king. Would you do less for your future?"

Every bone in his body felt heavy. "Perhaps I grow weary of the fight."

Fritz took a step back. "And you think I don't? At least I remember what's important." He turned and strode from the room.

Leo could only watch him go. He knew he'd chosen the right path. Larissa deserved so much more than he was capable of giving at the moment. He ought to be glad she'd realized the truth.

Even if every part of him cried out in loss.

CHAPTER EIGHTEEN

BELLE, CALLIE, AND Tuny met in Larissa's bedchamber that night after the rest of the family was in bed. Her friend had apparently arranged the meeting.

"You were pale as blanc mange most of the afternoon," Tuny told Larissa as she pulled the dressing table chair closer to the bed. Callie and Belle were already snuggled in pillows piled against the carved headboard, and Larissa was sitting on the end, knees tucked up under her nightgown.

"What happened?" Belle asked.

Callie wrapped her arms about her waist and spoke before Larissa could decide how to explain. "Prince Otto asked for time alone with Father. He wants to marry one of us."

Belle perked up. "It must be Larissa."

"It was," Larissa confirmed, throat still tight.

Belle squealed and clapped her hands, but Callie turned white.

"I thought you favored the captain," Tuny said with a frown.

"I do," Larissa agreed. "Which is why I told Father to send my regrets to the prince. Father asked him not to call again for a time."

"Oh," Callie said, dropping her arms. "Well, that's the end of that, then."

Belle made a face. "I'll be sorry to see him go. He was

good fun."

Tuny snorted. "And spoiled. Like the whole lot of them cavorting around London, if you ask me."

"There are some perfectly fine young men on the *ton* this year," Belle insisted. "You only have to open your eyes to see them."

Tuny looked to Larissa, who smiled in commiseration.

"I'm glad you find them delightful, Belle," Larissa told her sister. "And I'm sorry to have to deprive you of the prince's company, but it's probably for the best."

"Is it?" Tuny asked. "His Royal High and Mighty might pitch a fit at being denied. He could tell the captain not to call either."

Larissa tugged a cover closer. "Leo told me he might not be able to call the next few days in any regard, and that was before Father turned down the prince."

"He'll call," Belle said, ever the voice of optimism. "He cares about you. You can see it in his eyes when he looks your way. Nothing the prince does will keep him from your side for long."

Larissa wanted to believe that.

Even though Leo wasn't expected, Larissa couldn't help perking up every time the door knocker sounded the next day. They had a steady stream of callers, from young ladies happy to share confidences about the Season to young men delighted to further their acquaintance. Leo was not among them. Neither was the prince. He seemed to have taken their father's advice to heart.

But that didn't stop him from approaching Larissa at Lady Carrolton's soiree that evening.

The Earl of Carrolton had a large house at the other end of Clarendon Square, set off from the main square by a circular carriage drive. Inside and out, it was well regarded as one of the most elegantly appointed residences in London. He and his wife regularly entertained, and an invitation to one of the countess's soirees was highly coveted. It should have come as no surprise that she would include the prince.

The greater surprise was that Leo was not accompanying him.

Belle spotted Prince Otto across the gallery as they entered, and she quickly pulled Larissa, Callie, and Tuny away from the duke and Jane to stop along one of the painted silk walls as the other guests moved among groups, chatting and laughing.

"He's here," she said, nodding to a knot of men across the room. Lord Carrolton stood head and shoulders above most of them, but the prince's scarlet coat was still evident.

"Thank goodness it's as crowded as usual," Tuny said, waving her fan in front of her face. "He may not even notice us."

"Or he may heed Father's request," Callie added, "and not approach us."

Larissa wasn't sure the prince was that much of a gentleman, but he proved himself more interested in talking with the other cabinet members in attendance, and she could only hope that meant he was tending to his father's plans for once.

Callie nodded to Tuny. "I think that fellow who passed us as we came in trod on your hem."

Tuny twisted to look over the back of her sky-blue silk gown. Some of the soutache that edged the hem was dangling on the floor behind her. "Oh no! I only have two evening gowns as it is!"

Larissa linked arms with her. "We'll find the ladies retiring room and have it stitched in place."

Tuny shot her a grateful smile. She gathered her dragging trim as best she could, and the two made for the entrance.

The ladies' retiring room was a little chamber off the corridor. The maid in attendance quickly went to work on Tuny's trim. Larissa looked at her reflection in the gilt-framed mirror hanging on one wall. Her hair was curled in clusters around her face. Her modest neckline crossed from shoulder to shoulder and was edged in white lace. She looked her usual serene self, a credit to her family. A shame her heart felt bruised.

"There," she said, after Tuny had thanked the maid for her work. "You're all put back together."

"And you're not," Tuny said, giving her arm a squeeze as they stepped out into the corridor. "I'm sorry he isn't here tonight. Perhaps your father could speak to the king about holding a military review in Hyde Park. That would bring out your captain."

Larissa laughed. "It might at that."

Someone stepped into the corridor to bar their way. The glow from the chandelier glinted on sandy hair. Prince Otto broadened his stance, gold sash running from one shoulder to the opposite hip.

"A word, Lady Larissa," he said. It was not a request.

"Good evening, Your Highness," she said, putting the right amount of chill in her voice. "I do not believe we have anything that must be said. If you will excuse us."

"She means take yourself off and be quick about it," Tuny explained.

The prince raised a brow at her, then directed his gaze at Larissa. How had she ever taken him for Leo? Instead of the warmth she was used to seeing, those bright eyes positively sizzled with frustration. Tuny had claimed he'd pitch a fit. Apparently, she'd been right.

"This will take only a few moments," he said. "And I would prefer to have the discussion in private." He crossed his arms over his chest as if refusing to budge until she agreed.

"Stuff that," Tuny said, moving closer to Larissa. "I'm

not leaving."

"Yes, you are," Larissa told her, keeping an eye on him. "You're going to tell my father, His Grace the Duke of Wey, that the Crown Prince of Batavaria is making a nuisance of himself."

Tuny grinned. "Right. Back in a moment." She hurried down the corridor for the gallery where the soiree was being held.

Larissa raised her chin. "You have less than five minutes before they return."

"Just long enough to ask you why," he said. "Why refuse my suit?"

"I don't love you," Larissa said. "I'm not sure I even like you."

He took a step closer. She refused to retreat. "You have fallen in love with someone else, then," he said.

She kept her mouth closed, but he nodded. "Yes, I can see it in your face. My traitor of a captain, perhaps."

Larissa stiffened. "Don't you blame him for your defects! You have been capricious, duplicitous, and even unkind at times."

"Guilty," he agreed. "That is my role, you see, as it is his role to be noble, loyal, and stalwart. I would never do anything to harm a hair on his head, I assure you. I only ask that you tell him how you feel."

Larissa stood her ground. "That is not a lady's place."

He leaned closer. "If being a lady is that important to you, you don't deserve him." He bowed, pivoted, and strode off, leaving her alone with her conflicting emotions.

The king swung into the private salon at the palace that night and headed for the liquor cabinet before stopping as his gaze hit on Leo at the desk.

"Still at it?" he demanded. "Ask Lawrence to draft

that letter if it proves so difficult. As chamberlain, he was trained in such matters."

So was he. "This is something I must write," Leo said, rising and staring down at the fourth blank piece of parchment he'd faced that evening. The other three were wadded up on the floor, the words deemed too pedestrian to explain himself to Larissa.

"And so you tell your brother to take your place again at the Earl of Carrolton's soiree." His father shook his head.

Leo frowned. "Fritz went out? He never told me. I thought we agreed to remain together for now."

Their father leveled a finger at him. "Fritz no doubt went because you were expected to attend. You cannot keep avoiding your responsibilities this way. You are the crown prince, not your brother."

Leo drew in a breath. "Perhaps I am merely following your example."

His finger fell. "Was that intended as an insult?"

More than he had once felt comfortable giving. But he could remain silent no longer, not with Larissa, and not with his father.

"Should it be?" Leo challenged. "I cannot keep up your pretense, Father. We are not wealthy. We may never regain our kingdom. Surely there is more to life than posturing."

"Posturing has served us well so far," the king said with a shrug. "I see no need to change that."

"And that," Leo said, "is entirely the problem." All the frustrations, all the concerns, all the arguments he'd had with himself rose up in front of him. He had told Fritz he was tired of fighting. Perhaps he merely needed something more noble for which to fight.

He bowed to the king. "I tender my resignation. I am done."

His father blinked. "What?"

"I abdicate," Leo explained. "My position, my stake

in whatever questionable fortune remains, my rank in the Imperial Guard. I will be merely Mr. Leopold Archambault, once of a quaint little kingdom in the Alps, now a petitioner for asylum in England."

"No," the king barked, striding to meet him, blue eyes blazing. "I refuse to accept. You are my heir."

"To what?" Leo asked, spreading his hands. "You have left me with nothing, Father. At the moment, I cannot even be sure of my honor."

His mouth worked a moment, color deepening. A storm was likely coming. Leo would not back down. Indeed, for the first time in a long time, he felt as if he was breathing the cool, clean air of Batavaria again.

"What do you want?" the king asked at last.

Leo cocked his head. "The Lion of the Alps, willing to concede?"

"I never concede," his father snapped. "But I might be willing to negotiate."

Leo pounced on the offer. "The truth, about the jewels, our income, and our standing with King George."

Again he hesitated. Then he stalked to the sofa and threw himself down on it. "Oh, why not? You were dangerously close to the truth in any event. Sit."

Knowing obedience might gain him the information he sought at last, Leo sat.

"It takes a great deal of income to maintain the consequence of a king," his father said. "We have enough to last for some time, but your future concerns me."

The future concerned Leo as well, which was why he had been advocating change, but he merely nodded in understanding. "Then you arranged to have the jewels stolen, so you could make a claim."

His father shifted on the sofa. "And to cover the fact that they were paste. I sold them to pay our way to England. We ran up debt in the German confederation. It seemed the wisest course."

"Why?" Leo asked, trying to make sense of what he'd just heard. "You brought us all here, but you never approached King George."

"He will refuse any request," his father said, leaning back with a sigh. "They all refuse. Liverpool's instructions helped negotiate the terms that took our kingdom. He was unlikely to renegotiate now, especially not with Canning as Foreign Secretary."

"So we came here merely to escape creditors?" Leo asked, the words tasting foul in his mouth.

"And to find you both wealthy brides," the king said as if that was a worthy goal. "The English love a prince. Those dowries could go a long way toward keeping us solvent."

Leo stood. "No. You bartered my home, my history, and my honor. I will not allow you to barter my love as well."

His father gazed up at him. "So you love your little duke's daughter."

"More than anything."

His brows rose. "A strong vow. How do you think she will take matters when she learns you no longer wish to be a prince?"

"She thinks me your second son, a captain," Leo said. "And I doubt she will care if I resign that commission either."

"But she will care you cannot support her," his father pointed out. "All you need do is say nothing to the insurance agency. I will have Lawrence work with her father to win you a dowry worthy of a prince. Between the two, you will be set for life."

He was right. If Leo went along with his father's schemes, he could support Larissa in style.

But he would lose himself in the process. And he could well lose her love if she ever discovered his perfidy.

"No," he repeated. "Larissa deserves better, and so do I. Besides, we are no closer to determining who holds our birth records."

He shook his head. "That fool of a thief I hired must have taken them. I told him to steal only the jewels."

"Who is he?" Leo asked. "How can we locate him?"

"No idea," his father said. "I found him trying to pick the lock on the door to the garden and enlisted his aid. You nearly caught him the night of the reception, but I made sure he had an easier way in the night of the ball. He was good enough to leave the key to the safe under my pillow when he was done. But I have not seen him since. Likely he threw the birth records away when he realized he could get nothing for them."

Leo could only hope his father was right. "Negotiations are concluded then, Father. I resign. I will approach Lord Liverpool and request a position in the War Office. I know enough about military matters on the Continent that I might be of some use to him there. I might also be of use to our people."

His father rose to stand with head high and back straight, every inch the King of Batavaria. "My son," he spat, "will not be a spy for England."

"You have left me with little choice, Father," Leo said.

His lips curled. "Go, then. That piece of paper that proves which of you is crown prince has conveniently disappeared, and few will be bothered to dig up the original. Fritz can be my heir."

"I wish the two of you well," Leo said with a bow. "I will retrieve my things. And I will tell the insurance agent that we are withdrawing our claim on the jewels. Larissa and her friend Miss Bateman appear to have found them in the Covent Garden market in all their paste glory."

His father slammed his fist down on the arm of the sofa so hard it tilted. "You will do no such thing. I forbid it."

"I am no longer your heir," Leo said, turning for the door. "I don't have to care what you forbid."

"Wait."

The word held desperation. Surprised, Leo turned to meet his father's gaze. The commanding look had faded, and the lines around his eyes were all the more evident.

"Tell the insurance agent we discovered a servant who only worked the night of the party found the safe left open and moved the Crown Jewels somewhere else for safekeeping," he told Leo. "We only now discovered they are secure."

It was still a lie, but he recognized the gambit as a way to salvage his father's reputation. "I can do that. It would help if you reinstated Mr. Mayes. He has some standing here."

His father nodded. "As you wish. We could say he discovered the truth."

He had, and Leo could only bless him for it. "Agreed. But I still intend to offer my services to Lord Liverpool. Perhaps when he sees my good work, he may be willing to listen to your request for an audience with the king."

His father nodded slowly. "England could use the services of a crown prince."

Leo inclined his head. "Thank you, Father."

"And your princess?" he asked. "Will you marry her?"

"I will," Leo said, "provided she agrees. And I will have Mr. Mayes draw up the marriage arrangements, in her favor, not yours."

His father straightened once more. "Agreed. Negotiations concluded. I taught you well."

He had learned a great deal from his father, but perhaps not the lessons his father had intended. Before he could say as much, the chamberlain stumbled into the salon. Face blanched, hand shaking, he brought a note to the king. "Your Majesty, terrible news."

The king snatched the note away from him. Leo stepped closer to read it over his father's arm.

We have the crown prince. Unless you sign a document that you and all your descendants disavow any future rights to the

*lands of Batavaria and swear never to enter the region again on
pain of death, your heir will disappear.* Bring the document to
the Great Pagoda in Kew Gardens tomorrow when you tour.
Tell no one else, or the prince dies.*

"Cowards!" the king thundered, crushing the note in
his fist. "They dare not face me on the battlefield or even
in the courts that they resort to this."

Fritz would have known how to react if it had been
Leo who had been kidnapped. His brother would be
questioning all those involved, gathering the guards,
taking action. What did Leo have except strategy and
diplomacy?

He raised his head and met the chamberlain's troubled
gaze. "Who brought this? Is the messenger still on the
grounds?"

"The coachman," Lawrence explained, hair so out
of place great swaths of skin showed through. "He was
waiting for the prince outside the Earl of Carrolton's
residence and grew concerned when the event appeared
to be over and the prince had not called for him. No
one in the house saw the prince leave, but a footman
had been ordered to give the note to anyone who came
asking. He did not, apparently, recognize the man who
handed it to him. I swore the coachman to silence."

"Then my brother took no guardsmen with him?" Leo
pressed.

Lawrence frowned. "Not to my knowledge, but I
shall confirm that immediately." He glanced at the king.
"Unless you had a more urgent request, my liege?"

The king waved a hand, and Lawrence bowed before
backing from the room.

"This is my fault," Leo said, feet carrying him from one
side of the salon to the other. "I should never have started
this charade."

"No," his father said, moving to the desk Leo had
vacated and lowering himself onto the chair. "Fritz has

been trained since he was a child to be your protector. He would have wanted it this way."

Leo skidded to a stop to stare at him. "You sound as if you have lost all hope of saving him."

"I have not given up on saving Fritz," the king said, dipping the quill in ink. "I am giving up on Batavaria. I will not allow either of my sons to come to harm. I will draft this document they want and sign it. You will stand as my witness."

He felt so heavy he could have sunk through the thick carpet and the wood floor beneath. "Father, no. Think of our people."

"I have thought of our people most of my life," he said, the scritch of the pen against the parchment loud in the room. "It is time I thought of my family first."

It was as if his own blood was pouring from that quill. "There must be a way to rescue Fritz and keep our rights. Fritz would know."

The king glanced up. "What do you propose?"

Leo drew a breath. "Write the note for us to take. But tomorrow, we will make sure Fritz is alive, then we will discover our enemies and show them the House of Archambault refuses to bow."

CHAPTER NINETEEN

LARISSA'S CONVERSATION WITH Prince Otto haunted her the rest of the evening. Did he have no understanding of the proper way of doing things in England? Even on the Continent, she'd heard, a lady did not pursue a gentleman. Men proposed. Women accepted. That was the way it was done. Oh, sometimes families arranged marriages with little involvement from the couple, but those days, happily, were nearly behind them. She could marry who she wished.

A gentleman suitable for the daughter of a duke.

She had known that rule her entire life. Never had she thought she'd fail to live up to it. She shivered imagining the look of disgust on her mother's face, the sorrow in her grandmother's eyes. Her father and Jane might have given their blessing to a captain of the Imperial Guard, but she knew he was not what would have been expected of her under other circumstances.

Even if he was more than she had ever expected.

Most of the gentlemen who approached her talked of commonplaces. Leo asked about her past, her plans for the future. Many fellows preened to have her, the daughter of a duke, on their arm, as if she were meant as nothing more than an adornment to their consequence. Leo involved her in his most urgent concerns and treated her as if her contributions mattered. A few gentlemen looked down on Callie for being so shy in company,

Tuny for being the daughter of a tradesman, and Jane for having been their governess. Leo treated them all with respect and affection.

When Leo looked at her, she knew she was beautiful, valued.

Maybe even loved.

Was she to turn her back on all that because of her mother's and grandmother's expectations?

"My room," she whispered to Callie as they came back into Weyfarer House that night. "Tell the others."

Callie nodded, eyes wide.

They filed in shortly after the maid had retired for the night. This time all four squeezed onto the big bed.

"I have made a decision," Larissa announced. "I'm going to tell Leo I love him."

Belle pressed both fists to her mouth, eyes shining. Callie grinned.

"Good for you," Tuny said.

Belle dropped her hands. "He'll propose. I know it."

"Perhaps not," Larissa warned. "I don't think I've mistaken his feelings for me, but he owes a duty to his king. He may feel he cannot marry me without the blessing of his liege. I'm not sure of Batavarian law, but you know it's a requirement here in England that the king approve any marriages within the royal family."

"Then we'll have to convince King Frederick to give his blessing," Belle said.

"Even *you* might have trouble convincing a king to do something he doesn't want to do," Callie pointed out.

Belle wrinkled her nose. "I doubt it."

Larissa laughed. "Well, let's hope your talents aren't necessary. I could use your help finding a way to speak to Leo, though. Father told the prince not to call, and I doubt we'd be welcome to call on them after the way I talked to him tonight."

"Kew," Callie said. "I heard the Earl of Carrolton talking

with another guest about the matter. You know how he loves gardening. The king, the Imperial Guard, and the prince will be touring the Royal Botanic Gardens at Kew tomorrow."

"The *Royal* Botanic Gardens," Tuny pointed out. "They require special permission to enter, and you'd have to take a carriage out from London to reach it. Not easy for most."

Larissa drew in a breath. "But possible for the daughter of a duke."

Callie nodded. "I'll ask Mother to apply for permission."

"No time to wait for the request to go through the process," Larissa told her. "I will simply have to brazen it out."

"If you ask Father for a carriage, he'll require you to take a chaperone," Belle said.

Larissa sighed. Must she throw off every precaution, act like some hoyden with no idea of propriety?

A lady did what must be done for those she loved. Her mother and grandmother hadn't taught her that.

Jane had, and Larissa believed it with all her heart.

"I'll take Thalston," she said. "He can help convince the gardeners or their guards to let me in. If only I could be assured Leo will listen."

"He'll listen," Tuny told her. "He likes you, Larissa, just as Belle said. Anyone can see that." She dropped her gaze and plucked at the coverlet. "I know. I looked the same way my first Season."

Belle wiggled on the bed. "You had a beau!"

Tuny's head came up. "I never had a beau. I had a fascination for a fellow, but he didn't return it. A shame everyone else falls short in comparison."

Callie sighed. "I know what you mean."

Larissa looked to her sister. "You too! I was afraid you were growing fond of Prince Otto."

Callie reddened. "His name doesn't matter."

Larissa reached out a hand to her sister. "If you tell us, we can look for opportunities to draw out his regard."

"Leave her be," Tuny told them all. "Loving and knowing he doesn't return your admiration is bad enough. Being forced into trying to catch his eye is worse. Better to keep looking for someone who loves you back." She turned to Larissa. "Go talk to your captain. He'll see reason. Leave it to the rest of us to find our own true loves."

She could not know what she asked. For most of her life, Larissa had been taking care of Callie and Belle. She had been able to give a great deal of the responsibility to Jane, who had loved and nurtured them, but when it came to suitable matches, Larissa hadn't been sure whether to trust her stepmother. Jane might have married a duke, but that had been more Fortune's doing than any kind of strategy.

But as she looked around at their faces—from Callie's brave smile to Belle's conspiratorial grin to Tuny's spirited determination—she realized they had grown. They knew what they wanted and were willing to work together to see it done. Why else agree to their wedding vow? Perhaps, perhaps, she didn't have to bear all the responsibility for their futures. Perhaps she could look to her own future and where she was called to be.

At Kew tomorrow, and at Leo's side, always.

Thalston was amenable to Larissa's plan when she approached him after breakfast the next morning.

"A secret meeting at Kew, eh?" he asked, green eyes lighting. "For the Crown, no doubt."

She couldn't lie to him. "For a chance at a real future, for me and Captain Archambault. Father may be disappointed I didn't pursue a prince, but I must do what I believe to be right."

"And Mother will always champion love," Thal said

with a grin. "I'm game. What must we do?"

They strategized, but in the end, her brother managed to convince Jane that he required the carriage to go to Kew to study specimens related to one of his courses in school and that he had previously gained permission for such a trip. He neatly turned aside her offer to come with them.

"I must learn to deal with matters myself, Mother, if I'm to be a good duke," he told her. "Larissa has graciously agreed to accompany me."

Jane smiled at Larissa. "Well, that's settled, then."

Belle gave them two thumbs up behind Jane's back.

Which was why, shortly before one that afternoon, Larissa found herself stepping down in front of the Lion Gate at the Royal Botanic Gardens at Kew. The golden stone arch in the wrought-iron fence, topped by a stone lion staring at the greenery beyond, looked formidable enough to bar her from her goals. The guard on the other side, face hard and eyes wary, looked even worse.

"The gardens are not open to the public," he said, glancing from Thalston to Larissa and back.

Thal stood at his full height, which put his head only slightly lower than the brim of her straw hat, and raised his chin. "I am Lord Thalston, heir to the Duke of Wey, and this is my sister, Lady Larissa. We have been told we may view the gardens."

The guard thawed enough to incline his head. "Your lordship, your ladyship. I'm afraid I wasn't given word of your intention to visit."

Thal frowned, but Larissa stepped forward. "That is neither here nor there, my good man. Our gracious Majesty would never refuse the family of one of his closest advisors. He would be most displeased to hear you had turned us back."

The guard glanced from the crest prominently displayed on the carriage, to the liveried coachman and groom staring at him, to Larissa. "Sorry, your ladyship. I have my duty."

Duty, expectations. Was everyone bound by them? She wanted to throw them all in the Thames.

Larissa wrapped her hands around two of the wrought-iron bars and gazed at the guard.

"Please," she said. "The man I love is in there. This may be my only chance to tell him how I feel and to see if he feels the same."

Thal was staring at her as if he'd never seen her before. The guard regarded her another moment. Then he reached for the gate latch.

"Welcome to Kew, my lord, my lady. You'll find one of the gardeners near the Great Pagoda, awaiting the arrival of the King of Batavaria and his court. He may be able to point out the whereabouts of your young man."

"Thank you," Larissa said. Her voice might have trembled a little, but she picked up her green plaid skirts and glided past him, head high and Thal at her side.

They managed to reach the closest copse of trees before Thal broke away from her and let out a peal of laughter. "That was a lark! You should go on the stage. What now?"

"We look for that gardener he mentioned," Larissa said, fighting a smile at her own boldness, "so we can locate Leo."

It wasn't hard to find the Great Pagoda. Built of stone, it rose ten stories above the grass of the gardens, towering over the firs surrounding it. A man in a rough tweed coat and trousers was standing by one of the red-painted columns that held up the first floor roof. Likely he was the gardener. She'd certainly never seen him with the Batavarian contingent before. He pulled off his cap as they approached, then bowed when Thal told him their names.

"So sorry I cannot be of more help, my lord," he said, slipping the cap back on his russet hair. "We're expecting important visitors today. You'll find a nice ruin off that way." He nodded beyond the greenwood.

"We know about your visitors," Thal told him as Larissa looked this way and that, trying to catch a glimpse of Leo. "My sister is a great favorite with the Batavarian court."

"Is she now?"

Both his tone and the look he sent her made Larissa feel as if she'd stepped out of the coach into a mudpuddle.

"Yes," she told him, chin up. "His Royal Highness is a frequent caller at our home."

"Offered to marry her," Thal supplied.

Larissa glared at him.

He cringed. "Callie told me."

"Sweet on you, is he?" the gardener sneered.

Larissa speared him with a look that had never failed her grandmother in making someone cringe. "I'm certain I would never presume upon His Highness's opinion. Suffice it to say, when he and the king visit, I believe they will be pleased to see me."

"In that case," he said, a hand snaking out to grab her arm, "you're coming with me."

The sun might be shining, but Leo felt as if a dark cloud hovered over the Royal Botanic Gardens as he and the king approached the Great Pagoda. He had never deployed his diplomacy to greater cause than when he'd used it to convince the gardeners and Lord Wellmanton, who had sponsored their tour, to allow them to continue this far without their escort. His only comfort was that the Imperial Guardsmen were stationed among the trees, ready to come to the king's aid at Leo's signal.

The chamberlain's questions had already alerted the guards to the problem. Once they had understood that it was Fritz who had been kidnapped, nothing would have stopped them from helping to rescue him.

"Where are they?" the king fumed now, glancing around the base of the ornate building. "Are they keeping him inside?"

As if in response, Mercutio slipped out from behind the nearest bush and bent in a bow. "Your most gracious Majesty, my dear captain, how it distresses me to see you this way."

"Stop your groveling," the king ordered. "Where is my son?"

Mercutio pressed a hand to his chest. "First, you must allow me to apologize. I would never have involved myself in such matters, but my associates in Württemberg wish their concerns to be resolved. I trust you brought the document?" His dark brows went up in question as he looked from the king to Leo.

Leo patted the leather satchel that hung by a strap from his shoulder. "We have it. First, show us the prince."

Mercutio gestured toward the building. "This way."

Leo refused to glance about to see if the guards were advancing. He followed the courtier around the curve of the cylindrical building to where a red door opened in its side.

"The king requires proof that we hold His Highness," Mercutio called.

Fritz came through the opening. His hands were behind his back, likely tied, and his coat was rumpled, but Leo couldn't spot any bruises or swelling. He drew in a breath only to puff it out again when another man pulled Larissa out the door too.

Leo started forward, and the king put out his hand, stopping him. His father shook his head once before looking to Mercutio.

"What is this?" the king demanded.

Mercutio frowned. "I do not know, gracious king."

A young man, perhaps twelve years of age, came out of the pagoda behind Larissa. He was pale and thin, with a shock of dark hair, but he held his head high, reminding Leo of her.

"You don't recognize your future queen and her brother," the man beside Larissa called.

The boy must be Lord Thalston. And, if Leo wasn't mistaken, the man holding them was the same fellow who had lunged at him and Fritz out of the darkness the night of Mrs. Netherbough's ball.

"Forgive me, Father," Fritz called. "They discovered the crown prince's fondness for Lady Larissa when she came looking for him."

Larissa shook off her captor's hold on her arm. "I did not come looking for Prince Otto. I came looking for Captain Archambault."

Leo's heart leapt up, and fear for her shot it down.

"Harm Lady Larissa or Lord Thalston, and their father the Duke of Wey will hunt you to the ends of the earth," Leo told the man. "And so will I."

"Signor Potterby, perhaps you should listen to the good captain," Mercutio suggested, shifting on his feet as if keen to be gone from this place.

Potterby seized Larissa's arm again. "No need for concern, Mercutio. So long as we get what we want, there will be no reason to harm anyone."

Mercutio eased closer to Leo and the king. "So very, very sorry, Your Majesty. If you would be so kind?" He held out his hand.

The king nodded, and Leo slipped the satchel off his shoulder. But he kept his grip on the strap. "First, release them."

"When we have the document," Potterby insisted.

He couldn't give them the satchel and the letter inside. His hope had been for the Imperial Guard to surround them before he had to turn it over. Yet if he didn't hand it over, they might harm Larissa before he or the guards could reach her. He hesitated.

Mercutio darted forward and yanked the bag out of his hand.

"I have it!" he cried, scampering back.

Once more, his father caught his arm. "Signal the guards."

"No," Leo grit out. "They cannot reach Fritz and the others in time."

He shook off his father and strode forward. "You are surrounded! If you want to escape, take me hostage. I am the real Crown Prince Otto Leopold. Let the others go!"

Larissa's gaze veered from the man beside her to the man she loved. Though the breeze ruffled Leo's sandy curls, his face was set, determined. She would not want to be one of the men facing him. He was simply magnificent.

"He's lying," the man she had come to know as the prince told Potterby, their captor. "He's trying to protect me."

And her. She'd seen the anguish cross Leo's face when the villain had marched her out of the pagoda. She'd hoped he cared for her. Now she knew. Leo was willing to exchange his life to keep her safe.

"I *am* trying to protect you," Leo called. "All of you. You have always been at my service, Fritz. Let me be the prince I should have been."

Mr. Mercutio was also glancing from Leo to his brother. Then he looked to his compatriot. "You seized the wrong one?"

Potterby was shaking his head. "This is a trick. Someone's going to pay." He raised the knife in his free hand.

"No!" Larissa cried, shoving against him.

The prince—the captain—whoever was standing beside her whirled and slammed his shoulder into the fellow, sending him staggering.

A lady should have screamed and collapsed in a faint. Larissa brought the heel of her half-boot down on the villain's instep, grabbed Thal's hand, and ran.

Right into Leo's arms.

He held her only a moment before setting her aside and dashing to help his brother. From the trees all around, the Imperial Guard stormed into the fray. In a thrice, they had Potterby and Mercutio in custody.

Her heart was jerking in her chest. "Are you all right, Thal?"

Her brother nodded. "You?"

"Yes," she said, drawing a stuttering breath. "I know my behavior just now wasn't the best example to you, but..."

"What are you talking about?" her brother cried. "Defying our parents, risking your reputation, fighting your way to your beloved's side? It's right out of a Scotch novel! I'm honored to witness it."

Larissa hugged him close, trying to find some semblance of calm. Her poise, her wits, seemed to have deserted her.

As she released her brother, Leo strode back to them. His gaze swept over her as if he was starving and she was a nice leg of mutton. "Are you unhurt?"

"Yes," she assured him. "Allow me to present my brother, Lord Thalston."

Thal inclined his head with every bit of the dignity their father showed to King George. "Captain, or should I say Your Highness?"

Larissa caught her breath.

"Prince Otto Leopold Augustus," he said. "Those closest to me call me Leo."

"Oh," Larissa said.

His face softened. "Please forgive me, Larissa. I was going to tell you. All I can say in my own defense is that the lie felt necessary at the time."

"Apparently it was," she acknowledged with a nod to where his brother was being released from the ropes that had held his hands bound. "Your life was in danger. You did what you must to protect yourself."

He glanced to the real Captain Archambault. "*Fritz* did what he must to protect me, and I fear I abused his trust at times. But no more."

She swallowed. "So it was all a fabrication, everything you said, everything you did?" If he answered yes, she thought she might never find calm again.

"No," he told her, taking her hand in his. "We are trying to see the kingdom restored, someone did break into the palace, and the Crown Jewels were stolen. So was my heart."

CHAPTER TWENTY

L EO WATCHED, WAITING, hoping. Larissa's lovely hazel eyes, the woodland colors of home, widened. Her rosy lips parted. He was bending his head when her brother moved.

"Excuse me," he said, face reddening. "I believe I'll go study plants now." He wandered to the closest bush as if prepared to give it his full attention.

"Plants?" Leo asked, nonplussed.

Color was climbing in her cheeks, but her eyes held a sparkle. "That's what we told our parents, that Thal must come to Kew Gardens to study plants for a class at Eton. It was only an excuse. I wanted to see you. I was afraid you'd heard that I refused your brother's advances. I didn't realize he was the captain. I thought he was the prince."

He wasn't sure what she was trying to tell him. "And now that you know?" Leo asked.

"It makes no difference," she said. "I couldn't marry him, Leo. I don't love him. I love you."

She said something else, but he was never sure afterward what it was. The entire world shifted, brightened, warmed at her words.

I don't love him. I love you.

He seized her about the waist and twirled her around as he had in the Batavarian waltz.

"Leo!" she cried, and he made himself lower her, though he kept his hands on her waist.

"You cannot know what this means to me," he told her. "I love you too, Larissa."

Her eyes were shining. "Oh, Leo."

There was nothing for it but that he kiss her, fully knowing they were in view of his father, his brother, her brother, and the majority of the Imperial Guard. She melted into him, so sweet, his very world. Her lashes fluttered against her cheeks as he released her.

"What about your father?" she whispered as if afraid to hear his answer.

"He has already given his blessing," Leo assured her. "As has your father."

She searched his face. "You spoke to my father?"

"No, my brother did, on my behalf." Leo glanced to where Fritz was questioning Potterby. "My brother has always been put in the position of protecting me, even in love, it seems."

She nodded, fingers fiddling with the fringe on one of her cuffs. "I can understand that. I've always felt it my role to protect my sisters. But I'm learning they can protect themselves."

"And so you gave me credit for pretending to be the captain so I could protect myself," he told her. "That was not my intention, at first. I envied Fritz his freedom and his ability to act. Sometimes, it felt as if all I did was talk—negotiating, persuading, begging, and never gaining ground. It seemed I had not earned the right to call myself prince. Perhaps I am growing into the role. I will spend the rest of my life attempting to live up to the title, regardless of whether we regain the kingdom."

She took his hand and gave it a squeeze. "Despite what I told you earlier, I can see now that I too have played a role at times, thinking propriety and my family's expectations were more important than what I felt, what I believed. It is no way to live, Leo. We must follow our hearts."

The pressure he'd felt for so long eased, drifting away on the cool summer breeze. Follow his heart? That he was capable of doing. Indeed, that might make him a king worthy of Batavaria.

"Then perhaps," he said, "we can continue to grow into our roles, following our hearts, together."

Her lips were trembling as he dropped to one knee and gazed up at her. "I have fought for my country, in word and deed, all my life, and seldom have I admitted defeat, but you have captured me, Larissa, and I have no desire to ever break free. I am unsure of what the future holds. I may always remain a prince in name only. But all that I am, all that I will ever be, I pledge to you. Will you do me the honor of marrying me?"

He loved her and wanted to spend the rest of his life with her. It was all she could ever have dreamed.

"Yes," Larissa said, conviction making the single word a solemn vow. "Yes, Leo. I will marry you."

He stood and pulled her back into his arms then. The way he held her, the way he talked with her, she would never call him a prince in name only.

He was the prince of her heart.

From a distance, she heard applauding. Breaking their kiss, she turned with Leo to find the king, Leo's brother, and Thal approaching them from opposite directions. Beyond them, a group of Imperial Guards was marching Potterby and Mercutio away. The latter sent her a soulful gaze.

"I take it you're going to do right by my sister," Thal said to Leo. "She took some risks to come here. Will an engagement be announced soon, or do I need to find a second?"

Leo raised his brows, but his brother laughed. "I like

this one."

Thal merely eyed him, which made the fellow laugh all the more.

"My liege," Leo said to the king, "Lady Larissa has done me the honor of agreeing to be my bride."

The king drew himself up, and Larissa raised her chin to meet his gaze.

"Welcome to the family," he boomed. "May this be a true sign of friendship and unity between our kingdoms." Larissa looked to Leo. "I believe it will."

"And who will you be marrying?" his brother asked, glancing between them. "The dashing captain or the reticent prince?"

"Both," Larissa said proudly.

Leo grinned.

"So, you will resume your mantle, Brother?" he asked. Was that resignation or disappointment in his tone? Leo had worn the mantle of second son well. She struggled to see his brother do the same. He would want center stage, to be in command, always.

"I will," Leo said as if he hadn't noticed the shadow crossing his brother's face. "And I will trust you to help me. Did you learn anything of use from the men who captured you?"

He glanced after their retreating forms. "The one who held us is English. Mercutio apparently hired him on behalf of our enemies in Württemberg. He convinced someone on the staff of the Württemberg Envoy to England to obtain the right to enter the gardens."

Leo nodded. "Secretary von Grub, perhaps?"

"Possibly," his brother allowed. "But we cannot accuse him without proof. And Mercutio may have misled him, making him think he did us a favor."

"I doubt Mr. von Grub would seek to do you a favor," Larissa told him, remembering her uncomfortable conversation with the fellow.

"Either way," he said, "I take it the idea was to hold the crown prince for ransom to stop us from pursuing our cause. Our enemies will only be satisfied, it seems, if we give up our birthrights."

Leo snorted. "And to think I was contemplating doing just that."

His brother started, but Larissa put a hand on his arm. "Leo, you cannot allow these villains to win."

He removed her hand but brought it to his lips for a kiss. "That determined to pursue a prince, are you?"

"That determined to see justice done," she said primly, though the pressure of his lips made her knees wobble.

The king cleared his throat. "These are thoughts for another day. Young dukeling, walk with me. I would like your perspective on a matter. You too, Frederick. Leopold, escort Lady Larissa home. I will return her brother shortly."

"With pleasure, Your Majesty," Leo said, clapping his fist to his chest and inclining his head. Then he offered Larissa his arm.

Together, they strolled through the green of the gardens, as if the lush landscape hadn't just been a scene that could have ended in tragedy. She couldn't help clinging to his arm, walking so close to him that her skirts brushed his boots. They were safe. They were alive. And they had a future, together.

Thomas was waiting with the family coach at the Lion Gate. The guard tipped his cap to her as she and Leo exited.

"I see you caught your fellow," he said with a grin. "You're a lucky man, my lad."

"I certainly am," Leo told him.

Larissa was blushing as he waved off the footman, handed her into the coach himself, then jumped in beside her.

"So you are truly the crown prince," she marveled as

Thomas took them back to Mayfair.

"I am," he said. "After we marry, I can prove it to you. The midwife cut my heel to show which child was the firstborn. I still carry the scar." He slipped his arm around her waist. "But it would have been nothing to the scar I would have carried had I been forced to leave you behind. I promise to put as much effort into our future as I did into attempting to retake Batavaria."

"Then I will be very well loved indeed," Larissa said.

He leaned closer and brushed his lips across hers, stealing her breath. "I wish I could have given you the queen's crown and cuffs."

"You never found the jewels," she said sadly.

He leaned back, twinkle in his diamond eyes. "Ah, but we did. You have them in your possession. You and your friend found them in the Covent Garden market."

Larissa frowned. "But they were paste."

"Why yes," Leo said. "Yes, they are."

She pressed a hand to her lips. "Oh, Leo, I'm so sorry."

"No more than we are," he assured her. "A shame we never learned the location of the royal birth records."

"Birth records?"

"The records that show which of us was born first," Leo explained. "The originals were archived in Batavaria, but the king carries duplicates in case they are needed. They were stolen along with the jewels."

Larissa started. "The prince with a mark on his heel. She knew!"

Leo looked at her askance. "She? Who?"

"The woman who sold me those jewels," Larissa said. "She said something about a prince with a mark on his heel. How would she know if she hadn't seen the birth records as well?"

"Could you find her again?" Leo pressed.

"Very likely," Larissa said. "And if I can't, then Tuny and her family certainly can. They visit Covent Garden market frequently."

"Then there is only one thing more I must do at the moment," he said. "As crown prince, I have a responsibility to see those who have helped us rewarded. We will hold a ceremony at the palace."

"For our wedding?" Larissa asked, heart starting to pound faster again.

"No," Leo told her. "I intend to wed you in an English cathedral, as befits the daughter of a duke and a princess of Batavaria. This is another sort of ceremony. Will you ask Mr. and Mrs. Mayes to join us tomorrow afternoon, say three? Fortune is welcome as well."

He was up to something, but she couldn't mind. She was simply too happy.

"We'll be there," she promised. She could hardly wait.

Larissa returned home to congratulations. Thal, the king, and Leo's brother had arrived before her and Leo and told everyone the good news. Jane hugged her, Belle squealed, Callie clasped her hands in front of her, Tuny shouted a hallelujah, and Peter stared at them all as if they'd gone mad.

Her father took her hands. "So you *are* marrying a prince," he said with a smile.

After Leo and his family left, she made sure to call on Meredith as well. The woman who had introduced her mother and her father merely smiled and told her how happy she was for her, until Larissa mentioned the ceremony at the palace tomorrow.

"Does the king plan to apologize for discharging Julian?" she asked, with a tone that said anything less was unacceptable.

"I don't know," Larissa told her. "But Crown Prince Otto Leopold was most insistent."

In the end, they all gathered at the palace: the duke and

Jane, Belle and Callie, Tuny and Larissa, Thal and Peter, and Meredith and Julian. Fortune came along on her jeweled collar, looking none too pleased by the matter.

They followed the footman past all twenty golden medallions of the gallery to the reception hall, where the Imperial Guards lined the walls like ebony statues in their black uniforms. King Frederick sat upon his throne, with Leo standing on one side and his brother on the other. Neither was smiling.

At least the king was wearing his crown, which Larissa had sent over the night before. She and Tuny were two of a few who knew the jewels glittering in it were not the originals. Tuny's brother had also sent word that he and Charlotte were on the case to find the woman who had sold Larissa the jewels and hoped to have the birth records back to His Majesty shortly.

His chamberlain stepped forward. "His Royal Majesty, Frederick Otto Leopold of the House of Archambault, King of Batavaria, is honored you would join him and his sons on this auspicious occasion and bids you welcome."

Her father inclined his head, as was his right as duke. Julian bowed. The ladies all curtseyed, Larissa lowest of all.

"And *you* didn't need help rising," Tuny whispered to her.

Larissa made sure none of her laughter broke free.

The chamberlain brought forth a scroll with golden finials and unrolled it. "Julian Mayes, come forward."

Julian started, but he moved away from Meredith and went to stand below the dais. He offered the king another bow. "Your Majesty, Your Highness, Captain."

"It has been brought to His Majesty's attention that you have rendered his kingdom a great service," the chamberlain said. "Your intelligence, quick-thinking, devotion, and loyalty are commended."

The king cleared his throat, and the chamberlain

stopped to gaze at him, brows up in surprise.
"I can take it from here, Lawrence," he said.

With the faintest of sniffs at being dismissed, Lawrence returned to his place against the wall just behind the throne.

King Frederick rose, resplendent in his ermine-lined robe, jewels flashing in the light. The Lion of the Alps was preparing to roar.

"I have been remiss in thanking you," he said, voice echoing in the long room. "Through your efforts, we have the Crown Jewels restored to us, and I have both my sons at my side."

Leo cracked a smile, then quickly swallowed it.

"Therefore, I ask you to kneel before me and swear your allegiance to our most noble cause."

Julian hesitated, then dropped to one knee. "Your cause, certainly, Your Majesty."

Again, Leo quirked a smile.

The king's look darkened, but he came to stand over Julian. "As it is in my power, I award you with the title of count in my court." He clapped his hands down on Julian's shoulders, nearly oversetting him. "Arise, Lord Belfort, Count of Batavaria."

As he stepped back, Julian blinked, then slowly stood. Meredith crossed both arms over her chest as if to hold in her wonder. Larissa thought she might be the only human who noticed the leash drop from her fingers.

Fortune noticed. She stalked up to the king and gave him her best stare. The king frowned at her.

Leo's brother broke away from the throne. "Allow me, Father." He bent and scooped up Fortune.

The gasps around the room were audible.

Fortune's eyes narrowed on his face for a moment, and Larissa stepped forward, to do what, she wasn't sure. But Fortune rubbed her head against his chest and suffered herself to be carried back to Meredith.

"Allow me to be the first to congratulate you, Lady Belfort," he said gallantly, offering Meredith her pet. "What are you doing?" the king barked. "I am not finished."

Again, everyone froze, Julian halfway back to Meredith's side.

"Frederick Leopold Augustus," the king thundered. "Approach your liege."

Larissa glanced to Leo, who was now smiling outright. This must be a good thing.

His brother didn't seem to think so. His steps were even slower than Julian's as he returned to his father's side, and his face was a mask. She thought all ten of the Imperial Guards had stiffened.

"Kneel," his father ordered.

He knelt. Head up and back straight, as if facing the guillotine.

"Whatever he's done," a squeaky voice called, "I'm sure he'll apologize."

Every gaze turned to Callie, who stood next to Jane, twisting her hands together. Her gaze was fixed on Leo's brother, and she bobbed her head as if encouraging him.

He returned his gaze to the king. "I have done nothing wrong."

"That sure, are you?" the king asked, face reddening. "Impersonating your brother, to the point that you offer his hand in marriage? Allowing yourself to be kidnapped so that you put the entire kingdom in jeopardy? Some would find those actions worthy of treason."

"I have given my life to protect the king and his crown prince," he said.

The king nodded. "And for that reason, I am here today awarding you with your own title." He brought his hands down on his son's shoulders. The captain did not so much as wince.

"Arise, Frederick, Count Montalban, my chief advisor."

He rose, swaying just the slightest as if stunned. Grins flashed on his guardsmen's faces.

"I have one more announcement to make," the king said, glancing around at them all. "Lord Liverpool has consented to arrange a meeting between my representatives and King George."

Once more Belle clapped her hands, but Leo stepped down from the dais to approach his father. "Your representatives?"

"You, your brother, and Lord Belfort," the king clarified. "I have decided to beard our enemies in their den. I will take four of the Imperial Guards with me and travel to Württemberg. I will ensure our people are well cared for, and we will settle this matter once and for all."

"Father," the new Count Montalban started, taking a step forward.

The king held up one hand. "This is my duty, Fritz. You and Leo are doing yours. It is time I did mine."

Leo glanced at Larissa before straightening his shoulders. "We will go with you, my liege."

"No," his father said. "It is time Württemberg realizes why I am called the Lion of the Alps." He nodded to his chamberlain, who inclined his head before looking to a door in the far wall.

Footmen began bringing in trays of food and drink then, and everyone except the guards moved forward to congratulate Julian and the count on their elevations. Both looked a bit bemused by the matter.

"So," Meredith said, joining her husband with Fortune once more secured. "You will be Lord Belfort now, official representative of the House of Archambault."

"I suppose I will." His smile looked a bit crooked. "And you will be Lady Belfort."

"That," she said, "will take some getting used to."

Leo moved closer to Larissa. "Does his lordship's elevation please you?"

"Very," she told him. "Mother said Uncle Julian was always a bit saddened that he lacked the title so many of his friends possessed. You remedied that for him."

He brought her hand to his lips and pressed a kiss against her knuckles. "I would solve any problem for you."

"I'm fairly good at solving my own problems," she said. "But help now and then would be greatly appreciated. You see, I made a vow with my sisters and Tuny that we would all see each other wed by harvest." She glanced to where Tuny, Callie, Belle, and the new count were talking. Belle was flirting, by the way her lashes were fluttering. Callie once more looked as if she wanted to disappear into the wallpaper.

"I see," he said. "I know only a few English gentlemen, but I would be delighted to further their acquaintances if that would help."

Larissa nodded. "We'll consider the options after you speak to Liverpool and King George. I have a feeling there will be little we cannot accomplish together."

Leo laughed. "Liverpool beware! England is about to be overtaken by the Prince and Princess of Batavaria."

"We will be more circumspect," Larissa promised him. "After all, a lady should never pursue her aims so openly."

"Even when she pursues a prince?" Leo asked.

"Only then," she told him before lifting her chin for his kiss.

"It seems you've changed your mind about Count Montalban," Meredith murmured to her pet as she let Fortune off her leash in their own home that evening. Julian was upstairs changing, and Meredith planned to join him shortly. To think, he had finally achieved his most cherished dream. Lord and Lady Belfort.

Tail high, Fortune stalked up to the sofa and ran her fur along it as if pleased to be back in her own environment.

Then she glanced at Meredith and hopped up onto the seat.

"I can't join you long, love," Meredith said, sinking down beside her to run her hand over the cat's silky back. "But I am pleased to know the count has changed his tune. Belle seems rather pleased as well."

Fortune wiggled away from her touch and went to the opposite side of the sofa to glance back at her over her shoulder.

"Not Belle?" Meredith stuck out her lower lip. "Callie?"

Fortune rolled over on her back and offered her stomach for a rub.

"Well," Meredith mused, accepting the invitation. "I wasn't sure Callie was ready, though she did jump to his defense this afternoon. This could be interesting."

Fortune began to purr.

THANK YOU FOR choosing Larissa and Leo's story. Larissa always dreamed of marrying a prince. I simply had to find one for her!

If you missed the earlier books featuring Meredith and Fortune, I suggest starting with *Never Doubt a Duke*, which tells the story of how Jane and Larissa's father fell in love.

If you enjoyed this book, there are several things you could do:

Sign up for my newsletter at *www.subscribe.reginascott.com* so you'll be the first to know when a new book is out or on sale. I offer my subscribers exclusive, free short stories and behind-the-scenes glimpses. Don't miss out.

Post a review on a bookseller site, BookBub, or Goodreads to help others find the book.

Discover my many other books on my website at *www.reginascott.com*.

Do you think Fortune is right about Callie and Fritz? Turn the page for a sneak peek of their story, *Never Court a Count*.

SNEAK PEEK:

THE WEDDING VOW

BOOK
TWO

REGINA SCOTT

CHAPTER ONE

London, England, June 1825

LADY CALANTHA DRYDEN, daughter of the Duke of Wey, had a unique talent: she could turn invisible. She'd noticed it as a child, when the servants would pass by her without so much as a smile. The governesses would laud her older sister, Larissa, and her younger sister, Belle, while never mentioning her own accomplishments. And if she was very, very careful, she could avoid her grandmother's censorious comments about her looks and intelligence by simply sitting very still and silent. The trait had only become more apparent as she'd reached the age to come out in Society.

She wasn't entirely sure how she did it. Maybe her pale blond hair or light blue eyes, like a reflection in a pond, made it easy to disappear. Maybe her slight frame and preference for light colors like pink and white allowed her to blend into the background. Maybe her nature was too quiet and self-effacing. Whatever the reason, people tended to overlook her, look past her, or look through her while in her company.

And they said the most outrageous things as a result.

This ball being given in Belle's honor was no exception. Callie had been retreating to the safety of the paneled wall when a group of young ladies on their first Season had stopped directly in her path. Huddled near a bank of potted palms that covered the door to the terrace, fans plying in front of their satin ballgowns, they hadn't paid her the least mind.

"He's ever so handsome," one of the young ladies was saying, head bent toward the others and curls dancing about her face. "And so charming."

Hadn't that been said of most of the young men on the *ton* this year? Callie sailed past, determined not to eavesdrop, until the next young lady spoke.

"And now he's a count in the Batavarian court, not to mention the brother of a prince and the son of a king."

Oh. *That* handsome, charming gentleman. Her cheeks heated at the very thought of Frederick Archambault, Count Montalban—Fritz as he preferred—recently arrived in London with the Batavarian court and elevated to the position of count. Fritz had been a frequent caller at her family's London address, but mostly because he was accompanying his brother, Crown Prince Otto Leopold, who had fallen in love with Larissa. He wasn't the sort of man Callie should admire as much as she did. Her hope for the future was a quiet life, book in hand, cat in her lap, pup at her side. He preferred the limelight and intrigue.

"I hear he decided to pursue Lady Calantha," another of the young women said, voice disdainful. "He'll learn soon enough he ought to steer clear."

"She's so odd," the fourth agreed.

Callie couldn't breathe. She turned away from her goal and slipped behind the palms. The cool shadows couldn't stop the heat spreading through her.

Shy.

Quiet.

Odd.

Invisible.

She shuddered. Why had she bothered coming?

Well, she had had a reason. Belle had wrung a vow from her, Larissa, and their best friend, Petunia Bateman, that they would all work to see each other happily wed by harvest. This was Belle's first Season, and she was determined to make it the best. This was the third long, painful Season for Callie, but she'd thought her sister might just be able to accomplish the impossible. Belle was like that. Few were proof against her whims.

Now, two months later, the brief hope she'd felt from her sister's optimistic encouragement had faded. Larissa was engaged, and Belle was admired. Even Tuny seemed to be making progress in finding a love, for she hinted of a man she admired. Callie alone had no prospects. And when she thought about Fritz, any hope she had of changing that positively plummeted.

It was difficult seeking a plain, quiet gentleman when perfection came calling on a regular basis.

Beyond her oasis, the four young ladies moved on. Others secured partners, and the next set began. Her sisters and Tuny were all dancing. Her father was with their mother. Ivy, the Marchioness of Kendall, Tuny's sister and their hostess for the evening, was on her husband's arm. Callie could have named every couple in line, in fact. Many had known her since she was a girl. A few of the others probably didn't know she existed.

The Duke of Wey has three daughters? Who else besides the elegant Lady Larissa and the adorable Lady Abelona?

She puffed out a sigh.

Two men stopped just beyond the palms, their backs to her. Dressed in the requisite black eveningwear, they both had slim physiques and straight blond hair just touching their collars. Callie pressed herself against the glass paned doors behind her and tried not to intrude on their conversation. But it proved impossible not to overhear them.

"Your plan came to naught," one said, voice low and deep. "Still they pursue their aims."

"For a time only," the other said. His voice hinted of

an accent. Not the lyrical lilt that rang in Fritz's often sarcastic drawl. She could not place it.

"Then you have decided your next steps?" The first man sounded decidedly eager about the matter.

"I have. Direct action failed us, but I am confident we can ruin them legally and socially." The cool calculation in his voice chilled her.

"Only tell me my part," the other begged. "You know I long to be of service to Württemberg."

Württemberg? Nothing could have stopped her from listening now. Württemberg was a kingdom on the Continent. Ten years ago, after a decision at the Congress of Vienna, it had subsumed the tiny mountain country of Batavaria, leaving King Frederick and his two sons without a home. Since the Batavarian court had arrived in England, men representing Württemberg had been determined to stop them from approaching King George to request aid in returning their kingdom to them. Crown Prince Otto Leopold, Count Montalban, and Callie's Uncle Julian, legal representation to the court, had an audience with the king only next week.

Were these men trying to stop it?

"My superior is most appreciative of all you have done for us thus far," the fellow with the accent assured the other. "I will pass along instructions once the plan is in place. Quickly now. We should not be seen talking overly long together."

They parted and moved off. Callie squeezed closer to the last palm in the row in hopes of catching sight of at least one of them. Instead, someone else was bearing down on her. She shoved herself back into the very corner of the space and held her breath, heart stuttering.

If ever there was a moment to be invisible, it was now.

The palm branches rustled as another body pushed its way through. The man hunkered low as if trying to prevent anyone from noticing.

Callie found her voice. "This spot is taken, sir. Move along."

He stiffened, and the light filtering through the leaves caught on the curly blond hair of Fritz, Count Montalban. "Callie?" he asked, voice colored with confusion.

She wanted to dive into one of the pots and burrow her way into the dirt. "It doesn't matter. Leave. Now."

His body deflated, and she heard a sigh that sounded positively relieved. "It *is* you. Be a friend and help me. I need to be invisible for a while."

His first luck of the evening. Despite her words to the contrary at the moment, Lady Calantha—Callie as she allowed him and his brother to call her—was a surprisingly sweet, shy young lady who would in no way impede his plans for the evening. If only he could say that about the other unmarried ladies at the ball.

He couldn't remember a time when he had had to actively hide at events. Since he'd reached his full height and been praised by his trainers in the military arts, he'd always stood in protection of the king, his father, and the crown prince, his brother. Leo in the scarlet and gold of the House of Archambault would take center stage, as was his birthright. Fritz would watch from the wall. Captain Archambault, head of the Imperial Guard. Only a few members of that guard knew the day he had let them all down, and he had done everything he could to prevent his lapse from ever happening again.

But since his father had seen fit to hand him a title of his own, he felt as if someone had painted an archery target on his back and every unmarried lady in London was taking aim. His father had joked that all young ladies wanted to be princesses. Apparently being a countess was just as coveted, especially now that his brother had announced his engagement to Lady Larissa, Callie's older sister. How was he to do his duty when he had to keep dodging attempts to ensnare him?

"You cannot be invisible," Callie hissed beside him. "That black coat with all the gold braid is entirely too noticeable."

At least he was back in his uniform tonight. There was a comfort in the familiar coat, the loose-fitting trousers that allowed for quick movement. For the last few weeks, he'd had to pretend he was the crown prince to give his twin brother the ability to determine who was trying to stop them from approaching King George. Leo believed the miscreants had been captured, but Fritz remained on guard.

As two young ladies promenaded past, he bent to keep his head below the tops of the palms.

"I don't see him anywhere," one complained, pausing directly in front of him. "He looks perfectly fit. Why won't he dance?"

"We must be persistent," the other said, gaze darting about. "He was trained to be a gentleman. If we make it appear he asked us to dance, Count Montalban will be honor-bound to take our arms."

He looked to Callie, and she nodded as if realizing why he might need to hide.

She was clever that way.

"Well, at least he hasn't asked Lady Calantha yet," the first said. "We still have a chance to turn his head."

Callie let out the tiniest of squeaks and pressed herself so far back against the door it was a wonder she didn't break the glass.

A door.

Fritz's hand was on the latch a moment later. He jerked his head at Callie to indicate she should accompany him, then slipped out onto the terrace that ran along the back of the Marquess of Kendall's town home. She followed.

He closed the door behind them, shutting off all

conversation. Only the faint music from the ball hovered in the air.

She drew in a deep breath. "You might have noticed that rumor has it you are courting me. Rubbish."

"Decided rubbish," he agreed.

She raised her chin. "Well, you needn't be so sure of the matter."

Fritz gave her his most disarming smile. "It is rubbish because I am not courting any young lady, even one so winsome as yourself."

The moonlight showed her pretty pink lips tightening. That was one thing he'd noticed about Callie. She had a preference for pink. Tonight, her ballgown was of a fine matte satin in a soft pink, with roses decorating the hem.

"And you can cease the flattery as well," she said. "We both know you don't mean it."

"Of course I mean it," Fritz said. "Unlike my brother, who must veil his opinions in diplomatic platitudes, I have the luxury of saying what I like. You are pretty, intelligent, and delightfully original. I like you."

Her mouth dropped open before she recovered herself. "You do?"

He went to lean a hip on the balustrade at the edge of the terrace, drawing a breath of the cool night air and savoring his few moments of freedom before he must return to the ball. "I do. I see no reason why we cannot be friends. After all, your sister is marrying my brother. It would be unseemly if we took each other in dislike."

"I suppose there's that," she allowed. One arm stole around her waist.

Fritz straightened. "Are you cold?" He started unbuttoning his coat.

She held up her other hand. "No. I'm fine. It's just a habit I have." She purposely dropped her arm.

"A habit like hiding behind potted palms?" he guessed.

She lowered her gaze. "It seemed expedient. I'm sure

you don't mind the number of people, but sometimes I find it a bit overwhelming."

"Focus on your goal," he advised. "That's what I do. I have had to attend events with more than six hundred people, most of whom thought themselves better than me, since I was fifteen. But I know why I'm there—to keep my father, the king, and Leo safe."

"Oh!" She hurried closer, face turned up to his. "You will need to be on your guard. I overhead the most horrid conversation just before you joined me. Two men were plotting with Württemberg to harm your family."

"What?" Fritz closed the last distance between them and put his hands on her shoulders to peer into her face. "When? What did they say?"

Behind her, the door opened, and a tall, slender man stepped out onto the terrace. Even in the moonlight, his bearing was noble, his movement confident. His gaze narrowed in on Fritz and Callie. His nose looked like a dagger aimed in their direction.

"Calantha," he said, striding toward them. "Your mother is worried about you."

Fritz dropped his hold, and she turned to face the door. "Father. I'm so sorry. I just needed a moment alone."

The Duke of Wey's gaze fell on Fritz like an anvil. "Apparently not alone. I expect to receive a call from you tomorrow, Count Montalban."

"Father, no!" she cried.

It was one of the few times Fritz had heard her assert herself in company. Every part of her lithe form vibrated with the same anguish that rang in her voice. He wanted to put her behind him, challenge her father to a duel, anything to keep her from harm.

What was he thinking? She wasn't his to protect. He wasn't looking for a bride. Courting would only hinder him from doing his duty. And a wife would want to know too many things about a past he tried so hard to forget.

Her father's look softened as she ran to him, and he put his arm about her shoulder. "You must leave this to me, Callie. It is my duty to keep you safe." As he glanced at Fritz, his face hardened once more. "I will see you tomorrow at eleven, my lord."

The king would not thank him for alienating one of their only allies. Fritz inclined his head. "Of course, Your Grace."

Callie sent him one last look before her father took her inside.

And Fritz knew he was well and truly trapped.

Learn more at
www.reginascott.com/nevercourtacount.com.

OTHER BOOKS BY REGINA SCOTT

Fortune's Brides Series

Never Doubt a Duke
Never Borrow a Baronet
Never Envy an Earl
Never Vie for a Viscount
Never Kneel to a Knight
Never Marry a Marquess
Always Kiss at Christmas

Grace-by-the-Sea Series

The Matchmaker's Rogue
The Heiress's Convenient Husband
The Artist's Healer
The Governess's Earl
The Lady's Second-Chance Suitor
The Siren's Captain

Uncommon Courtships Series

The Unflappable Miss Fairchild
The Incomparable Miss Compton
The Irredeemable Miss Renfield
The Unwilling Miss Watkin
An Uncommon Christmas

Lady Emily Capers

Secrets and Sensibilities
Art and Artifice
Ballrooms and Blackmail
Eloquence and Espionage
Love and Larceny

Marvelous Munroes Series
My True Love Gave to Me
The Rogue Next Door
The Marquis' Kiss
A Match for Mother

Spy Matchmaker Series
The Husband Mission
The June Bride Conspiracy
The Heiress Objective

And other books for Revell, Love Inspired Historical,
and Timeless Regency collections.

ABOUT THE AUTHOR

Regina Scott started writing novels in the third grade. Thankfully for literature as we know it, she didn't sell her first novel until she learned a bit more about writing. Since her first book was published in 1998, her stories have traveled the globe, with translations in many languages including Dutch, German, Italian, and Portuguese. She now has more than fifty published works of warm, witty romance.

Alas, she cannot have a cat of her own, as her husband is allergic to them. Fortune the cat belongs to her critique partner and dear friend Kristy J. Manhattan, who supports pet rescue groups and spoils her four-footed family members. If Fortune resembles any cat you know, credit Kristy.

Regina Scott and her husband of 30 years reside in the Puget Sound area of Washington State. She has dressed as a Regency dandy, driven four-in-hand, learned to fence, and sailed on a tall ship, all in the name of research, of course.

Learn more about her at her website at
www.reginascott.com.

Made in the USA
Coppell, TX
25 January 2022